HIGH
FIVE

HIGH FIVE

A STEPHANIE PLUM NOVEL

Janet Evanovich

QPD

Quality Paperbacks Direct
London

First published in the United States of America
in 1999 by St Martin's Press, New York

This edition published 1999 by QPD by arrangement with
Macmillan Publishers Ltd
25 Eccleston Place, London SW1W 9NF
Basingstoke and Oxford
www.macmillan.co.uk

Associated companies throughout the world

CN 2836

A CIP catalogue record for this book is available
from the British Library.

Printed and bound in Great Britain by
Mackays of Chatham plc, Chatham, Kent

ACKNOWLEDGMENTS

Thanks to Mary Anne Day, Joy Gianolio, Nancy Hunt, Merry Law, Lisa Medvedev, Catherine Mudrak, Fran Rak, Hope Sass, Karen Swee, Elaine Vliet, Joan Walsh, and Vicki Wiesner, The Women Mystery Writers Reading Group, for suggesting the title for this book.

HIGH

FIVE

ONE

WHEN I WAS a little girl I used to dress Barbie up without underpants. On the outside, she'd look like the perfect lady. Tasteful plastic heels, tailored suit. But underneath, she was naked. I'm a bail enforcement agent now—also known as a fugitive apprehension agent, also known as a bounty hunter. I bring 'em back dead or alive. At least I try. And being a bail enforcement agent is sort of like being bare-bottom Barbie. It's about having a secret. And it's about wearing a lot of bravado on the outside when you're really operating without underpants. Okay, maybe it's not like that for all enforcement agents, but I frequently feel like my privates are alfresco. Figuratively speaking, of course.

At the moment I wasn't feeling nearly so vulnerable. What I was feeling at the moment was desperate. My rent was due, and Trenton had run out of scofflaws. I had my hands palms down on Connie Rosolli's desk, my feet planted wide, and hard as I tried, I couldn't keep my voice from sounding like it was coming out of Minnie Mouse. "What do you mean, there are no FTAs? There are always FTAs."

"Sorry," Connie said. "We've got lots of bonds posted, but nobody's jumping. Must have something to do with the moon."

FTA is short for failure to appear for a court date. Going FTA is a definite no-no in the criminal justice system, but that doesn't usually stop people from doing it.

Connie slid a manila folder over to me. "This is the only FTA I've got, and it's not worth much."

Connie is the office manager for Vincent Plum Bail Bonds. She's a couple of years older than me, which puts her in her early thirties. She wears her hair teased high. She takes grief from no one. And if breasts were money, Connie'd be Bill Gates.

"Vinnie's overjoyed," Connie said. "He's making money by the fistful. No bounty hunters to pay. No forfeited bonds. Last time I saw Vinnie in a mood like this was when Madame Zaretsky was arrested for pandering and sodomy and put her trained dog up as collateral for her bond."

I cringed at the mental image this produced because not only is Vincent Plum my employer, he's also my cousin. I blackmailed him into taking me on as an apprehension agent at a low moment in my life and have come to sort of like the job . . . most of the time. That doesn't mean I have any illusions about Vinnie. For the most part, Vinnie is an okay bondsman. But privately, Vinnie is a boil on the backside of my family tree.

As a bail bondsman Vinnie gives the court a cash bond as a securement that the accused will return for trial. If the accused takes a hike, Vinnie forfeits his money. Since this isn't an appealing prospect to Vinnie, he sends me out to find the accused and drag him back into the system. My fee is 10 percent of the bond, and I only collect it if I'm successful.

I flipped the folder open and read the bond agreement. "Randy Briggs. Arrested for carrying concealed. Failed to appear at his court hearing." The bond amount was seven hundred dollars. That meant I'd get seventy. Not a lot of money for risking my life by going after someone who was known to carry.

"I don't know," I said to Connie, "this guy carries a knife."

Connie looked at her copy of Briggs' arrest sheet. "It says here it was a small knife, and it wasn't sharp."

"How small?"

"Eight inches."

"That isn't small!"

"Nobody else will take this," Connie said. "Ranger doesn't take anything under ten grand."

Ranger is my mentor and a world-class tracker. Ranger also never seems to be in dire need of rent money. Ranger has other sources of income.

I looked at the photo attached to Briggs' file. Briggs didn't look so bad. In his forties, narrow-faced and balding, Caucasian. Job description was listed as self-employed computer programmer.

I gave a sigh of resignation and stuffed the folder into my shoulder bag. "I'll go talk to him."

"Probably he just forgot," Connie said. "Probably this is a piece of cake."

I gave her my *yeah, right* look and left. It was Monday morning and traffic was humming past Vinnie's storefront office. The October sky was as blue as sky gets in New Jersey, and the air felt crisp and lacking in hydrocarbons. It was nice for a change, but it kind of took all the sport out of breathing.

A new red Firebird slid to curbside behind my '53 Buick. Lula got out of the car and stood hands on hips, shaking her head. "Girl, you still driving that pimpmobile?"

Lula did filing for Vinnie and knew all about pimpmobiles firsthand since in a former life she'd been a 'ho. She's what is gently referred to as a big woman, weighing in at a little over two hundred pounds, standing five-foot-five, looking like most of her weight's muscle. This week her hair was dyed orange and came off very autumn with her dark brown skin.

"This is a classic car," I told Lula. Like we both knew I really gave a fig about classic cars. I was driving The Beast because my Honda had caught fire and burned to a cinder, and I didn't have any money to replace it. So here I was, borrowing my uncle Sandor's gas-guzzling behemoth . . . again.

"Problem is, you aren't living up to your earning potential," Lula said. "We only got chickenshit cases these days. What you need is to have a serial killer or a homicidal rapist jump bail. Those boys are worth something."

"Yeah, I'd sure like to get a case like that." Big fib. If Vinnie ever gave me a homicidal rapist to chase down I'd quit and get a job selling shoes.

Lula marched into the office, and I slid behind the wheel and reread the Briggs file. Randy Briggs had given the same address for home and work. Cloverleaf Apartments on Grand Avenue. It wasn't far from the office. Maybe a mile. I pulled into traffic, made an illegal U-turn at the intersection, and followed Hamilton to Grand.

The Cloverleaf Apartments building was two blocks down Grand. It was redbrick-faced and strictly utilitarian. Three stories. A front and a back entrance. Small lot to the rear. No ornamentation. Aluminum-framed windows that were popular in the fifties and looked cheesy now.

I parked in the lot and walked into the small lobby. There was an elevator to one side and stairs to the other. The elevator looked claustrophobic and unreliable, so I took the stairs to the second floor. Briggs was 2B. I stood outside his door for a moment, listening. Nothing drifted out. No television. No talking. I pressed the doorbell and stood to the side, so I wasn't visible through the security peephole.

Randy Briggs opened his door and stuck his head out. "Yeah?"

He looked exactly like his photo, with sandy blond hair that was neatly combed, cut short. He was unbearded, unblemished. Dressed in clean khakis and a button-down shirt. Just like I'd expected from his file . . . except he was only three feet tall. Randy Briggs was vertically challenged.

"Oh, shit," I said, looking down at him.

"What's the matter?" he said. "You never see a short person before?"

"Only on television."

"Guess this is your lucky day."

I handed him my business card. "I represent Vincent Plum Bail Bonds. You've missed your court date, and we'd appreciate it if you'd reschedule."

"No," Briggs said.

"Excuse me?"

"No. I'm not going to reschedule. No. I'm not going to court. It was a bogus arrest."

"The way our system works is that you're supposed to tell that to the judge."

"Fine. Go get the judge."

"The judge doesn't do house calls."

"Listen, I got a lot of work to do," Briggs said, closing his door. "I gotta go."

"Hold it!" I said. "You can't just ignore an order to appear in court."

"Watch me."

"You don't understand. I'm appointed by the court and Vincent Plum to bring you in."

"Oh, yeah? How do you expect to do that? You going to shoot me? You can't shoot an unarmed man." He stuck his hands out.

"You gonna cuff me? You think you can drag me out of my apartment and down the hall without looking like an idiot? Big bad bounty hunter picking on a little person. And that's what we're called, Toots. Not midget, not dwarf, not a freaking Munchkin. Little person. Get it?"

My pager went off at my waist. I looked down to check the read-out and *slam*. Briggs closed and locked his door.

"Loser," he called from inside.

Well, that didn't go as smoothly as I'd hoped. I had a choice now. I could break down his door and beat the bejeezus out of him, or I could answer my mother's page. Neither was especially appealing, but I decided on my mother.

My parents live in a residential pocket of Trenton nicknamed the Burg. No one ever really leaves the Burg. You can relocate in Antarctica, but if you were born and raised in the Burg you're a Burger for life. Houses are small and obsessively neat. Televisions are large and loud. Lots are narrow. Families are extended. There are no pooper-scooper laws in the Burg. If your dog does his business on someone else's lawn, the next morning the doo-doo will be on your front porch. Life is simple in the Burg.

I put the Buick into gear, rolled out of the apartment building lot, headed for Hamilton, and followed Hamilton to St. Francis Hospital. My parents live a couple blocks behind St. Francis on Roosevelt Street. Their house is a duplex built at a time when families needed only one bathroom and dishes were washed by hand.

My mother was at the door when I pulled to the curb. My grandmother Mazur stood elbow to elbow with my mother. They were short, slim women with facial features that suggested Mongol ancestors . . . probably in the form of crazed marauders.

"Thank goodness you're here," my mother said, eyeing me as I got out of the car and walked toward her. "What are those shoes? They look like work boots."

"Betty Szajak and Emma Getz and me went to that male dancer place last week," Grandma said, "and they had some men parading around, looking like construction workers, wearing boots just like those. Then next thing you knew they ripped their clothes off and all they had left was those boots and these little silky black baggie things that their ding-dongs jiggled around in."

My mother pressed her lips together and made the sign of the cross. "You didn't tell me about this," she said to my grandmother.

"Guess it slipped my mind. Betty and Emma and me were going to bingo at the church, but it turned out there wasn't any bingo on account of the Knights of Columbus was holding some to-do there. So we decided to check out the men at that new club downtown." Grandma gave me an elbow. "I put a fiver right in one of those baggies!"

"Jesus H. Christ," my father said, rattling his paper in the living room.

Grandma Mazur came to live with my parents several years ago when my grandpa Mazur went to the big poker game in the sky. My mother accepts this as a daughter's obligation. My father has taken to reading *Guns & Ammo*.

"So what's up?" I asked. "Why did you page me?"

"We need a detective," Grandma said.

My mother rolled her eyes and ushered me into the kitchen. "Have a cookie," she said, setting the cookie jar on the small Formica-topped kitchen table. "Can I get you a glass of milk? Some lunch?"

I lifted the lid on the cookie jar and looked inside. Chocolate chip. My favorite.

"Tell her," Grandma said to my mother, giving her a poke in the side. "Wait until you hear this," she said to me. "This is a good one."

I raised my eyebrows at my mother.

"We have a family problem," my mother said. "Your uncle Fred is missing. He went out to the store and hasn't come home yet."

"When did he go out?"

"Friday."

I paused with a cookie halfway to my mouth. "It's Monday!"

"Isn't this a pip?" Grandma said. "I bet he was beamed up by aliens."

Uncle Fred is married to my grandma Mazur's first cousin Mabel. If I had to guess his age I'd have to say somewhere between seventy and infinity. Once people start to stoop and wrinkle they all look alike to me. Uncle Fred was someone I saw at weddings and funerals and once in a while at Giovichinni's Meat Market, ordering a quarter pound of olive loaf. Eddie Such, the butcher, would have the olive loaf on the scale and Uncle Fred would say, "You've got the olive loaf on a piece of waxed paper. How much does that piece of waxed paper weigh? You're not gonna charge me for that waxed paper, are you? I want some money off for the waxed paper."

I shoved the cookie into my mouth. "Have you filed a missing persons report with the police?"

"Mabel did that first thing," my mother said.

"And?"

"And they haven't found him."

I went to the refrigerator and poured out a glass of milk for myself. "What about the car? Did they find the car?"

"The car was in the Grand Union parking lot. It was all locked up nice and neat."

"He was never right after that stroke he had in ninety-five," Grandma said. "I don't think his elevator went all the way to the top anymore, if you know what I mean. He could have just wandered off like one of those Alzheimer's people. Anybody think to check the cereal aisle in the supermarket? Maybe he's just standing there 'cause he can't make up his mind."

My father mumbled something from the living room about my grandmother's elevator, and my mother slid my father a dirty look through the kitchen wall.

I thought it was too weird. Uncle Fred was missing. This sort of thing just didn't happen in our family. "Did anybody go out to look for him?"

"Ronald and Walter. They covered all the neighborhoods around the Grand Union, but nobody's seen him."

Ronald and Walter were Fred's sons. And probably they'd enlisted their kids to help, too.

"We figure you're just the person to take a crack at this," Grandma said, "on account of that's what you do . . . you find people."

"I find criminals."

"Your aunt Mabel would be grateful if you'd look for Fred," my mother said. "Maybe you could just go over and talk to her and see what you think."

"She needs a detective," I said. "I'm not a detective."

"Mabel asked for you. She said she didn't want this going out of the family."

My internal radar dish started to hum. "Is there something you're not telling me?"

"What's to tell?" my mother said. "A man wandered off from his car."

I drank my milk and rinsed the glass. "Okay, I'll go talk to Aunt Mabel. But I'm not promising anything."

UNCLE FRED AND Aunt Mabel live on Baker Street, on the fringe of the Burg, three blocks over from my parents. Their ten-year-old Pontiac station wagon was parked at the curb and just about spanned the length of their rowhouse. They've lived in the rowhouse for as long as I can remember, raising two children, entertaining five grandchildren, and annoying the hell out of each other for over fifty years.

Aunt Mabel answered my knock on her door. She was a rounder, softer version of Grandma Mazur. Her white hair was perfectly permed. She was dressed in yellow polyester slacks and a matching floral blouse. Her earrings were large clip-ons, her lipstick was a bright red, and her eyebrows were brown crayon.

"Well, isn't this nice," Aunt Mabel said. "Come into the kitchen. I got a coffee cake from Giovichinni today. It's the good kind, with the almonds."

Certain proprieties were observed in the Burg. No matter that your husband was kidnapped by aliens, visitors were offered coffee cake.

I followed after Aunt Mabel and waited while she cut the cake. She poured out coffee and sat opposite me at the kitchen table.

"I suppose your mother told you about your uncle Fred," she said. "Fifty-two years of marriage, and *poof*, he's gone."

"Did Uncle Fred have any medical problems?"

"The man was healthy as a horse."

"How about his stroke?"

"Well, yes, but everybody has a stroke once in a while. And that stroke didn't slow him down any. Most of the time he remembered things no one else would remember. Like that business with the garbage. Who would remember a thing like that? Who would even care about it? Such a fuss over nothing."

I knew I was going to regret asking, but I felt compelled. "What about the garbage?"

Mabel helped herself to a piece of coffee cake. "Last month there was a new driver on the garbage truck, and he skipped over our house. It only happened once, but would my husband forget a thing like that? No. Fred never forgot anything. Especially if it had to do with money. So at the end of the month Fred wanted two dollars back on account of we pay quarterly, you see, and Fred had already paid for the missed day."

I nodded in understanding. This didn't surprise me at all. Some men played golf. Some men did crossword puzzles. Uncle Fred's hobby was being cheap.

"That was one of the things Fred was supposed to do on Friday," Mabel said. "The garbage company was making him crazy. He went there in the morning, but they wouldn't give him his money without proof that he'd paid. Something about the computer messing up some of the accounts. So Fred was going back in the afternoon."

For two dollars. I did a mental head slap. If I'd been the clerk Fred had talked to at the garbage company I'd have given Fred two dollars out of my own pocket just to get rid of him. "What garbage company is this?"

"RGC. The police said Fred never got there. Fred had a whole list of errands he was going to do. He was going to the cleaners, the bank, the supermarket, and RGC."

"And you haven't heard from him."

"Not a word. Nobody's heard anything."

I had a feeling there wasn't going to be a happy ending to this story.

"Do you have any idea where Fred might be?"

"Everyone thinks he just wandered away, like a big dummy."

"What do you think?"

Mabel did an up-and-down thing with her shoulders. Like she didn't know what to think. Whenever I did that, it meant I didn't want to *say* what I was thinking.

"If I show you something, you have to promise not to tell anyone," Mabel said.

Oh boy.

She went to a kitchen drawer and took out a packet of pictures. "I found these in Fred's desk. I was looking for the checkbook this morning, and this is what I found."

I stared at the first picture for at least thirty seconds before I realized what I was seeing. The print was taken in shadow and looked underexposed. The perimeter was a black plastic trash bag, and in the center of the photo was a bloody hand severed at the wrist. I thumbed through the rest of the pack. More of the same. In some the bag was spread wider, revealing more body parts. What looked like a shinbone, part of a torso maybe, something that might have been the back of the head. Hard to tell if it was man or woman.

The shock of the pictures had me holding my breath, and I was getting a buzzing sensation in my head. I didn't want to ruin my bounty-hunter image and keel over onto the floor, so I concentrated on quietly resuming breathing.

"You have to give these to the police," I said.

Mabel gave her head a shake. "I don't know what Fred was doing with these pictures. Why would a person have pictures like this?"

No date on the front or the back. "Do you know when they were taken?

"No. This is the first I saw them."

"Do you mind if I look through Fred's desk?"

"It's in the cellar," Mabel said. "Fred spent a lot of time down there."

It was a battered government-issue desk. Probably bought at a Fort Dix yard sale. It was positioned against a wall opposite the washer and dryer. And it was set on a stained piece of wall-to-wall carpet that I assumed had been saved when new carpet was laid upstairs.

I pawed through the drawers, finding the usual junk. Pencils and pens. A drawer filled with instruction booklets and warranty cards for household appliances. Another drawer devoted to old issues of *National Geographic*. The magazines were dog-eared, and I could see Fred down here, escaping from Mabel, reading about the vanishing rain forests of Borneo.

A canceled RGC check had been carefully placed under a paperweight. Fred had probably made a copy to take with him and had left the original here.

There are parts of the country where people trust banks to keep their checks and to simply forward computer-generated statements each month. The Burg isn't one of those places. Residents of the Burg aren't that trusting of computers or banks. Residents of the Burg like paper. My relatives hoard canceled checks like Scrooge McDuck hoards quarters.

I didn't see any more photos of dead bodies. And I couldn't find any notes or sales receipts that might be connected to the pictures.

"You don't suppose Fred killed this person, do you?" Mabel asked.

I didn't know what I supposed. What I knew was that I was very creeped out. "Fred didn't seem like the sort of person to do something like this," I told Mabel. "Would you like me to pass these on to the police for you?"

"If you think that's the right thing to do."

Without a shadow of a doubt.

I had phone calls to make, and my parents' house was closer than my apartment and less expensive than using my cell phone, so I rumbled back to Roosevelt Street.

"How'd it go?" Grandma asked, rushing into the foyer to meet me.

"It went okay."

"You gonna take the case?"

"It's not a case. It's a missing person. Sort of."

"You're gonna have a devil of a time finding him if it was aliens," Grandma said.

I dialed the central dispatch number for the Trenton Police Department and asked for Eddie Gazarra. Gazarra and I grew up together, and now he was married to my cousin Shirley the Whiner. He was a good friend, a good cop, and a good source for police information.

"You need something," Gazarra said.

"Hello to you, too."

"Am I wrong?"

"No. I need some details on a recent investigation."

"I can't give you that kind of stuff."

"Of course you can," I said. "Anyway, this is about Uncle Fred."

"The missing Uncle Fred?"

"That's the one."

"What do you want to know?"

"Anything."

"Hold on."

He was back on the line a couple minutes later, and I could hear him leafing through papers. "It says here Fred was reported missing on Friday, which is technically too early for a missing person, but we always keep our eyes open anyway. Especially with old folks. Sometimes they're out there wandering around looking for the road to Oz."

"You think that's what Fred's doing? Looking for Oz?"

"Hard to say. Fred's car was found in the Grand Union parking lot. The car was locked up. No sign of forced entry. No sign of struggle. No sign of theft. There was dry cleaning laid out on the backseat."

"Anything else in the car? Groceries?"

"Nope. No groceries."

"So he got to the dry cleaner but not the supermarket."

"I have a chronology of events here," Gazarra said. "Fred left his house at one o'clock, right after he ate lunch. Next stop that we know of was the bank, First Trenton Trust. Their records show he withdrew two hundred dollars from the automatic teller in the lobby at two thirty-five. The cleaner, next to Grand Union in the same strip mall, said Fred picked his cleaning up around two forty-five. And that's all we have."

"There's an hour missing. It takes ten minutes to get from the Burg to Grand Union and First Trenton."

"Don't know," Gazarra said. "He was supposed to go to RGC Waste Haulers, but RGC says he never showed up."

"Thanks, Eddie."

"If you want to return the favor, I could use a baby-sitter Saturday night."

Gazarra could always use a baby-sitter. His kids were cute but death on baby-sitters.

"Gee, Eddie, I'd love to help you out, but Saturday's a bad day. I promised somebody I'd do something on Saturday."

"Yeah, right."

"Listen, Gazarra, last time I baby-sat for your kids they cut two inches off my hair."

"You shouldn't have fallen asleep. What were you doing sleeping on the job, anyway?"

"It was one in the morning!"

My next call was to Joe Morelli. Joe Morelli is a plainclothes cop who has skills not covered in the policeman's handbook. A couple months ago, I let him into my life and my bed. A couple weeks ago, I kicked him out. We'd seen each other several times since then on chance encounters and arranged dinner dates. The chance encounters were always warm. The dinner dates took the temperature up a notch and more often than not involved loud talking, which I called a discussion and Morelli called a fight.

None of these meetings had ended in the bedroom. When

you grow up in the Burg there are several mantras little girls learn at an early age. One of them is that men don't buy goods they can get for free. Those words of wisdom hadn't stopped me from giving my goods away to Morelli, but they *did* stop me from *continuing* to give them away. That plus a false pregnancy scare. Although I have to admit, I had mixed feelings about not being pregnant. There was a smidgen of regret mixed with the relief. And probably it was the regret more than the relief that made me take a more serious look at my life and my relationship with Morelli. That and the realization that Morelli and I don't see eye-to-eye on a lot of things. Not that we'd entirely given up on the relationship. It was more that we were in a holding pattern with each of us staking out territory . . . not unlike the Arab-Israeli conflict.

I tried Morelli's home phone, office number, and car phone. No luck. I left messages everywhere and left my cell phone number on his pager.

"Well, what did you find out?" Grandma wanted to know when I hung up.

"Not much. Fred left the house at one, and a little over an hour later he was at the bank and the cleaner. He must have done something in that time, but I don't know what."

My mother and my grandmother looked at each other.

"What?" I asked. "What?"

"He was probably taking care of some personal business," my mother said. "You don't want to bother yourself with it."

"What's the big secret?"

Another exchange of looks between my mother and grandmother.

"There's two kinds of secrets," Grandma said. "One kind is where nobody knows the secret. And the other kind is where everybody knows the secret, but *pretends* not to know the secret. This is the second kind of secret."

"So?"

"It's about his honeys," Grandma said.

"His honeys?"

"Fred always has a honey on the side," Grandma said. "Should have been a politician."

"You mean Fred has affairs? He's in his seventies!"

"Midlife crisis," Grandma said.

"Seventy isn't midlife," I said. "Forty is midlife."

Grandma slid her uppers around some. "Guess it depends how long you intend to live."

I turned to my mother. "You knew about this?"

My mother took a couple deli bags of cold cuts out of the refrigerator and emptied them on a plate. "The man's been a philanderer all his life. I don't know how Mabel's put up with it."

"Booze," Grandma said.

I made myself a liverwurst sandwich and took it to the table. "Do you think Uncle Fred might have run off with one of his girlfriends?"

"More likely one of their husbands picked Fred up and drove him to the landfill," Grandma said. "I can't see cheapskate Fred paying for the cleaning if he was going to run off with one of his floozies."

"You have any idea who he was seeing?"

"Hard to keep track," Grandma said. She looked over at my mother. "What do you think, Ellen? You think he's still seeing Loretta Walenowski?"

"I heard that was over," my mother said.

My cell phone rang in my shoulder bag.

"Hey, Cupcake," Morelli said. "What's the disaster?"

"How do you know it's a disaster?"

"You left messages on three different phones plus my pager.

It's either a disaster or you want me bad, and my luck hasn't been that good today."

"I need to talk to you."

"Now?"

"It'll only take a minute."

THE SKILLET IS a sandwich shop next to the hospital and could be better named the Grease Pit. Morelli got there ahead of me. He was standing, soda in hand, looking like the day was already too long.

He smiled when he saw me . . . and it was the nice smile that included his eyes. He draped an arm around my neck, pulled me to him, and kissed me. "Just so my day isn't a complete waste," he said.

"We have a family problem."

"Uncle Fred?"

"Boy, you know everything. You should be a cop."

"Wiseass," Morelli said. "What do you need?"

I handed him the packet of pictures. "Mabel found these in Fred's desk this morning."

He shuffled through them. "Christ. What is this shit?"

"Looks like body parts."

He tapped me on the head with the stack of pictures. "Comedian."

"You have any ideas here?"

"They need to go to Arnie Mott," Morelli said. "He's in charge of the investigation."

"Arnie Mott has the initiative of a squash."

"Yeah. But he's still in charge. I can pass them on for you."

"What does this mean?"

Joe shook his head, still studying the top photo. "I don't know, but this looks real."

I MADE AN illegal U-turn on Hamilton and parked just short of Vinnie's office, docking the Buick behind a black Mercedes S600V, which I suspected belonged to Ranger. Ranger changed cars like other men changed socks. The only common denominator with Ranger's cars was that they were always expensive and they were always black.

Connie looked over at me when I swung through the front door. "Was Briggs really only three feet tall?"

"Three feet tall and uncooperative. I should have read the physical description on his application for appearance bond before I knocked on his door. Don't suppose anything else came in?"

"Sorry," Connie said. "Nothing."

"This is turning into a real bummer of a day. My uncle Fred is missing. He went out to run errands on Friday, and that was the last anyone's seen him. They found his car in the Grand Union parking lot." No need to mention the butchered body.

"I had an uncle do that once," Lula said. "He walked all the way to Perth Amboy before someone found him. It was one of them senior moments."

The door to the inner office was closed, and Ranger was nowhere to be seen, so I guessed he was talking to Vinnie. I cut my eyes in that direction. "Ranger in there?"

"Yeah," Connie said. "He did some work for Vinnie."

"Work?"

"Don't ask," Connie said.

"Not bounty hunter stuff."

"Not nearly."

I left the office and waited outside. Ranger appeared five minutes later. Ranger's Cuban-American. His features are Anglo, his eyes are Latino, his skin is the color of a mocha latte, and his body is as good as a body can get. He had his black hair pulled back into a ponytail. He was wearing a black T-shirt that fit him like a tattoo and black SWAT pants tucked into black high-top boots.

"Yo," I said.

Ranger looked at me over the top of his shades. "Yo yourself."

I gazed longingly at his car. "Nice Mercedes."

"Transportation," Ranger said. "Nothing fancy."

Compared to what? The Batmobile? "Connie said you were talking to Vinnie."

"Transacting business, babe. I don't *talk* to Vinnie."

"That's sort of what I'd like to discuss with you . . . business. You know how you've kind of been my mentor with this bounty hunter stuff?"

"Eliza Doolittle and Henry Higgins Do Trenton."

"Yeah. Well, the truth is, the bounty huntering isn't going all that good."

"No one's jumping bail."

"That too."

Ranger leaned against his car and crossed his arms over his chest. "And?"

"And I've been thinking maybe I should diversify."

"And?"

"And I thought you might help me."

"You talking about building a portfolio? Investing money?"

"No. I'm talking about *making* money."

Ranger tipped his head back and laughed softly. "Babe, you don't want to do that kind of diversifying."

I narrowed my eyes.

"Okay," he said. "What did you have in mind?"

"Something legal."

"There's all kinds of legal."

"I want something entirely legal."

Ranger leaned closer and lowered his voice. "Let me explain my work ethic to you. I don't do things I feel are morally wrong. But sometimes my moral code strays from the norm. Sometimes my moral code is inconsistent with the law. Much of what I do is in that gray area just beyond entirely legal."

"All right then, how about steering me toward something mostly legal and definitely morally right."

"You sure about this?"

"Yes." No. Not at all.

Ranger's face was expressionless. "I'll think about it."

He slipped into his car, the engine caught, and Ranger rolled away.

I had a missing uncle who quite possibly had butchered a woman and stuffed her parts into a garbage bag, but I also was a month overdue on my rent. Somehow I was going to have to manage both problems.

TWO

I WENT BACK to Cloverleaf Apartments and parked in the lot.
I got a black nylon web utility belt from the back of the Buick
and strapped it on, arming it with a stun gun, pepper spray, and
cuffs. Then I went in search of the building superintendent. Ten
minutes later I had a key to Briggs' apartment and was at his
door. I rapped twice and yelled, "Bail enforcement." No answer.
I opened the door with the key and walked in. Briggs wasn't
there.

Patience is a virtue bounty hunters need and I lack. I found
a chair facing the door and sat down to wait. I told myself I'd
stay for as long as it took, but I knew it was a lie. To begin with,
being in his apartment like this was a little illegal. And then there
was the fact that I was actually pretty scared. Okay, so he was
only three feet tall . . . that didn't mean he couldn't shoot a gun.
And it didn't mean he didn't have friends who were six-foot-four
and nuts.

I'd been sitting for a little over an hour when there was a
knock at the door, and I realized a piece of paper had been slipped
under the doorjamb.

"Dear Loser, I know you're there," the message on the paper said, "and I'm not coming home until you leave."

Great.

MY APARTMENT BUILDING bears a striking resemblance to Cloverleaf. Same blocky brick structure, same minimalist attention to quality. Most of the tenants in my building are senior citizens with a few Hispanics thrown in to make things interesting. I'd come directly home after vacating Briggs' apartment. I'd gotten my mail when I'd passed through the lobby, and I didn't have to open the envelopes to know the contents. Bills, bills, bills. I unlocked my door, tossed the mail on the kitchen counter, and checked my answering machine for messages. None. My hamster, Rex, was asleep in his soup can in his cage.

"Hey, Rex," I said. "I'm home."

There was a slight rustling of pine shavings but that was it. Rex wasn't much for small talk. I went to the refrigerator to get him a grape and found a sticky note tacked to the door. "I'm bringing dinner. See you at six." The note wasn't signed, but I knew it was from Morelli by the way my nipples got hard.

I threw the note into the trash and dropped the grape into Rex's cage. There was a major upheaval of shavings. Rex appeared butt-first, stuffed the grape into his cheek pouch, blinked his shiny black eyes, twitched his whiskers at me, and scooted back into the can.

I took a shower, did the gel-and-blow-dry thing with my hair, dressed in jeans and a denim shirt, and flopped onto the bed facedown to think. My usual thinking position is on my back, but I didn't want to wreck my hair for Morelli.

The first thing I thought about was Randy Briggs and how it would feel good to drag him by his little feet down the stairs of his apartment building, with his stupid melon head going bump, bump, bump on the steps.

Then I thought about Uncle Fred, and I got a sharp pain in my left eyeball. "Why me?" I said, but there was no one around to answer.

Truth is, Fred wasn't exactly Indiana Jones, and I couldn't imagine anything other than an Alzheimer's attack happening to Fred, in spite of the gory photographs. I searched my mind for memories of him, but found very little. When he smiled it was big and phony, and his false teeth made a clicking sound. And he walked with his toes pointed out . . . like a duck. That was it. Those were my memories of Uncle Fred.

I dozed off while walking down memory lane, and suddenly I awoke with a start, all senses alert. I heard the front door to my apartment click open, and my heart started knocking around in my chest. I'd locked the door when I'd gotten home. And now someone had opened it. And that someone was in my apartment. I held my breath. Please, God, let it be Morelli. I didn't much like the idea of Morelli sneaking into my apartment, but it was a lot more palatable than coming face-to-face with some ugly, droolly guy who wanted to squeeze my neck until my tongue turned purple.

I scrambled to my feet and searched for a weapon, settling for a stiletto-heeled pink-satin pump left over from a stint as bridesmaid for Charlotte Nagy. I crept out of my bedroom, through the living room, and peeked into the kitchen.

It was Ranger. And he was dumping the contents of a large plastic container into a bowl.

"Jesus," I said, "you scared the hell out of me. Why don't you try knocking next time."

"I left you a note. I thought you'd be expecting me."

"You didn't sign the note. How was I supposed to know it was you?"

He turned and looked at me. "Were there any other possibilities?"

25

"Morelli."

"You back with him?"

Good question. I glanced at the food. Salad. "Morelli would have brought sausage sandwiches."

"That stuff'll kill you, Babe."

We were bounty hunters. People shot at us. And Ranger was worried about trans fats and nitrates. "I'm not sure our life expectancy is all that good anyway," I said.

My kitchen is small, and Ranger seemed to be taking up a lot of space, standing very close. He reached around me and snagged two salad bowls from the over-the-counter cabinet. "It's not length of life that's important," he said. "It's the quality. The goal is to have purity of mind and body."

"Do you have a pure mind and body?"

Ranger locked eyes with me. "Not right now."

Hmm.

He filled a bowl with salad and handed it to me. "You need money."

"Yes."

"There are lots of ways to make money."

I stared down into my salad, pushing greens around with my fork. "True."

Ranger waited for me to look up at him before he spoke. "You sure you want to do this?"

"No, I'm not sure. I don't even know what we're talking about. I don't actually know what it is that you *do*. I'm just searching for a second profession that'll supplement my income."

"Any restrictions or preferences?"

"No drugs or illegal gun sales."

"Do you think I'd deal drugs?"

"No. That was thoughtless."

He helped himself to salad. "What I have going now is a renovation job."

This sounded appealing. "You mean like interior decorating?"

"Yeah. Guess you could call it interior decorating."

I tried the salad. It was pretty good, but it needed something. Croutons fried in butter. Big chunks of fattening cheese. And beer. I looked in vain for another bag. I checked the refrigerator. No beer there either.

"This is the way it works," Ranger said. "I send a team in to renovate, and then I place one or two people in the building to take care of long-term maintenance." Ranger looked up from his food. "You're keeping in shape, right? You run?"

"Sure. I run all the time." I run *never*. My idea of exercise is to barrel through a shopping mall.

Ranger gave me a dark look. "You're lying."

"Well, I *think* about running."

He finished his food and put the bowl in the dishwasher. "I'll pick you up tomorrow at five A.M."

"Five A.M.! To start an interior decorating job?"

"It's the way I like to do it."

A warning message flashed through my brain. "Maybe I should know more—"

"It's routine. Nothing special." He checked his watch. "I have to go. Business meeting."

I didn't want to speculate on the nature of his business meeting.

I BUZZED THE television on, but couldn't find anything to watch. No hockey. No fun movies. I went to my shoulder bag and pulled out the large envelope from the copier. I'm not sure why, but I'd made color copies of the pictures before meeting Morelli. I'd been able to fit six photos to a page and had filled four pages. I spread the pages on my dining-room table.

Not nice stuff to look at.

When the photos were laid out side-by-side, certain things became evident. I was pretty sure there was only one body and that it wasn't the body of an old person. No gray hair. And the skin was firm. Difficult to tell if it was a woman or a young man. Some of the pictures had been taken quite close. Some were from further away. It didn't look like the parts were ever rearranged. But the bag was sometimes pulled down to reveal more.

Okay, Stephanie, put yourself in the photographer's shoes. Why are you taking these pictures? Trophy shots? I didn't think so, because none showed the face. And there were twenty-four pictures here, so the roll was intact. If I wanted a remembrance of this grisly act, I'd want a face shot. Ditto for proof that the job had been done. Proof of a kill required a face shot. What was left? A visual record by someone who didn't want to disturb the evidence. So maybe Uncle Fred happened on a bag of body parts and ran out and got himself a point-and-shoot. And then what? Then he put the pictures in his desk drawer and disappeared while running errands.

That was my best guess, as weak as it was. The truth is, the pictures could have been taken five years ago. Someone could have given them to Fred for safekeeping or as a macabre joke.

I stuffed the prints back into their envelope and grabbed my shoulder bag. I thought searching the neighborhood around Grand Union would be wasted effort, but I felt the need to do it anyway.

I drove to a residential area behind the strip mall and parked on the street. I grabbed my flashlight and set out on foot, walking streets and back alleys, looking behind bushes and trash cans, calling Fred's name. When I was a kid I had a cat named Katherine. She showed up on our doorstep one day and refused to leave. We started feeding her on the back porch, and then somehow she found her way into the kitchen. She went out at night to roam the neighborhood, and slept curled up in a ball on my bed during the day. One night Katherine went out and never came back. For days I walked the streets and alleys, looking behind bushes and trash cans, calling her name, just like I was doing now for Fred. My mother said cats sometimes wander off like that when it's their time to die. I thought it was a lot of hooey.

I STUMBLED OUT of bed at four-thirty, staggered into the bathroom and stood in the shower until my eyes opened. After a while my skin started to shrivel, and I figured I was done. I toweled off and shook my head by way of styling my hair. I didn't know what I was supposed to wear for interior decorating, so I wore what I always wore . . . jeans and a T-shirt. And then to dress it up, just in case this actually turned out to be interior decorating, I added a belt and a jacket.

Ranger was waiting in the parking lot when I swung out the back door. He was driving a shiny black Range Rover with tinted side windows. Ranger's cars were always new and their point of purchase was never easy to explain. Three men took up the backseat. Two were black, one was of indeterminate origin. All three men had Marine buzz cuts. All were wearing black SWAT pants and black T-shirts. All were heavily muscled. Not an ounce of fat among them. None of them looked like interior decorators.

I buckled myself into the seat next to Ranger. "Is that the interior decorating team in the backseat?"

Ranger smiled in the predawn darkness and cruised out of the lot.

"I'm dressed different from everybody else," I said.

Ranger stopped at the light on Hamilton. "I've got a jacket and a vest for you in the back."

"This isn't interior decorating, is it?"

"There's all kinds of interior decorating, Babe."

"About the vest—"

"Kevlar."

Kevlar was bulletproof. "Rats," I said. "I hate getting shot at. You know how I hate getting shot at."

"Just a precaution," Ranger said. "Probably no one will get shot."

Probably?

We rode in silence through center city. Ranger was in his zone. Thinking private thoughts. The guys in back looking like they had no thoughts at all—ever. And me, debating jumping out of the car at the next light and running like hell back to my apartment. And at the same time, as ridiculous as it sounds, I was keeping an eye peeled for Fred. He was stuck in my brain. It was like that with my cat, Katherine, too. She'd been gone fifteen years, but I always looked twice when I caught a glimpse of a black cat. Unfinished business, I guess.

"Where are we going?" I finally asked.

"Apartment building on Sloane. Gonna do some house cleaning."

Sloane Street runs parallel and two blocks over from Stark. Stark is the worst street in the city, filled with drugs and despair and feed-lot housing. The ghetto gentrifies as the blocks march south, and much of Sloane is the demarcation line between the lawless and the law-abiding. It's a constant struggle to hold the line and keep the pushers and hookers off Sloane. And word is that lately Sloane's been losing the battle.

Ranger drove three blocks up Sloane and parked. He nodded at the yellow-brick building across the street, two doors down. "That's our building. We're going to the third floor."

The building was four stories tall, and I guessed there were two or three small apartments on each floor. Ground-level brick was covered with gang graffiti. Windows were dark. No street traffic. Wind-blown trash banked against curbs and collected in doorways.

I glanced from the building to Ranger. "You sure this is legal?"

"Been hired by the landlord," Ranger said.

"Does this housecleaning involve people or is it just . . . things?"

Ranger looked at me.

"There's a legal process involved in getting people and their possessions out of an apartment," I said. "You need to present an eviction notice and—"

"The legal process is moving a little slow," Ranger said. "And in the meantime, the kids in this building are being harassed by the people who come to shoot up in 3C."

"Think of this as community service," one of the guys in the back said.

The other two nodded. "Yeah," they said. "Community service."

I cracked my knuckles and chewed on my lower lip.

Ranger angled from behind the wheel, walked to the rear of the Range Rover, and opened the door. He gave everyone a flak vest, and then he gave everyone a black windbreaker that had SECURITY printed in large white letters on the back.

I strapped my vest on and watched while everyone else buckled on black nylon web utility belts and holstered guns.

"Let me take a wild guess here," Ranger said, slinging an arm around my shoulder. "You forgot to bring your gun."

"Interior decorators don't use guns."

"They do in this neighborhood."

The men were lined up in front of me.

"Gentlemen," Ranger said, "this is Ms. Plum."

The indeterminate-origin guy put his hand out. "Lester Santos."

The next man in line did the same. "Bobby Brown."

The last man was Tank. It was easy to see how he'd come by the name.

"I better not get into trouble for this," I said to Ranger. "I'm going to be really bummed if I get arrested. I hate getting arrested."

Santos grinned. "Man, you don't like to get shot. You don't like to get arrested. You don't know how to have fun at all."

Ranger shrugged into his jacket and set off, crossing the street with the band of merry men closing ranks behind him.

We entered the building and climbed two flights of stairs. Ranger went to 3C and listened at the door. The rest of us flattened against the wall. No one spoke. Ranger and Santos stood, guns in hand. Brown and Tank held flashlights.

I braced myself, expecting Ranger to kick the door down, but instead, he took a key from his pocket and inserted it in the lock. The door started to open but caught on a security chain. Ranger took two steps back and threw himself at the door, catching the door at chain height with his shoulder. The door popped open, and Ranger was in first. Then everyone was in except me. Lights flashed on. Ranger shouted, "Security!" and everything was chaos. Half-naked people were scrambling off floor mattresses. Women were shrieking. Men were swearing.

Ranger's team went room by room, cuffing people, lining them up against the living room wall. Six people in all.

One of the men was berserk, waving his arms to avoid getting cuffed. "You can't do this, you fuckers," he was yelling. "This is my apartment. This is private property. Somebody call the fucking police." He pulled a knife from his pants pocket and flicked it open.

Tank grabbed the guy by the back of his shirt, lifted him off his feet, and threw him out the window.

Everyone went still, staring dumbstruck at the shattered glass. My mouth was open and my heart had gone dead in my chest.

Ranger didn't look all that disturbed. "Have to replace that window," he said.

I heard a groan and some scraping sounds. I crossed the room to the window and looked out. The guy with the knife was spread-eagle on the fire escape, making feeble attempts to right himself.

I clapped a hand to my heart, relieved to find it had started beating again. "He's on the fire escape! God, for a minute there I thought you dumped him three stories."

Tank looked out the window with me. "You're right. He's on the fire escape. Sonovagun."

It was a small apartment. One small bedroom, one small bath, small kitchen, small living room. Kitchen counters were littered with fast-food wrappers and bags, empty soda cans, food-encrusted plates, and cheap, dented pots. The Formica was scarred with burn marks from cigarettes and crack cookers. Used syringes, half-eaten bagels, filthy dish towels, and unidentifiable garbage clogged the sink. Two stained and torn mattresses had been pushed against the wall in the living room. No lamps, no tables, no chairs, no sign that civilized man occupied the apartment. Just filth and clutter. The same refuse that banked against gutters outside filled the rooms of 3C. The air was stale with the odors of urine and pot and unwashed bodies and something nastier.

Santos and Brown herded the bedraggled occupants into the hall and down the stairs.

"What happens to them now?" I asked Ranger.

"Bobby'll drive them over to the meth clinic and drop them off. They're on their own from there."

"No arrests?"

"We don't do arrests. Not unless someone's FTA."

Tank returned from the car with a cardboard box filled with interior decorating supplies, which in this case consisted of disposable gloves, trash bags, and a coffee can for syringes.

"This is the deal," Ranger said to me. "We strip the apartment of everything not nailed down. Tomorrow the landlord will bring someone in to clean and do repairs."

"What's to stop the tenant from returning?"

Ranger just stared at me.

"Right," I said. "Stupid question."

IT WAS MIDMORNING when we went through with the broom. Santos and Brown had positioned themselves on folding chairs in the small vestibule downstairs. They were to take the first security shift. Tank was on his way to the landfill with the mattresses and bags of garbage. Ranger and I were left to lock up the apartment.

Ranger angled the brim of a Navy SEALs ball cap to shade his eyes. "So," he said, "what do you think of security work? You want to be on the team? I can let you take the graveyard shift with Tank."

"He isn't going to throw any more people out windows, is he?"

"Hard to say, Babe."

"I don't know if I'm cut out for this."

Ranger took his SEALs hat off and put it on me, tucking my hair behind my ears, letting his hands linger a moment too long. "You have to believe in what you're doing."

That could be a problem. And Ranger could be a problem. I was feeling much too attracted to him. Ranger wasn't listed under *potential boyfriends* in my Rolodex. Ranger was listed under *crazed mercenaries*. An attraction to Ranger would be like chasing after the doomsday orgasm.

I took a steadying breath. "I guess I could try a shift," I said. "See how it goes."

I WAS STILL wearing the hat when Ranger dropped me off at my apartment. I removed the cap and held it out to him. "Don't forget your SEALs hat."

Ranger looked at me from behind dark glasses. His eyes hidden. His thoughts unreadable. His voice soft. "Keep it. Looks good on you."

"It's a righteous hat."

He smiled. "Live up to it, Babe."

I pushed through the double glass doors into the lobby. I was about to take the stairs when the elevator opened and Mrs. Bestler leaned out. "Going up," she said. "Step to the rear of the car."

Mrs. Bestler was eighty-three and had an apartment on the third floor. When things got boring she played elevator operator.

"Morning, Mrs. Bestler," I said. "Second floor."

She hit the two button and eyeballed me. "Looks like you've been working. Catch any bad guys today?"

"Helped a friend clean an apartment."

Mrs. Bestler smiled. "What a good girl." The elevator stopped and the doors opened. "Second floor," Mrs. Bestler sang out. "Better dresses. Designer suits. Ladies' lounge."

I let myself into my apartment and went straight to the phone machine and its blinking red light.

I had two messages. The first was from Morelli, and it was for dinner. Miss Popularity, that's me.

"Meet you at Pino's at six," Morelli said.

Morelli's invitations always produced mixed emotions. The initial reaction was a sexual rush at the sound of his voice, the rush was followed by a queasy stomach while I considered his motives, and the queasy stomach eventually gave way to curiosity and anticipation. Ever the optimist.

The second message was from Mabel. "A man just came asking about Fred," Mabel said. "Something about a business deal, and he needed to find Fred right away. I explained how I couldn't help him, but I said you were on the job, so he shouldn't worry. I thought you might want to know."

I called Mabel back and asked who the man was and what he looked like.

"He was about my height," she said. "And he had brown hair."

"Caucasian?"

"Yes. And now that you mention it, he didn't give me his name."

"What kind of business deal was he talking about?"

"I don't know. He didn't say."

"Okay," I said. "Let me know if he bothers you again."

I checked in with the office to see if there were any new FTAs and was told no luck. I called my best friend, Mary Lou, but she couldn't talk because her youngest kid was sick with a cold, and the dog had eaten a sock and had just pooped it out on the living room rug.

I was contemplating Rex's soup can with new appreciation when the phone rang.

"I got it," Grandma said. "I got a name for you. I was at the beauty parlor this morning getting a set, and Harriet Schnable was there for a perm, and she said she heard at bingo that Fred's been paying calls on Winnie Black. Harriet isn't one of those to make something of nothing."

"Do you know Winnie Black?"

"Only through the seniors' club. She goes on the bus trip to Atlantic City sometimes. Her and her husband, Axel. I guess that's how Fred meets most of his honeys these days . . . at the seniors' meetings. A lot of those women are real hot to trot, if you know what I mean. I even got Winnie's address," Grandma said. "I called Ida Lukach. She's the club's membership chairman. She knows everything."

I took down the address and thanked Grandma.

"Personally, I'm hoping it was aliens," Grandma said. "But then I don't know what they'd want with an old fart like Fred."

I settled my new hat on my brown bear cookie jar and traded my jeans for a beige suit and heels. I didn't know Winnie Black, and I thought it wouldn't hurt to look professional. Sometimes people responded better to a suit than to jeans. I grabbed my shoulder bag, locked the apartment, and joined Mrs. Bestler in the elevator.

"Did he find you?" Mrs. Bestler wanted to know.

"Did who find me?"

"There was a man looking for you. Very polite. I let him off on your floor about ten minutes ago."

"He never knocked on my door. I would have heard him. I was in the kitchen almost the whole time."

"Isn't that odd." The elevator door opened to the lobby, and Mrs. Bestler smiled. "First floor. Ladies' handbags. Fine jewelry."

"What did the man look like?" I asked Mrs. Bestler.

"Oh, dear, he was big. Very big. And dark-skinned. African-American."

Not the man Mabel just called about. That guy was short and Caucasian.

"Did he have long hair? Maybe pulled back into a ponytail?"

"No. He almost didn't have any hair at all."

I did a fast check of the lobby. No big guy lurking in the corners. I exited the building and looked around the lot. Nobody there either. My visitor had disappeared. Too bad, I thought. I'd love an excuse not to visit Winnie Black. I'd talk to a census taker, a vacuum-cleaner salesman, a religious zealot. All preferable to

Winnie Black. It was bad enough knowing cheapskate Uncle Fred had a girlfriend. I really didn't want to *see* her. I didn't want to confront Winnie Black and have to imagine her in the sack with duck-footed Fred.

WINNIE LIVED IN a little bungalow on Low Street. White clap-board with blue shutters and a red door. Very patriotic. I parked, marched up to her front door, and rang the bell. I hadn't any idea what I was going to say to this woman. Probably something like, Excuse me, are you going around the block with my uncle Fred?

I was about to ring a second time when the door opened and Winnie Black peered out at me.

She had a pleasant, round face and a pleasant, round body, and she didn't look like the sort to boff someone's uncle.

I introduced myself and gave her my card. "I'm looking for Fred Shutz," I said. "He's been missing since Friday, and I was hoping you might be able to give me some information."

The pleasant expression froze on her face. "I'd heard he was missing, but I don't know what I can tell you."

"When did you see him last?"

"The day he disappeared. He stopped by for some coffee and cake. He did that sometimes. It was right after lunch. And he stayed for about an hour. Axel, my husband, was out getting the tires rotated on the Chrysler."

Axel was getting his tires rotated. Unh! Mental head slap. "Did Fred seem sick or worried? Did he give any indication that he might be going off somewhere?"

"He was . . . distracted. He said he had something big going on."

"Did he say any more about it?"

"No. But I got the feeling it had to do with the garbage com-pany. He was having a problem with his account. Something

about the computer deleting his name from the customer list. And
Fred said he had the goods on them, and he was going to make out
in spades. Those were his exact words—'make out in spades.' I
guess he never got to the garbage company."

"How do you know he never got to the garbage company?"
I asked Winnie.

Winnie seemed surprised at the question. "Everyone knows."

No secrets in the Burg.

"One other thing," I said. "I found some photographs on
Fred's desk. Did Fred ever mention any photographs to you?"

"No. Not that I can think of. Were these family photographs?"

"They were pictures of a garbage bag. And in some of the
pictures you could see the bag's contents."

"No. I would have remembered something like that."

I looked over her shoulder into the interior of her neat little
house. No husband in sight. "Is Axel around?"

"He's at the park with the dog."

I got back in the Buick and drove two blocks to the park. It
was a patch of well-tended grass, two blocks long and a block
wide. There were benches and flower beds and large trees, and
there was a small kids' play area at one end.

It wasn't hard to spot Axel Black. He was sitting on a bench,
lost in thought, with his dog at his side. The dog was a small
mutt type, sitting there, eyes glazed, looking a lot like Axel. The
difference was that Axel had glasses and the dog had hair.

I parked the car and approached the two. Neither moved,
even when I was standing directly in front of them.

"Axel Black?" I asked.

He looked up at me. "Yes?"

I introduced myself and gave him my card. "I'm looking for
Fred Shutz," I said. "And I've been talking to some of the seniors
who might have known Fred."

"Bet they've been giving you an earful," Axel said. "Old Fred was a real character. Cheapest man who ever walked the earth. Argued over every nickel. Never contributed to anything. And he thought he was a Romeo, too. Always cozying up to some woman."

"Doesn't sound like you thought much of him."

"Had no use for the man," Axel said. "Don't wish him any harm, but don't like him much either. The truth is, he was shifty."

"You have any idea what happened to him?"

"Think he might have paid too much attention to the wrong woman."

I couldn't help thinking maybe he was talking about Winnie as being the wrong woman. And maybe he ran Fred over with his Chrysler, picked him up, shoved him in the trunk, and dumped him into the river.

That didn't explain the photographs, but maybe the photographs had nothing to do with Fred's disappearance.

"Well," I said, "if you think of anything, let me know."

"You bet," Axel said.

Fred's sons, Ronald and Walter, were next on my list. Ronald was the line foreman at the pork roll factory. Walter and his wife, Jean, owned a convenience store on Howard Street. I thought it wouldn't hurt to talk to Walter and Ronald. Mostly because when my mother asked me what I was doing to find Uncle Fred I needed to have something to say.

Walter and Jean had named their store the One-Stop. It was across the street from a twenty-four-hour supermarket and would have been driven out of business long ago were it not for the fact that in one stop customers could purchase a loaf of bread, play the numbers, and put down twenty dollars on some nag racing at Freehold.

Walter was behind the register reading the paper when I

walked into the store. It was early afternoon, and the store was empty. Walter put the paper down and got to his feet. "Did you find him?"

"No. Sorry."

He took a deep breath. "Jesus. I thought you were coming to tell me he was dead."

"Do you think he's dead?"

"I don't know what I think. In the beginning I figured he just wandered off. Had another stroke or something. But now I can't figure it. None of it makes sense."

"Do you know anything about Fred having problems with his garbage company?"

"Dad had problems with everyone," Walter said.

I said good-bye to Walter, fired up the Buick, and drove across town to the pork roll factory. I parked in a visitor slot, went inside, and asked the woman at the front desk to pass a note through to Ronald.

Ronald came out a few minutes later. "I guess this is about Dad," he said. "Nice of you to help us look for him. I can't believe he hasn't turned up by now."

"Do you have any theories?"

"None I'd want to say out loud."

"The women in his life?"

Ronald shook his head. "He was a pip. Cheap as they come and could never keep his pecker in his pants. I don't know if he can still fire up the old engine, but he's still running around. Christ, he's seventy-two years old."

"Do you know anything about a disagreement with the garbage company?"

"No, but he's had a year-long feud with his insurance company."

THREE

I LEFT THE pork roll factory's parking lot and headed across town. It was almost five and government workers were clogging the roads. That was one of the many good things about Trenton. If you needed to practice Italian hand signals, there was no shortage of deserving bureaucrats.

I made a fast stop back at my apartment for some last-minute beautifying. I added an extra layer of mascara, fluffed my hair, and headed out.

Morelli was at the bar when I got to Pino's. He had his back to me, and he was lost in thought, elbows on the bar, head bent over his beer. He wore jeans and running shoes and a green plaid flannel shirt unbuttoned over a Gold's Gym T-shirt. A woman at the opposite end of the bar was watching him in the behind-the-bar mirror. Women did that now. They watched and wondered. When he was younger and his features were softer, women did more than watch. When he was younger, mothers statewide warned their daughters about Joe Morelli. And when he was younger, daughters statewide didn't give a darn what their mothers told them. Morelli's features were more angular these days.

His eyes were less inviting to strangers. Women included. So women watched and wondered what it would be like to be with Morelli.

I knew, of course, what it was like to be with Morelli. Morelli was magic.

I took the stool next to him and waved a "beer, please" signal to the bartender.

Morelli gave me an appraising look, his eyes dilated black in the dim bar light. "Business suit and heels," he said. "That means you've either been to a wake, a job interview, or you tried to trick some nice old lady out of information she shouldn't be giving you."

"Door number three."

"Let me guess . . . this has to do with your uncle Fred."

"Bingo."

"Having any luck?"

"Hard to say. Did you know Fred fooled around? He had a girlfriend."

Morelli grinned. "Fred Shutz? Hell, that's encouraging."

I rolled my eyes.

He took our beer glasses off the bar and motioned to the area set aside for tables. "If I was Mabel I'd be happy Fred was going elsewhere," he said. "I don't think Fred looks like a lot of fun."

"Especially since he collects pictures of dismembered bodies."

"I gave the pictures to Arnie. He didn't look happy. I think he was hoping Fred would turn up hitching a ride down Klockner Boulevard."

"Is Arnie going to do anything on this?"

"He'll probably go back and talk to Mabel some more. Run the photos through the system to see what comes up."

"Did you already run them through?"

"Yeah. And I didn't get anything."

There was nothing fancy about Pino's. At certain times of the day the bar was filled with cops unwinding after their shift. And at other times of the day the tables set aside for diners were filled with hungry Burg families. In between those times, Pino's was home to a few regular drunks, and the kitchen was taken over by cockroaches as big as barn cats. I ate at Pino's in spite of the roach rumor because Anthony Pino made the best pizza in Trenton. Maybe in all of Jersey.

Morelli gave his order and tipped back in his chair. "How friendly are you feeling toward me?"

"What'd you have in mind?"

"A date."

"I thought *this* was a date."

"No. This is dinner, so I can ask you about the date."

I sipped at my beer. "Must be some date."

"It's a wedding."

I sat up straighter in my chair. "It isn't *my* wedding, is it?"

"Not unless there's something going on in your life that I don't know about."

I blew out a sigh of relief. "Wow. For a minute there I was worried."

Morelli looked annoyed. "You mean if I asked you to marry me, that's the reaction I'd get?"

"Well, yeah."

"I thought you wanted to get married. I thought that was why we stopped sleeping together . . . because you didn't want sex without marriage."

I leaned forward on the table and cocked a single eyebrow at him. "Do you want to get married?"

"No, I don't want to get married. We've been all through this."

"Then my reaction doesn't matter, does it?"

"Jesus," Morelli said. "I need another beer."

"So what's with the wedding?"

"My cousin Julie's getting married on Saturday, and I need a date."

"You're giving me four days' notice to go to a wedding? I can't be ready for a wedding in four days. I need a new dress and shoes. I need a beauty parlor appointment. How am I going to do all this with four days' notice?"

"Okay, fuck it, we won't go," Morelli said.

"I guess I could do without the beauty parlor, but I definitely need new shoes."

"Heels," Morelli said. "High and spiky."

I fiddled with my beer glass. "I wasn't your last choice, was I?"

"You're my only choice. If my mother hadn't called this morning I wouldn't have remembered the wedding at all. This case I'm on is getting to me."

"Want to talk about it?"

"That's the last thing I want to do."

"How about Uncle Fred, want to talk about him some more?"

"The playboy."

"Yeah. I don't understand how he could just disappear."

"People disappear all the time," Morelli said. "They get on a bus and start life over. Or they jump off a bridge and float out with the tide. Sometimes people help them disappear."

"This is a man in his seventies who was too cheap to buy a bus ticket and would have had to walk miles to find a bridge. He left his cleaning in the car. He disappeared in the middle of running errands."

We both momentarily fell silent while our pizza was placed on the table.

"He'd just come from the bank," Morelli said when we were alone. "He was an old man. An easy mark. Someone could have driven up to him and forced him into their car."

"There were no signs of struggle."

"That doesn't mean one didn't take place."

I chewed on that while I ate my pizza. I'd had the same thought, and I didn't like it.

I told Morelli about my conversation with Winnie Black.

"She know anything about the pictures?"

"No."

"One other thing," Morelli said. "I wanted to tell you about Benito Ramirez."

I looked up from the pizza. Benito Ramirez was a heavy-weight professional boxer from Trenton. He liked to punish peo-ple and didn't limit the punishing to inside the ring. He liked to beat up on women. Liked to hear them beg while he inflicted his own brand of sick torture. And in fact, I knew some of that torture had ended in death, but there'd always been camp fol-lowers who'd gotten posthumous credit for the worst of Ramirez's crimes. He'd been involved in my very first case as a bounty hunter, and I'd been instrumental in putting him behind bars. His incarceration hadn't come soon enough for Lula. Ramirez had almost killed her. He'd raped her and beat her and cut her in terrible places. And then he'd left her naked, bloody body on my fire escape for me to find.

"What about Ramirez?" I asked Morelli.

"He's out."

"Out where?"

"Out of jail."

"*What?* What do you mean, he's out of jail? He almost killed Lula. And he was involved in a whole bunch of other murders." Not to mention that he'd stalked and terrorized *me*.

"He's released on parole, doing community service, and get-ting psychiatric counseling." Morelli paused to pull off another piece of pizza. "He had a real good lawyer."

Morelli had said this very matter of fact, but I knew he didn't feel matter of fact. He'd put on his cop face. The one that shut out emotion. The one with the hard eyes that gave nothing away.

I made a display of eating. Like I wasn't too bothered by this news either. When in fact, nausea was rolling through my stomach. "When did this happen?" I asked Morelli.

"Yesterday."

"And he's in town?"

"Just like always. Working out in the gym on Stark."

A big man, Mrs. Bestler had said. African-American. Polite. Prowling in my hall. Sweet Jesus, it might have been Ramirez.

"If you even *suspect* he's anywhere near you, I want to know," Morelli said.

I'd shoved another piece of pizza into my mouth, but I was having a hard time swallowing. "Sure."

We finished the pizza and dawdled over coffee.

"Maybe you should spend the night with me," Morelli said. "Just in case Ramirez decides to look you up."

I knew Morelli had other things in mind beyond my safety. And it was a tempting offer. But I'd already taken that bus, and it seemed like a ride that went nowhere. "Can't," I said. "I'm working tonight."

"I thought things were slow."

"This isn't for Vinnie. This is for Ranger."

Morelli did a little grimace. "I'm afraid to ask."

"It's nothing illegal. It's a security job."

"It always is," Morelli said. "Ranger does all kinds of security. Ranger keeps small Third World countries secure."

"This has nothing to do with gunrunning. This is legitimate. We're doing front-door security for an apartment building on Sloane."

"Sloane? Are you crazy? Sloane's at the edge of the war zone."

"That's why the building needs policing."

"Fine. Let Ranger get someone else. Trust me, you don't want to be out looking for a parking place on Sloane in the middle of the night."

"I won't have to look for a parking place. Tank's picking me up."

"You're working with a guy named Tank?"

"He's big."

"Jesus," Morelli said. "I had to fall in love with a woman who works with a guy named Tank."

"You love me?"

"Of course I love you. I just don't want to marry you."

I STEPPED OUT of the elevator and saw him sitting on the floor in the hall, next to my door. And I knew he was Mabel's visitor. I stuck my hand in my shoulder bag, searching for my pepper spray. Just in case. I rooted around in the bag for a minute or two, finding lipsticks and hair rollers and my stun gun, but no pepper spray.

"Either you're searching for your keys or your pepper spray," the guy said, getting to his feet. "So let me help you out, here." He reached into his pocket, pulled out a canister of pepper spray, and tossed it to me. "Be my guest," he said. And then he pushed my door open.

"How'd you do that? My door was locked."

"God-given talent," he said. "I thought it would save time if I searched your apartment before you got home."

I shook the spray to make sure it was live.

"Hey, don't get all bent out of shape," he said. "I didn't wreck anything. Although, I have to tell you, I did have fun in your panty drawer."

Instinct said he was playing with me. There was no doubt in my mind he'd gone through my apartment, but I doubted he lingered with my lingerie. Truth is, I didn't have a lot and what I had wasn't especially exotic. I felt violated all the same, and I would have sprayed him on the spot, but I didn't trust the spray in my hand. It was his, after all.

He rocked back on his heels. "Well, aren't you going to ask me in? Don't you want to know my name? Don't you want to know why I'm here?"

"Talk to me."

"Not here," he said. "I want to go in and sit down. I've had a long day."

"Forget it. Talk to me here."

"I don't think so. I want to go inside. It's more civilized. It would be like we were friends."

"We're not friends. And if you don't talk to me right now, I'm going to gas you."

He was about my height, five-foot-seven, and built like a fire-plug. It was hard to tell his age. Maybe late thirties. His brown hair was receding. His eyebrows looked like they'd been fed steroids. He was wearing ratty running shoes, black Levi's, and a dark gray sweatshirt.

He gave a big sigh and hauled a .38 out from under the sweatshirt. "Using the pepper spray wouldn't be a good idea," he said, "because then I'd have to shoot you."

My stomach dropped an inch and my heart started banging in my chest. I thought about the pictures and how someone had gotten themselves killed and mutilated. Fred had gotten involved somehow. And now I was involved, too. And there was a reasonable chance that I was being held at gunpoint by a guy who was on a first-name basis with the photographed garbage bag.

"If you shoot me in the hall, my neighbors will be all over you," I said.

"Fine. Then I'll shoot them, too."

I didn't like the idea of him shooting someone, especially me, so we both went into my apartment.

"This is much better," he said, heading for the kitchen, opening the refrigerator and getting a beer.

"Where'd that beer come from?"

"It came from me. Where do you think, the beer fairy? Lady, you need to go food shopping. It's unhealthy to live like this."

"Who *are* you?"

He shoved the gun under his waistband and stuck his hand out. "I'm Bunchy."

"What kind of a name is Bunchy?"

"When I was a kid I had this underwear problem."

Ugh. "You have a real name?"

"Yeah, but you don't need to know it. Everybody calls me Bunchy."

I was feeling better now that the gun wasn't pointed at me. Feeling good enough to be curious. "So what's this business deal with Fred?"

"Well, the truth is, Fred owes me some money."

"Uh-huh."

"And I want it."

"Good luck."

He chugged half a bottle of beer. "Now, see, that's not a good attitude."

"How did Fred come to owe you money?"

"Fred likes to play the ponies once in a while."

"Are you telling me you're Fred's bookie?"

"Yeah, that's what I'm telling you."

"I don't believe you. Fred didn't gamble."

"How do you know?"

"Besides, you don't look like a bookie," I said.

"How do bookies look?"

"Different." More respectable.

"I figure you're looking for Fred, and I'm looking for Fred, and maybe we can look for Fred together."

"Sure."

"See, that wasn't so difficult."

"Are you gonna go now?"

"Unless you want me to stay and watch television."

"No."

"I got a better television, anyway," he said.

AT 12:30 I was downstairs, waiting for Tank. I'd taken a nap, and I was feeling halfway alert. I was dressed in black jeans, black T-shirt, Ranger's SEALs hat, and the black SECURITY jacket. At Ranger's request, I had my gun clipped to my belt, and my shoulder bag held the other essentials—stun gun, pepper spray, flashlight, and cuffs.

The lot was eerie at this time of the night. The seniors' cars were fast asleep, their hoods and roofs reflecting light from the halogen floods. The macadam looked mercurial. The neighborhood of small single-family houses behind my building was dark and quiet. Occasionally there was the whir of traffic on St. James. Headlights flashed at the corner and a car turned into my lot. I had a moment of stomach-fluttering panic that this wasn't Tank, that this might be Benito Ramirez. I held my ground, thinking about the gun on my hip, telling myself I was cool, I was bad, I was a dangerous woman not to be messed with. Make my day, punk, I thought. Yeah, right. If it turned out to be Ramirez I'd wet my pants and run screaming back into the building.

The car was black and shiny. An SUV. It rolled to a stop in front of me, and the driver's side window slid down.

Tank looked out. "Ready to rock and roll?"

I took the seat beside him and buckled up. "Do you expect a lot of rockin' and rollin' tonight?"

"I expect none. Working this shift is like watching grass grow."

That was a relief. I had a lot to think about, and I didn't especially want to see Tank in action. Even more, I didn't want to see myself in action.

"I don't suppose you know a bookie named Bunchy, do you?"

"Bunchy? Nope. Never heard of him. He local?"

"Actually, I'm not sure."

The ride across town was quiet. One vehicle was parked at the curb in front of the Sloane Street apartment building. It was another new black SUV. Tank parked behind it. Beyond the building on either side and across the street, cars lined the curb.

"One of the things we like to enforce is a no-parking zone in front of the building," Tank said. "Keeps things clean. The tenants have parking behind the building. Only security vehicles are allowed here at the door."

"And if someone wants to park here?"

"We discourage it."

Master of understatement.

Two men were in the lobby. They were dressed in black, wearing the SECURITY jackets. One came forward when we approached and unlocked the door.

Tank stepped in and looked around. "Anything happening?"

"Nothing. Been quiet all night."

"When was the last time you walked?"

"Twelve."

Tank nodded.

The men gathered their belongings—a large Thermos, a book, and a gym bag—and pushed through the lobby door. They stood for a moment on the street, taking it in, before climbing into their SUV and motoring off.

A small table and two folding chairs had been placed against the far lobby wall, enabling the security team to watch both the door and the stairs. There were two walkie-talkies on the table.

Tank locked the front door, took one of the walkie-talkies, and clipped it to his belt. "I'm going to do a walk-through. You stay here and keep your eye on things. Call me if anyone approaches the door."

I sent him a salute.

"Snappy," he said. "I like that."

I sat in the folding chair and watched the door. No one approached. I watched the stairs. Nothing going on there, either. I checked out my manicure. Not great. I looked at my watch. Two minutes had gone by—478 minutes more and I could go home.

Tank ambled down the stairs and took his seat. "Everything's cool."

"Now what?"

"Now we wait."

"For what?"

"For nothing."

Two hours later, Tank was comfortably slouched in his chair, arms crossed, eyes slitted but vigilant, watching the door. His metabolism had dropped to reptilian. No rise and fall of his chest. No shifting of position—250 pounds of security in suspended animation.

I, on the other hand, had given up trying to keep from falling off my chair and was stretched out on the floor where I could doze without killing myself.

I heard Tank's chair creak. Heard him lean forward. I opened an eye. "Time for another walk-through?"

Tank was on his feet. "Someone's at the door."

I sat up to see, and *BANG!* There was the loud discharge of a gun, and then the sound of glass shattering. Tank pitched back, hit the table, and crashed to the floor.

The gunman rushed into the lobby, gun still in hand. It was the man Tank had thrown through the window, the occupant of apartment 3C. His eyes were wild, his face pale. "Drop the gun," he yelled at me. "Drop the fucking gun."

I looked down, and sure enough, I was holding my gun. "You aren't going to shoot me, are you?" I asked, my voice sounding hollow in my head.

He was wearing a long raincoat. He ripped the coat open and held it wide to show a bunch of packets duct-taped to his body. "You see this? These are explosives. You don't do what I say, and I'll blow us up."

I heard a clunk and realized the gun had slipped from my fingers and fallen onto the floor.

"I need to get into my apartment," he said. "I need to get in now."

"It's locked."

"So get a key."

"I don't have a key."

"Jesus," he said, "so kick the damn door down."

"Me?"

"You see anyone else here?"

I looked down at Tank. He wasn't moving.

The raincoat guy waved his gun in the direction of the stairs. "Move."

I edged around him and took the stairs to the third floor. I stood in front of the door to 3C and tried the handle. Locked, all right.

"Kick it in," the raincoat guy said.

I gave it a kick.

"Christ! That's not a kick. Don't you know anything? Don't you watch television?"

I took a couple of steps back and hurled myself at the door. I hit sideways and bounced off. Nothing happened to the door. "That worked when Ranger did it," I said.

The raincoat guy was sweating, and the gun was shaking in his hand. He turned to the door, aimed the gun with two hands, and squeezed the trigger twice. Wood splintered, and there was the sound of metal on metal. He kicked the door at lock height, and the door crashed open. He jumped in, hit the light switch, and looked everywhere at once. "What happened to my stuff?"

"We cleaned the apartment."

He ran into the bedroom and bathroom and back to the living room. He opened all the cabinet doors in the kitchen. "You had no right," he screamed at me. "You had no right to take my stuff."

"There wasn't much."

"There was a lot! Do you know what I had here? I had good stuff. I had pure. Jesus, do you know how bad I need a hit?"

"Listen, how about if I drive you to the clinic. Get you some help."

"I don't want the clinic. I want my stash."

The occupant of apartment 3A opened her door. "What's going on?"

"Get back in your apartment and lock your door," I said. "We have a little problem here."

The door slammed shut and the lock clicked.

The raincoat guy was running around in his apartment again. "Jesus," he was saying. "Jesus. Jesus."

Another woman appeared in the hall. She was frail and stooped. Her age had to be upwards of a hundred. Her short white hair stuck up in tufts. She was dressed in a worn pink flannel nightgown and big fuzzy slippers. "I can't sleep with all this racket," she said. "I've lived in this building for forty-three years, and I've never seen such goings-on. This used to be a nice neighborhood."

The raincoated guy whipped around, pointed his gun at the woman, and fired. The bullet tore into the wall behind her.

"Bite me," the old lady said, pulling a nickel-plated 9mm from somewhere in the folds of her nightgown, aiming the gun two-handed.

"*No!*" I yelled. "Don't shoot. He's wired with—"

Too late. The old lady drilled the guy, the sound of my voice lost in the blast.

I WOKE UP strapped to a gurney. I was in the apartment-house lobby, and the lobby was filled with people, mostly cops. Morelli's face swam into focus. He was moving his mouth, but he wasn't saying anything.

"What?" I yelled. "Speak up."

He shook his head, waved his hands, and I saw him mouth, "Take her away." A paramedic rolled the gurney out of the lobby into the night air. We clattered over the sidewalk, and then I felt myself lifted into the ambulance, the flashing strobes blinding against the black sky.

"Hey, wait a minute," I said. "I'm fine. Let me up. Untie these straps."

IT WAS MIDMORNING when I was released from the hospital. I was dressed and pacing when Morelli strode into my room with my discharge papers.

"They're letting you go," he said. "If I had my way, I'd move you upstairs to psychiatric."

I stuck my tongue out at him because I was feeling exceptionally mature. I grabbed my bag, and we fled the room before the nurse arrived with the mandatory wheelchair.

"I have a lot of questions," I said to Morelli.

He steered me toward the elevator. "I have a few of my own. Like, what the hell happened?"

"Me first. I need to know about Tank. No one will tell me anything. Is he, um, you know—?"

"Dead? No. Unfortunately. He was wearing a flak vest. The impact of the bullet knocked him back and stunned him. He hit his head when he fell and was out for a while, but he's fine. And by the way, where were you when he was shot?"

"I was stretched out on the floor. It was past my bedtime."

Morelli grinned. "Let me get this straight. You didn't get shot because you fell asleep on the job?"

"Something like that. It sounded better the way I phrased it. What about the guy with the bomb?"

"So far they've found a shoe and a belt buckle in the vicinity of what's left of the apartment—which, by the way, isn't much—and some teeth on Stark Street."

The elevator door opened, and we both stepped in.

"You're kidding about the teeth, right?"

Morelli grimaced and pushed the button.

"Nobody else hurt?"

"No. The old lady got knocked on her ass just like you. Can you corroborate her story that it was self-defense?"

"Yeah. The drug guy got a round off before she blew him up. It should be embedded in the wall . . . if the wall's still there."

We exited the downstairs lobby and crossed the street to Morelli's truck.

"Now what?" Morelli asked. "Your place? Your mother's house? My place? You're welcome to stay with me if you're feeling shaky."

"Thanks, but I need to go home. I want to take a shower and change my clothes." Then I wanted to go look for Fred. I was antsy to retrace Fred's steps. I wanted to stand in the parking lot where he'd disappeared and get psychic vibes. Not that I'd ever gotten psychic vibes from anything before, but hey, there's always a first time. "By the way, do you know a bookie named Bunchy?"

"No. What's he look like?"

"Average short Italian guy. Forty, maybe."

"Doesn't do anything for me. How do you know him?"

"He visited Mabel, and then he visited me. He claims Fred owes him money."

"Fred?"

"If Fred wanted to play the horses, why wouldn't he place his bets with his son?"

"Because he doesn't want anyone to know he's gambling?"

"Oh, yeah. I didn't think of that." Duh.

"I talked to your doctor," Morelli said. "He told me you're supposed to stay quiet for a couple days. And he said the ringing in your ears should diminish over time."

"The ringing's already a lot better."

Morelli glanced at me sideways. "You're not going to stay quiet, are you?"

"Define 'quiet.' "

"At home, reading, watching television."

"I might do some of that."

Morelli pulled into my parking lot and rolled to a stop. "When you're up to it, you need to stop in at the station and make a formal report."

I jumped out. "Okay."

"Hold it," Morelli said, "I'll go up with you."

"Not necessary. Thanks anyway. I'm fine."

Morelli was grinning again. "Afraid you might lose control in the hall and beg me to come in and make love to you?"

"In your dreams, Morelli."

When I got up to my apartment the red light on my phone machine was blinking, blinking, blinking. And Bunchy was asleep on my couch.

"What are you doing here?" I yelled at him. "Get up! Get out! This isn't the Hotel Ritz. And do you realize what you're doing is breaking and entering?"

"Boy, don't get your panties in a bunch," he said, getting to his feet. "Where have you been? I got worried about you. You didn't come home last night."

"What are you, my mother?"

"Hey, I'm concerned, that's all. You should be happy to have a friend like me." He looked around. "Do you see my shoes?"

"You are *not* my friend. And your shoes are under the coffee table."

He retrieved the shoes and laced them up. "So where were you?"

"I had a job. I was moonlighting."

"Must have been some job. Your mother called and said she heard you blew someone up."

"You talked to my mother?"

"She left a message on your machine." He was looking around again. "Do you see my gun?"

I turned on my heel and went in to the kitchen to play my messages.

"Stephanie, it's your mother. What's this about an explosion? Edna Gluck heard from her son, Ritchie, that you blew someone up? Is this true? Hello? Hello?"

Bunchy was right. Damn that big-mouth Ritchie.

I played the second message. Breathing. As was message number three.

"What's with the breathing?" Bunchy wanted to know, standing in the middle of my kitchen floor, hands stuck in his pockets, his rumpled, beyond-faded, plaid flannel shirt hanging loose.

"Wrong number."

"You'd tell me if you had a problem, right? Because, you know, I have a way of solving problems like that."

No doubt in my mind. He didn't look like a bookie, but I had no trouble at all believing he could solve *that* kind of problem. "Why are you here?"

He prowled through my cabinets, looking for food, finding nothing that interested him. Guess he wasn't crazy about hamster pellets.

"I wanted to know if you found anything," he said. "Like, do you have clues or something?"

"No. No clues. Nothing."

"I thought you were supposed to be this hotshot detective."

"I'm not a detective at all. I'm a bail enforcement agent."

"Bounty hunter."

"Yeah. Bounty hunter."

"So, that's okay. You go out and find people. That's what we want to have happen here."

"How much money did Fred owe you?"

"Enough that I want it. Not enough to make a man feel like he had to disappear. I'm a pretty nice guy, you know. It isn't like I go around breaking people's knees 'cause they don't pay up. Well, okay, so sometimes I might break a knee, but it's not like it happens every day."

I rolled my eyes.

"You know what I think you should do?" Bunchy said. "I think you should go check at his bank. See if he's taken any money out. I can't do things like that on account of I look like I might break people's knees. But you're a pretty girl. You probably got a friend works in the bank. People would want to do a favor for you."

"I'll think about it. Now go away."

Bunchy ambled to the door. He took a beat-up brown leather jacket from one of the pegs on the wall and turned to look at me. His expression was serious. "Find him."

What hung unsaid in the air was . . . or else.

I slipped the bolt behind him. First chance I had I was going to have to get a new lock. Surely someone made a lock that actually kept people out.

I called my mother back and explained to her that I hadn't blown someone up. He'd sort of blown himself up with some help from an old lady in a pink nightgown.

"You could have a good job," my mother said. "You could take lessons from that place that advertises on television and teaches you to be a computer operator."

"I have to go now."

"How about dinner. I'm making a nice pot roast with potatoes and gravy."

"I don't think so."

"Pineapple upside-down cake for dessert."

"Okay. I'll be there at six."

I erased the breathing messages and told myself they were wrong numbers. But in my heart, I knew the breather.

I double-checked all the locks on my door, and I checked to make sure my windows were secure and no one was hiding in a closet or under the bed. I took a long, hot shower, wrapped myself in a towel, stepped out of the bathroom . . . and came face-to-face with Ranger.

FOUR

"*YIKES!*" I JUMPED back and clapped my hand to my chest, tightening my towel. "What are you doing here?" I yelled at Ranger.

His eyes dropped to the towel and then back to my face. "Returning your hat, Babe." He put the SEALs hat on my head and adjusted it over my damp hair. "You left it in the lobby."

"Oh. Thanks."

Ranger smiled.

"What?" I asked.

"Cute," Ranger said.

I narrowed my eyes. "Anything else?"

"You doing the shift with Tank tonight?"

"You're still policing that building?"

"It's got a big hole in it, Babe. Gotta keep the bad guys out."

"I'll pass on that one."

"No problem. I have other jobs you can try on."

"Oh, yeah? Like what?"

Ranger shrugged. "Things turn up." He reached behind him and came up with a gun. My gun. "Found this in the lobby, too."

He tucked the gun under the top edge of my towel, wedging it between my breasts, his knuckles brushing against me.

My breath caught in my throat, and for a moment I thought my towel might catch fire.

Ranger smiled again. And I did more eye narrowing.

"I'll be in touch," Ranger said.

And then he was gone.

Dang. I carefully extracted the gun from the towel and put it in the cookie jar in the kitchen. Then I went back to my door to examine the locks. Worthless pieces of junk. I locked them anyway, including the bolt. I didn't know what more I could do.

I went into the bedroom, dropped the towel, and shimmied into a sports bra and Jockey bikinis. This wasn't going to be one of those silk and lace days. This was going to be a no-nonsense Jockey day all the way through.

Half an hour later, I was out the door, dressed in jeans and a denim shirt. I buckled myself into Big Blue and motored out of the lot. Two blocks later, I turned onto Hamilton and noticed a car close on my tail. I swiveled in my seat and looked at the driver. Bunchy. I pressed my lips together, getting a smile and a wave from him. This guy was unreal. He'd pulled a gun on me, and probably he had something to do with the body in the garbage bag, but I was having a hard time working up any real fear of him. In all honesty, he was sort of likeable . . . in an annoying kind of way.

I swerved to the curb, yanked the emergency brake up, got out, and stomped over. "What are you doing?" I shouted into his window.

"Following you."

"Why?"

"I don't want to miss anything. In case you get lucky and find Fred, I want to be there."

"I don't know how to break this to you, but between you and

me, I think it's unlikely that Fred is going to be in any shape to repay your money if and when I find him."

"You think he's fish food?"

"It's a possibility."

He shrugged. "Call me crazy, but I'm an optimist."

"Fine. Go be an optimist someplace else. I don't like you following me around. It's creepy."

"I won't be any bother. You won't even know I'm here."

"You're driving six inches from my rear. How am I going to not know you're here?"

"Don't look in your mirror."

"And I don't think you're a bookie, either," I said. "Nobody knows you. I've been asking around."

He smiled, like this was pretty funny. "Oh, yeah? Who do you think I am?"

"I don't know."

"Let me know when you find out."

"Asshole."

"Sticks and stones," Bunchy said. "And I bet your mother wouldn't like you using that language."

I huffed off to the Buick, jammed myself behind the wheel, and drove to the office.

"You see that guy parked behind me?" I asked Lula.

"The one in the piece-of-shit brown Dodge?"

"His name's Bunchy, and he says he's a bookie."

"He don't look like no bookie to me," Lula said. "And I never heard of anyone named Bunchy."

Connie squinted out the window, too. "I don't recognize him, either," she said. "And if he's a bookie, he's not doing all that good."

"He says Fred owes him money, and he's following me in case I find Fred."

"Does that float your boat?" Lula wanted to know.

"No. I need to get rid of him."

"Permanently? 'Cause I got a friend—"

"No! Just for the rest of the day."

Lula took another look at Bunchy. "If I shoot out his tires, will he shoot back?"

"Probably."

"I don't like when they shoot back," Lula said.

"I thought maybe I could trade cars with you."

"Trade my Firebird for that whale you drive? I don't think so. Friendship don't go *that* far."

"Fine! Great! Forget I asked!"

"Hold on," Lula said. "Don't have to go getting all snippy. I'll have a talk with him. I can be real persuasive."

"You aren't going to threaten him, are you?"

"I don't threaten people. What kind of woman you think I am?"

Connie and I watched her sashay out the office over to the car. We knew what kind of woman she was.

Lula was wearing a canary-yellow spandex miniskirt and a stretchy top that was at least two sizes too small. Her hair was orange. Her lipstick was bright pink. And her eyelids were gold glitter.

We heard her say, "Hello, handsome," to Bunchy, and then she lowered her voice, and we couldn't hear any more.

"Maybe you should try to sneak away while Lula's got his attention," Connie said. "Maybe you could roll the Buick back nice and easy, and he won't notice."

I thought chances of Bunchy not noticing were pretty slim, but I was willing to try. I quickly walked to the car, snuck in on the curb side, and slid behind the wheel. I released the emergency brake, held my breath, and turned the key in the ignition. *Varoooom.* A V8 does *not* sneak.

Bunchy and Lula both turned to look at me. I saw Bunchy

say something to Lula. And Lula grabbed Bunchy by the shirt-front and yelled *"Go!"* to me. "I got him," she said. "You can count on me!"

Bunchy slapped at her hand, and Lula squashed herself into the car window with her big yellow ass hanging out, looking from the outside like Pooh Bear stuck in the rabbit hole. She had Bunchy by the neck, and when I drove by I saw her plant a kiss square on his mouth.

MABEL WAS IN the kitchen making tea when I got there.

"Anything new in the investigation?" she asked.

"I talked to the man who was looking for Fred. He says he's Fred's bookie. Did you know Fred was gambling?"

"No." She paused with the tea bag in her hand. "Gambling," she said, testing the word. "I had no idea."

"He could be lying," I said.

"Why would he do that?"

Good question. If Bunchy wasn't a bookie, then what? What was his involvement?

"About those pictures," I said to Mabel. "Do you have any idea when they might have been taken?"

Mabel added water to her teapot. "I think it must have been recently because I never saw them before. I don't go into Fred's desk all the time, but every now and then I need something. And I never saw any pictures. Fred doesn't take pictures. Years ago, when the kids were little, we used to take pictures. Now Ronald and Walter bring us pictures of the grandchildren. We don't even own a camera anymore. Last year we had to take pictures of the roof for the insurance company, and we got one of those dispos-able cameras."

I left Mabel to her tea and got back behind the wheel. I looked up and down the street. So far, so good. No Bunchy.

My next stop was the strip mall where Fred did his shopping. I parked in the same area where Fred's car was found. It was about the same time of day. Weather was similar. Seventy and sunny. There were enough people moving around that a scuffle would be noticed. A man walking around dazed would probably be noticed too, but I didn't think that's what I was looking for.

First Trenton was located at the end of the strip mall. It was a branch office with a drive-through window outside and full-service banking inside. Leona Freeman was a teller at First Trenton. She was a second cousin on my mother's side, a couple years older than me, and she had a head start on the family thing, with four kids, two dogs, and a nice husband.

Business was slow when I walked in, and Leona waved at me from behind the counter. "Stephanie!"

"Hey, Leona, how's it going?"

"Pretty good. What's with you? You want some money? I gotta lot."

I grinned.

"Bank joke," Leona said.

"Did you hear about Fred going missing?"

"I heard. He was in here right before it happened."

"Did you see him?"

"Yeah, sure. He got money from the machine, and then he went in to see Shempsky."

Leona and I went to school with Allen Shempsky. He was an okay guy who'd worked his way up the ladder and was now a VP. And this was a new development. No one had said anything about Fred going to see Shempsky. "What'd Fred want with Allen?"

Leona shrugged. "Don't know. He was in there talking to Allen for about ten minutes. He didn't stop to say hello or anything when he came out. Fred was like that. Not the most sociable person."

Shempsky had a small private office tucked between two other small private offices. His door was open, so I stuck my head in.

"Knock, knock," I said.

Allen Shempsky looked at me blank-faced for a moment, and then I saw recognition kick in. "Sorry," he said, "my mind was someplace else. What can I do for you?"

"I'm looking for my uncle Fred. I understand he talked to you just before he disappeared."

"Yeah. He was thinking of taking out a loan."

"A loan? What kind of a loan?"

"Personal."

"He say what he needed the money for?"

"No. Wanted to know what interest rates were and how long would it take. That sort of thing. Preliminary stuff. No paperwork or anything. I think he was only in here for maybe five minutes. Ten tops."

"Did he seem upset?"

"Not that I remember. Well, not any more than usual. Fred was sort of a grumpy guy. The family ask you to look for Fred?"

"Yeah." I stood and gave Shempsky my card. "Let me know if you think of anything significant."

A loan. I couldn't help wondering if it was to pay off Bunchy. I didn't think Bunchy was a bookie, but I wouldn't be shocked to find he was a blackmailer.

The dry cleaner was in the middle of the strip of buildings, next to Grand Union. I knew the woman behind the counter by sight, but not by name. I brought my clothes here too, some-times.

She remembered Fred, but not much else. He'd picked up his clothes and that was it. No conversation. They'd been busy at the time. She hadn't paid a lot of attention to Fred.

I went back to the Buick and stood there, looking around,

trying to imagine what might have happened. Fred had parked in front of Grand Union, anticipating that he'd have groceries to carry. He'd laid the cleaning neatly on the backseat, then closed and locked the car. Then what? Then he'd disappeared. The mall opened to a four-lane highway on one side. Behind the mall was an apartment complex and the neighborhood of single-family houses where I'd searched for Fred.

The RGC office was down by the river, on the other side of Broad. It was an industrial area of warehouses and mom-and-pop factories. Not especially scenic. Perfect for a waste hauler.

I eased into traffic and pointed Big Blue's nose west. Ten minutes and seven lights later, I rolled down Water Street, squinting at the somber brick buildings, looking for numbers. The road was cracked and pocked with potholes. Parking lots associated with businesses were ringed by chain-link fences. Sidewalks were empty. Windows were dark and lifeless. I didn't need to see the numbers, RGC was easy to spot. Large sign. Lots of garbage trucks parked in the lot. There were five visitor slots next to the building. They were all empty. No surprise there. It didn't exactly smell like roses outside.

I parked in one of the slots and scurried inside. The office was small. Linoleum floor, death-pallor-green walls, and a counter cut the room in half. There were two desks and file cabinets in the back half of the room.

A woman got up from one of the desks and stood at the counter. A plaque on the counter read MARTHA DEETER, RE-CEPTIONIST, and I assumed this was Martha.

"Can I help you?" Martha asked.

I introduced myself as Fred's niece and told her I was looking for Fred.

"I remember speaking to him," she said. "He went home to get his canceled check and never returned. It never occurred to me that something might have happened to him. I just assumed he'd given up. We get a lot of people in here trying to get something for nothing."

"Go figure."

"Exactly. That's why I sent him home for the check. The old ones are the worst. They're all on fixed incomes. They'll say anything to hang on to a dollar."

There was a man sitting at the second desk. He got up and moved next to Martha. "Perhaps I can be of assistance here. I'm the bookkeeper, and I'm afraid this is my problem. Truth is, this has happened before. It's the computer. We just can't get it to recognize certain customers."

Martha tapped a finger on the counter. "It's *not* the computer. There are people out there who'll take advantage. People think it's okay to gyp big business."

The man gave me a tight smile and extended his hand. "Larry Lipinski. I'll make sure the account is set straight."

Martha didn't look happy. "We really should see the canceled check."

"For goodness' sakes," Lipinski said to Martha, "the man disappeared in the middle of his errands. He probably had the check on him. How do you expect them to show you the check?"

"Supposedly the Shutzes have been customers for years. They must have canceled checks from previous quarters," she said.

"I don't believe this," Lipinski said. "Give it a rest. It's the computer. Remember last month? We had the same problem."

"It isn't the computer."

"It is."

"Isn't."

"Is."

I backed out of the office and slipped out the door. I didn't want to be around for the bitch-slapping and hair-pulling. If Fred was going to "make out in spades," it seemed unlikely he'd make his killing with these two.

Half an hour later I was back at Vinnie's. His door was shut and there were no bond seekers at Connie's desk. Lula and Connie were discussing meatloaf.

"That's disgusting," Lula said, eyeballing Connie's sandwich. "Whoever heard of mayonnaise on meatloaf? Everybody knows you gotta put ketchup on meatloaf. You can't put no dumb-ass mayonnaise on it. What is that, some Italian thing?"

Connie gave Lula a stiff middle finger. "*This* is an Italian thing," she said.

I snitched a corn chip from the bag on Connie's desk. "So what happened?" I asked Lula. "You and Bunchy going steady now?"

"He's not such a bad kisser," Lula said. "He had a hard time giving it his full attention at first, but after a while I think he was into it."

"I'm going after Briggs," I said. "You want to ride shotgun?"

"Sure," Lula said, pulling a sweatshirt over her head. "Better than sitting around here. It's damn boring in here today." She had keys in her hand. "And I'm driving. You have a pipsqueak sound system in that Buick, and I need Dolby. I need mood music. I gotta get myself ready to kick some butt."

"We're not kicking butt. We're finessing."

"I could do that, too," Lula said.

I followed Lula out the door to her car. We buckled ourselves in, the CD player clicked on, and the bass almost lifted us off the ground.

"So what's the plan?" Lula asked, pulling into Briggs' parking lot. "We need a plan."

"The plan is that we knock on his door and lie."

"I could get into that," Lula said. "I like to lie. I could lie your ass off."

We crossed the lot and took the stairs. The hall was empty, and there was no noise coming from Briggs' apartment.

I flattened against the wall, out of sight, and Lula knocked twice on Briggs' door.

"How's this?" she asked. "I look okay? This here's my non-threatening look. This look says, Come on, motherfucker, open your door."

If I saw Lula on the other side of my apartment door, wearing her nonthreatening look, I'd hide under my bed. But hey, that's me.

The door opened with the security chain in place and Briggs peeked out at Lula.

"Howdy," Lula said. "I'm from downstairs, and I got a petition for you to sign on account of they're gonna raise our rent."

"I didn't hear anything about a rent raise," Briggs said. "I didn't get any notice."

"Well, they're gonna do it all the same," Lula said.

"Sons of bitches," Briggs said. "They're always doing something in this building. I don't know why I stay here."

"Cheap rent?" Lula asked.

The door closed, the chain slid off, and the door opened wide.

"Hey!" Briggs said when Lula and I pushed past him into the apartment. "You can't just barge in like this. You tricked me."

"Look again," Lula said. "We're bounty hunters. We can barge if we want to. We got rights."

"You have *no* rights," Briggs said. "It's a bogus charge. I was carrying a ceremonial knife. It was engraved."

"A ceremonial knife," Lula said. "Seems like a little dude like you should be able to carry a ceremonial knife."

"Exactly," Randy said. "I'm unjustly accused."

" 'Course it don't matter," Lula said. "You still gotta go to the pokey with us."

"I'm in the middle of a big project. I don't have time."

"Hmmm," Lula said. "Let me explain to you how this works. Bottom line is, we don't give a doody."

Briggs pressed his lips together and folded his arms tight across his chest. "You can't make me go."

"Sure we can," Lula said. "You're just a little pipsqueak. We could make you sing 'Yankee Doodle' if we wanted. 'Course, we wouldn't do that on account of we're professionals."

I pulled a pair of cuffs out of my back pocket and clamped one of the bracelets on Briggs.

Briggs looked at the cuff like it was the flesh-eating virus. "What's this?"

"Nothing to be alarmed about," I said. "Standard procedure."

"Eeeeeeeee," Briggs shrieked. "Eeeeeeeee."

"Stop that!" Lula yelled. "You sound like a girl. You're creeping me out."

He was running around the room now, waving his arms and still shrieking. "Eeeeeeeee."

"Get a grip!" Lula said.

"Eeeeeeee."

I made a grab for the cuff but missed. "Stand still," I ordered.

Briggs bolted past Lula, who was dumbstruck, rooted to the floor, and then ran out the door.

"Get him," I yelled, rushing at Lula. "Don't let him get away!" I pushed her into the hall, and we thundered down the stairs after Briggs.

Briggs sprinted through the small lobby, through the front door, and into the parking lot.

"Well, damn," Lula said, "I can hear his little feet going, but I can't see him. He's lost in between all these cars."

We separated and walked into the lot, Lula going one way and me the other. We stopped and listened for footsteps when we got to the outer perimeter.

"I don't hear him anymore," Lula said. "He must be going tippytoe."

We started to walk back when we saw Briggs round the corner of the apartment building and race inside.

"Holy cow!" Lula said. "He's going back to his apartment."

We ran across the lot, barreled through the door, and took the stairs two at a time. When we got to Briggs' apartment the door was closed and locked.

"We know you're in there," Lula yelled. "You better open this door."

"You can huff and you can puff, but you'll never get through this door," Briggs said.

"The hell we won't," Lula told him. "We could shoot the lock off. And then we're gonna come in there and root you out like a rodent."

No answer.

"Hello?" Lula called.

We listened at the door and heard the computer boot up. Briggs was going back to work.

"Nothing I hate more than a wise-ass dwarf," Lula said, hauling a .45 out of her purse. "Stand back. I'm gonna blast this door open."

Drilling Briggs' door held a lot of appeal, but probably it wasn't practical to shoot up an apartment building for a guy who was only worth seven hundred dollars.

"No shooting," I said. "I'll get the key from the super."

"That isn't gonna do you no good if you're not willing to shoot," Lula said. "He's still gonna have the security chain on."

"I saw Ranger pop a door open with his shoulder."

Lula looked at the door. "I could do that too," she said. "Only I just bought this dress with them little spaghetti straps, and I wouldn't want to have a bruise."

I looked at my watch. "It's almost five, and I'm having dinner with my parents tonight."

"Maybe we should do this some other time."

"We're leaving," I hollered through Briggs' door, "but we'll be back. And you'd better be careful of those handcuffs. They cost me forty dollars."

"We would have been justified to shoot our way in on account of he's in possession of stolen property," Lula said.

"Do you always carry a gun?" I asked Lula.

"Don't everybody?"

"They released Benito Ramirez two days ago."

Lula stumbled on the second step down. "That's not possible."

"Joe told me."

"Piece-of-shit legal system."

"Be careful."

"Hell," Lula said. "He already cut me. You're the one who has to be careful."

We swung through the door and stopped in our tracks.

"Uh-oh," Lula said. "We got company."

It was Bunchy. He was parked behind us in the lot. And he didn't look happy.

"How do you suppose he found us?" Lula asked. "We aren't even in your car."

"He must have followed us from the office."

"I didn't see him. And I was looking."

"I didn't see him either."

"He's good," Lula said. "He might be someone to worry about."

"HOW'S THE POT roast?" my mother wanted to know. "Is it too dry?"

"It's fine," I told her. "Just like always."

"I got the green bean casserole recipe from Rose Molinowski. It's made with mushroom soup and bread crumbs."

"Whenever there's a wake or a christening, Rose always brings this casserole," Grandma said. "It's her signature dish."

My father looked up from his plate. "Signature dish?"

"I got that from the shopper's channel on TV. All the big designers got signature this and that."

My father shook his head and bent lower over his pot roast.

Grandma helped herself to some of the casserole. "How's the manhunt going? You got any good leads on Fred yet?"

"Fred is a dead end. I've talked to his sons and his girlfriend. I've retraced his last steps. I've talked to Mabel. There's nothing. He's disappeared without a trace."

My father muttered something that sounded a lot like "lucky bastard" and continued to eat.

My mother rolled her eyes.

And Grandma spooned in some beans. "We need one of them psychics," Grandma said. "I saw on television where you can call them up, and they know everything. They find dead people all the time. I saw a couple of them on a talk show, and they were saying how they help the police with these serial murder cases. I was watching that show, and I was thinking that if I was a serial murderer I'd chop the bodies up in little pieces so those psychics wouldn't have such an easy job of it. Or maybe I'd drain all the blood out of the body and collect it in a big bucket. Then I'd bury a chicken, and I'd take the victim's blood and make a trail to the chicken. Then the psychic wouldn't know what to make of it when the police dug up a chicken." Grandma helped herself to the gravy boat and poured gravy over her pot roast. "Do you think that'd work?"

Everyone but Grandma paused with forks in midair.

"Well, I wouldn't bury a *live* chicken," Grandma said.

No one had much to say after that, and I felt myself nodding off halfway through my second piece of cake.

"You look all done in," Grandma said. "Guess getting blown up takes it out of you."

"I didn't get much sleep last night."

"Maybe you want to take a nap while your grandmother and I clean up," my mother said. "You can use the guest room."

Ordinarily, I'd excuse myself and go home early, but tonight Bunchy was sitting across the street, two houses down, in the Dodge. So leaving early didn't appeal to me. What appealed to me was to make Bunchy's night as long as possible.

My parents have three bedrooms. My grandma Mazur sleeps in my sister's room, and my room is used as a guest room. Of course, I'm the only guest who ever uses the guest room. All my parents' friends and family live within a five-mile radius and have no reason to stay overnight. I also live within five miles, but I've been known to have the occasional disaster that sends me in search of temporary residence. So my bathrobe hangs in the guest room closet.

"Maybe just a short nap," I said. "I'm really tired."

THE SUN WAS slanting through the break in the curtains when I woke up. I had a moment of disorientation, wondering if I was late for school, and then realized I'd been out of school for a lot of years, and that I'd crawled into bed for a short nap and ended up sleeping through the night.

I rolled out of bed fully dressed and shuffled down to the kitchen. My mother was making vegetable soup, and my grandmother was sitting at the kitchen table reading the paper, scrutinizing the obituaries.

Grandma looked up when I came in. "Weren't you at the garbage company yesterday, checking on Fred?"

I poured myself a cup of coffee and sat across from her. "Yep."

"It says here this woman, Martha Deeter, who was the receptionist at RGC, was shot to death last night. Says they found her in the parking lot of her apartment building." Grandma slid the paper over to me. "Got a picture of her and everything."

I stared goggle-eyed at the picture. It was Martha, all right. With the way she was going at it with her office mate, I'd expected she might have fingerprint marks on her neck. A bullet in the brain never occurred to me.

"Says she's being laid out at Stiva's tomorrow night," Grandma said. "We should go on account of it was our garbage company."

The Catholic church held bingo parties only twice a week, so Grandma and her friends enlarged their social life by attending viewings.

"No suspects," I said, reading the article. "The police think it was robbery. Her purse was missing."

THE BROWN DODGE was still parked down the street when I left my parents' house. Bunchy was asleep behind the wheel, his head back, mouth open. I rapped on the window, and he jumped awake.

"Shit," he said, "what time is it?"

"Were you here all night?"

"Sure looks like it."

Looked like it to me, too. He looked even worse than usual. He had dark circles under his eyes, he needed a shave, and his hair looked like it had been styled by a stun gun.

"So, you didn't kill anybody last night?"

Bunchy blinked at me. "Not that I remember. Who bought the farm?"

"Martha Deeter. She worked at RGC Waste Haulers."

"Why would I want to kill her?"

"I don't know. I saw it in the paper this morning and just thought I'd ask."

"Never hurts to ask," Bunchy said.

I LET MYSELF into my apartment and saw the light flashing on my phone machine.

"Hey, Babe," Ranger said, "got a job for you."

The second message was from Benito Ramirez. "Hello, Stephanie," he said. Quiet-voiced. Articulate, as always. "I've been away for a little while . . . as you know." There was a pause and in my mind I could see his eyes. Small for his face and terrifyingly insane. "I came by to see you, but you weren't at home. That's okay. I'll try some other time." He gave a small, girlish giggle and disconnected.

I erased Ranger's message and saved Ramirez's. Probably I should have a restraining order issued. Ordinarily I didn't hold much stock in restraining orders, but in this case, if Ramirez continued to harass me I might be able to get his parole revoked.

I connected with Ranger on his car phone. "What's the job?" I asked.

"Chauffeur. I have a young sheik flying in to Newark at five."

"He carrying drugs? Delivering guns?"

"Negative. He's visiting relatives in Bucks County. Long weekend. Probably he won't even blow himself up."

"What's the catch?"

"No catch. You wear a black suit and white shirt. You meet him at the gate and escort him safely to his destination."

"I guess that sounds okay."

"You'll be driving a Town Car. You can pick it up at the garage on Third and Marshall. Be there at three o'clock and talk to Eddie."

"Anything else?"

"Make sure you're dressed."

"You mean the suit—"

"I mean the gun."

"Oh."

I disconnected and went back to Fred's photos. I spread the color copies out on the table just as I did the first time. Two of the pictures were of the bag all tied up. I was guessing that was how Fred found it. He took a couple pictures, then he opened the bag. The big question was, did he know what was inside before he opened it, or was it a surprise?

I went upstairs to Mrs. Bestler, who had failing eyesight, and borrowed a magnifying glass. I returned to my apartment, took the pages closer to the window, and looked at them with the glass. The glass wasn't much help, but I was almost sure it was a woman. Short dark hair. No jewelry on her right hand. There seemed to be newspapers crumpled into the bag with her. A crime lab might be able to pick something out to help date the photo. The bag with the woman was sitting with other bags. I could count four. They were on asphalt. Garbage stacked outside a business, maybe. A business too small to need a Dumpster. Lots of those around. Or it could be a driveway belonging to a family who made tons of garbage.

Part of a building was visible in the background. Hard to tell what it was. It was out of focus and in shade. A stucco wall was my best guess.

That was all the pictures were going to offer up to me.

I took a shower, scrounged for lunch, and set off to talk to Mabel.

FIVE

I LEFT MY building with more caution than usual, keeping my eyes open for Ramirez. I reached the Buick and was almost disappointed not to have been accosted. On the one hand, it'd be good to get the confrontation over with. On the other hand . . . I didn't want to think about the other hand.

Bunchy wasn't there, either. I had mixed feelings about this, too. Bunchy was a pain in the behind, and I had no idea who he was, but I thought he might be good to have around if Ramirez attacked me. Better Bunchy than Ramirez. I don't know why I felt like that. For all I knew, Bunchy was the butcher.

I chugged out of the lot and drove on autopilot to Mabel's house, trying to prioritize projects. I had to neutralize Ramirez, get to the bottom of the Fred thing, chauffeur some sheik . . . And I felt uncomfortable about the dead garbage lady. Not to mention, I needed shoes for Saturday night. I lined everything up in my mind. The shoes were, hands down, top priority. Okay, so sometimes I wasn't the world's greatest bounty hunter. I wasn't a fabulous cook. I didn't have a boyfriend, much less a husband. And I wasn't a big financial success. I could live with all those failings as long as I knew that once in a while I looked really hot. And Saturday night I was going to look hot. So I needed shoes and a new dress.

Mabel was standing at the door when I drove up. Still on the lookout for Fred, I guess.

"I'm so glad you're here," she said, ushering me into the house. "I don't know what to think."

As if I could help her in that department.

"Sometimes I expect Fred to walk in the door, just like always. And then other times I know he'll never be back. And the thing is . . . I really need a new washer and dryer. In fact, I've needed them for years, but Fred was so cautious about spending money. Maybe I'll just go down to Sears and take a look. It doesn't hurt to look, does it?"

"Looking sounds good to me."

"I knew I could count on you," Mabel said. "Would you like some tea?"

"No thanks on the tea, but I have some more questions. I want you to think about places Fred might go that would have four or five garbage bags sitting outside on garbage day. The bags would be sitting on asphalt. And there might be a light-colored stucco wall behind them."

"This is about those photographs, isn't it? Let me think. Fred had a routine, you know. When he retired two years ago, he took over the errands. In the beginning we did the marketing together, but it was too stressful. So I started staying home and watching my television shows in the afternoon, and Fred took over the errands. He went to the Grand Union every day. And sometimes he'd go to Giovichinni's Meat Market. He didn't go there too often because he thought Giovichinni gypped him on the meat scale. He only went there if he wanted kielbasa. Once in a while he'd splurge on Giovichinni's olive loaf."

"Did he go to Giovichinni's last week?"

"Not that I know of. The only thing different about last week was that he went out in the morning to the garbage company. He didn't usually go out in the morning, but he was really in a state over that missed day."

"Did he ever go out at night?"

"We went to the seniors' club on Thursdays to play cards. And we went to special events sometimes. Like the Christmas party."

We were standing in front of the living room window, talking, when the RGC garbage truck rumbled up the street, bypassed Mabel's house, and stopped next door.

Mabel blinked in disbelief. "They didn't take my garbage," she said. "It's right out there on the curb, and they didn't take it." She threw the door open and trotted out to the sidewalk, but the truck was gone. "How could they do this?" she wailed. "What am I going to do with my garbage?"

I went to the Yellow Pages, found the number for RGC, and dialed the number. Larry Lipinski answered the phone.

"Larry," I said, "this is Stephanie Plum, remember me?"

"Sure," Larry said, "but I'm a little busy right now."

"I read about Martha—"

"Yeah, Martha. What's on your mind?"

"My aunt's garbage. The thing is, Larry, the truck went right by her house just now and didn't pick up her garbage."

There was a big sigh. "That's because she didn't pay her bill. There's no record of payment."

"We went through all that yesterday. You said you'd take care of it."

"Look, lady, I tried, okay? But there's no record of payment, and frankly I'm thinking Martha was right, and you and your aunt are trying to gyp us."

"Listen, Larry!"

Larry disconnected.

"You dumb fuck!" I yelled at the phone.

85

Aunt Mabel looked shocked.

"Sorry," I said. "I got carried away."

I went down to the cellar, got the canceled RGC check off Fred's desk, and dropped it into my shoulder bag.

"I'll take care of this tomorrow," I said. "I'd do it today, but I don't have time."

Mabel was wringing her hands. "That garbage is going to smell if I leave it sitting out there in the sun," she said. "What will the neighbors think?"

I did some mental head-banging. "No problem. Don't worry about it."

She gave me a tremulous smile.

I said good-bye, marched to the curb, extracted Mabel's nicely tied up plastic garbage bag from her container, and stuffed it into the trunk of my car. Then I drove to RGC, pitched the bag onto the sidewalk in front of their office, and raced away.

Am I a take-charge woman or what?

I drove away thinking about Fred. Suppose Fred saw someone do that? Well, not *exactly* what I just did. Suppose he saw someone take a garbage bag out of the trunk of their car and put it on the curb, alongside someone else's garbage. And suppose for one reason or another he got to wondering what was in the garbage bag?

This made a reasonable picture to me. I could see this happening. What I didn't understand, if in fact any of this occurred the way I imagined, was why Fred didn't report it to the police. Maybe he knew the person dumping the bag. But then why would he take pictures?

Hold on, let's reverse it. Suppose someone saw Fred dump the bag. They went to investigate, found the body and took pictures for evidence, then tried to blackmail Fred. Who would do such a thing? Bunchy. And maybe Fred all of a sudden got spooked and left for points south.

What's wrong with *this* picture? I couldn't see Fred taking a chain saw to some woman. And you'd have to be pretty dumb to blackmail Fred, because Fred didn't have any money.

THE SKIRT TO my black suit hit two inches above my knee. The jacket sat high on my hipbone. My stretchy white jersey tucked into the skirt. I was wearing sheer, barely black pantyhose and black heels. My .38 was in my black leather shoulder bag. And for this special occasion, I'd taken the time to put some bullets in the stupid thing . . . just in case Ranger showed up and gave me a pop quiz.

Bunchy was in the parking lot, parked behind my Buick. "Going to a funeral?"

"I have a job chauffeuring a sheik from Newark. It's going to take me out of town for the rest of the afternoon, and I'm worried about Mabel. Since you like to sit around and do nothing, I thought you might sit around and do nothing across from Mabel's house." Give him something to do, I thought. Keep the guy busy.

"You want me to protect the people I'm squeezing?"

"Yeah."

"It doesn't work that way. And what the hell are you doing going off on a chauffeuring job? You're supposed to be looking for your uncle."

"I need money."

"You need to find Fred."

"Okay, this is the honest-to-God truth . . . I don't know how to find Fred. I run down leads and they don't go anywhere. Maybe it would help if you told me what you were really after."

"I'm after Fred."

"Why?"

"You better get going," Bunchy said. "You're gonna be late."

THE GARAGE AT Third and Marshall didn't have a name. It was probably listed under something in the phone book, but on the outside of the building there was nothing. Just a redbrick building with a paved parking lot, enclosed by chain-link fencing. There were three bays in the side of the building, opening out to the lot. The bay doors were open and men worked on cars in each of the bays. A white stretch limo and two black Town Cars were parked in the lot. I pulled the Buick into a slot next to one of the Town Cars, locked the Buick, and dropped the keys into my shoulder bag.

A guy who looked like Antonio Banderas on an off day sauntered over to me.

"Nice car," he said, eyeing the Buick. "Man, they don't make cars like this anymore." He ran a hand over the back fender. "Cherry. Real cherry."

"Uh-huh." The cherry car got four miles to a gallon and cornered like a refrigerator. Not to mention it was all wrong for my self-image. My self-image called for fast and sleek and black, not bulbous and powder blue. Red would be okay, too. And I needed a sunroof. And a good sound system. And leather seats . . .

"Earth to Babe," Banderas said.

I dragged myself back to the moment. "You know where I can find Eddie?"

"You're looking at him, Cookie. I'm Eddie."

I extended my hand. "Stephanie Plum. Ranger sent me."

"I got a car ready and waiting." He rounded the nearest Town Car, opened the driver's side door, and took a large white envelope from behind the visor. "Here's everything you need. The keys are in the ignition. The car's gassed up."

"I don't need a chauffeur's license to do this, do I?"

He stared at me blank-faced.

"Yeah, right," I said. Probably nothing to worry about anyway. It wasn't easy to get a permit to carry concealed in Mercer County. And I wasn't one of the chosen. If I got stopped by a cop he'd be so overjoyed to be able to arrest me for illegally carrying concealed that he'd no doubt forget to charge me for the driving thing.

I took the envelope and slid behind the wheel. I adjusted the seat and leafed through the papers. Flight information, parking directions, some procedural instructions, name and brief description, and snapshot of Ahmed Fahed. No age was given, but he looked young in the photo.

I eased the Lincoln out of the lot and headed for Route 1. I picked up the turnpike in East Brunswick and glided along in my big, black, climate-controlled car, feeling very professional. Chauffeuring wasn't so bad, I thought. Today a sheik, tomorrow . . . who knows, maybe Tom Cruise. Definitely better than getting some computer nut out of his apartment. And if it wasn't for the fact that I couldn't stop thinking about that severed right hand and decapitated head, I'd really be enjoying myself.

I took the airport exit and found my way to Arrivals. My passenger was coming in from San Francisco, flying commercial. I parked in the area reserved for limos, crossed the road, entered the terminal, and checked the monitors for gate information.

A half hour later, Fahed strolled through the gate, wearing two-hundred-dollar sneakers and oversize jeans. His T-shirt advertised a microbrewery. His red plaid flannel shirt was wrinkled and unbuttoned, sleeves rolled to the elbow. I'd expected sheik clothes with the head thing and robe. Fortunately for me, he was the only arrogant Arab departing first class, so it wasn't hard to pick him out.

"Ahmed Fahed?" I asked.

His eyebrows raised ever so slightly in acknowledgment.

"I'm your driver."

He looked me over. "Where's your gun?"

"In my shoulder bag."

"My father always orders a bodyguard for me. He's afraid someone will kidnap me."

Now it was my turn to raise an eyebrow.

He shrugged. "We're rich. Rich people get kidnapped."

"Hardly ever in Jersey," I said. "Too much overhead. Hotel rooms and food bills. The payoff's better on extortion."

His gaze dropped to my chest. "You ever do it with a sheik?"

"Excuse me?"

"You could get lucky today."

"Yeah. And you could get shot. How old are you, anyway?"

He tipped his chin up an eighth of an inch. "Nineteen."

My guess would be closer to fifteen, but hey, what do I know about Arabs? "You have luggage?"

"Two bags."

I led the way to baggage, snagged his two pieces, and rolled them out of the building across the pick-up lanes to the parking garage. When I had my charge settled into the backseat, I cruised off into gridlocked traffic.

After a couple minutes of creeping along Fahed was antsy. "What's the problem?"

"Too many cars," I said. "Not enough road."

"Well, do something."

I glanced at him in the rearview mirror. "What did you have in mind?"

"I don't know. Just *do* something. Just *go*."

"This isn't a helicopter. I can't just *go*."

"Okay," he said. "I've got an idea. How about we do this?"

"What?"

"This."

I turned in my seat and looked at him. "What is *this*?"

He wagged his wonkie at me and smiled.

Great. A fifteen-year-old sex fiend, exhibitionist sheik.

"I can make it do tricks," he said.

"Not in *my* car, you can't. Put it back in your pants, or I'll tell your father."

"My father would be proud. Look at me . . . I'm hung like a horse."

I pulled a knife out of my shoulder bag and flipped it open. "I can make you hung like a hamster."

"American whore bitch."

I rolled my eyes.

"This is intolerable," he said. "I hate this traffic. And I hate this car. And I hate sitting here doing nothing."

Fahed wasn't the only one experiencing road rage. Other drivers were coming unglued. Men were swearing to themselves and tugging at ties. Fingers drummed impatiently on steering wheels. Someone behind me leaned on his horn.

"I'll give you one hundred dollars if you let me drive." Fahed said.

"No."

"A thousand."

"No."

"Five thousand."

I glanced at him in the rearview mirror. "No."

"You were tempted," he said, smiling, looking satisfied.

Ugh.

An hour and a half later we managed to reach the New Brunswick interchange.

"I need something to drink," Fahed said. "There's nothing to drink in this car. I'm used to having a stretch with a bar. I want you to find a place to get me a soda."

I wasn't sure if this was limo protocol, but I figured what the hell, it was his nickel. I picked up Route 1 and looked for fast food. Not much of a challenge. The first thing that came up was a McDonald's. It was dinnertime and the drive-through lane looked like the Jersey Turnpike, so I junked the drive-through and parked the car.

"I want a Coke," he said, sitting tight, clearly not interested in standing in line with the rest of New Jersey.

Don't freak out, I told myself. He's used to being waited on. "Anything else?"

"French fries."

Fine. I grabbed my bag and crossed the lot. I swung though the door and chose a line. Two people in front of me. I studied the menu over the counter. One person left in front of me. I hiked my bag higher on my shoulder and looked out the window. I didn't see my car. There was a small twinge of alarm just below my heart. I scanned the lot. No car. I left the line and pushed through the door into the cool air. The car was gone.

Shit!

My first fear was that he'd been kidnapped. I'd been hired as a chauffeur and bodyguard for the sheik, and the sheik's been kidnapped. The fear was short-lived. No one would want this rotten kid. Face it, Stephanie, that little snot took the car.

I had two choices. I could call the police. Or I could call Ranger.

I tried Ranger first. "Bad news," I said. "I sort of lost the sheik."

"Where did you lose him?"

"North Brunswick. He sent me into a McDonald's for a soda, and next thing I knew, he was gone."

"Where are you now?"

"I'm still at the McDonald's." Where else would I be?

"Don't move. I'll get back to you."

The connection was severed. "When?" I asked the dead phone. "When?"

Ten minutes later the phone rang.

"No problem," Ranger said. "Found the sheik."

"How'd you find him?"

"I called the car phone."

"Was he kidnapped?"

"Impatient. Said he got tired of waiting for you."

"That little jerk-off!"

Several people stopped in their tracks and stared.

I lowered my voice and turned, facing the phone. "Sorry, I got carried away," I said to Ranger.

"Understandable, Babe."

"He's got my jacket."

"Bones will get it when he gets the car. You need a ride home?"

"I can call Lula."

"YOU SHOULD HAVE taken me with you," Lula said. "This wouldn't have happened if you hadn't hauled your skinny ass off on your own."

"It seemed like such an easy job. Pick up a kid and drive him somewhere."

"Look at this," Lula said, "we're passing by the mall. I bet some shopping would cheer you right up."

"I *do* need shoes."

"See," Lula said, "there's a reason for everything. God meant for you to shop tonight."

We entered the mall through Macy's and blasted into the shoe department first thing.

"Hold on here!" Lula said. "Look at these shoes!" She'd pulled a pair of black satin shoes off the display. They had pointy toes and four-inch heels and a slim ankle strap. "These are hot shoes," Lula said.

I had to agree. The shoes were hot. I got my size from the salesperson and tried the shoes on.

"Those shoes are *you*," Lula said. "You gotta get those shoes. We'll take these shoes," Lula said to the salesclerk. "Wrap 'em up."

Ten minutes later, Lula was pulling dresses off the rack. "*Yow!*" Lula said. "Hold the phone. Here it is."

The dress she was holding was barely there. It was a shimmery black scrap of miracle fiber with a low-cut neck and a short skirt.

"This is a genuine hard-on dress," Lula said.

I suspected she was right. I looked at the price tag and sucked in some air. "I can't afford this!"

"You gotta at least try it on," Lula said. "Maybe it won't fit so good, and then you'll feel better about not being able to buy it."

It seemed like sound reasoning, so I dragged myself off to the dressing room. I did a fast computation of money left on my credit card and winced. If I caught Randy Briggs and I ate all my meals for the next month at my mother's house and I did my own nails for the wedding, I could *almost* afford the dress.

"Damn skippy," Lula said when I tottered out of the dressing room in the black shoes and black dress. "Holy shit."

I checked myself out in the mirror. It was definitely a "damn skippy, holy shit" outfit. And if I could lose five pounds in the next two days, the dress would fit.

"Okay," I said. "I'll take it."

"We need some french fries to celebrate with," Lula said after I bought the dress. "My treat."

"I can't have french fries. Another ounce and I won't get into the dress."

"French fries are a vegetable," Lula said. "They don't count when it comes to fat. And besides, we'll have to walk all the way down the mall to get to the food court, so we'll get exercise. In fact, probably we'll be so weak from all that walking by the time we get there we'll have to have a piece of crispy fried chicken along with the french fries."

It was dark when we left the mall. I had the button open on my skirt to accommodate the fried chicken and french fries, and I was having a panic attack over my new clothes.

"Look at this," Lula said, sidling up to her Firebird. "Somebody left us a note. It better not be that someone put a ding in my car. I hate when that happens."

I looked over her shoulder to read the note.

"I saw you in the mall," the note said. "You shouldn't tempt men by wearing dresses like that."

"Guess this is for you," Lula said. "On account of I wasn't wearing no dress."

I did a quick scan of the lot. "Unlock the car and let's get out of here," I said to Lula.

"It's just some pervert note," Lula said.

"Yeah, but it was written by someone who knew where our car was parked."

"Could have been someone who saw us when we first got here. Some little runt waiting for his wife to come out of Macy's."

"Or it could have been written by someone who tailed me out of Trenton." And I didn't think that someone was Bunchy. I'd been alert for Bunchy's car. And besides, I was pretty sure Bunchy would watch Mabel, like I asked.

Lula and I looked at each other and shared the same thought . . . Ramirez. We quickly jumped into the Firebird and locked the doors.

"Probably it wasn't him," Lula said. "You would have seen him, don't you think?"

MY NEIGHBORHOOD IS quiet after dark. All the seniors are tucked away in their apartments by then, settled in for the night, watching reruns of *Seinfeld* and *Cop Bloopers*.

Lula dropped me off at the back door to my building at a little after nine, and true to form, not a creature was stirring. We looked for headlights and listened for footfalls and car engines and came up empty.

"I'll wait until you get in the building," Lula said.

"I'll be fine."

"Sure. I know that."

I took the stairs, hoping they'd help out with the chicken and fries. When I'm scared, it's always a toss-up between the elevator and the stairs. I feel more in control on the stairs, but the stairwell feels isolating, and I know when the fire doors are closed, sound doesn't carry. I had a sense of relief when I reached my floor and there was no Ramirez.

I let myself into my apartment and called hello to Rex. I dropped my shopping bags on the kitchen counter, kicked my shoes off, and stripped out of the pantyhose. I did a fast room-by-room check, and no large men turned up there, either. Whew. I returned to the kitchen to listen to my phone messages and shrieked when someone knocked at my door. I squinted out the peephole with my hand over my heart.

Ranger.

"You never knock," I said, opening the door.

"I always knock. You never answer." He handed me my jacket. "The little sheik said you weren't any fun."

"Scratch chauffeuring off the list."

Ranger studied me for a moment. "Do you want me to shoot him?"

"No!" But it was a tempting idea.

He glanced down at the shoes and pantyhose on the floor. "Am I interrupting something?"

"No. I just got home. Lula and I went shopping."

"Recreational therapy?"

"Yeah, but I also needed a new dress." I held the dress up for him to see. "Lula sort of talked me into this. What do you think?"

Ranger's eyes darkened and his mouth tightened into a small smile. My face got warm and the dress slipped from my fingers and fell to the floor.

Ranger picked the dress up and handed it to me.

"Okay," I said, blowing a strand of hair off my forehead. "Guess I know what you think of the dress."

"If you knew, you wouldn't be standing here," Ranger said. "If you knew, you'd have yourself barricaded in the bedroom with your gun in your hand."

Gulp.

Ranger's attention strayed to the note on the counter. "Someone else shares my opinion of the dress."

"The note was left on the windshield of Lula's Firebird. We found it when we came out of the mall."

"You know who wrote it?"

"I have a couple ideas."

"You want to share them with me?"

"Could just be some guy who saw me at the mall."

"Or?"

"Or it could be Ramirez."

"You have reason to think it's Ramirez?"

"Touching it makes my skin crawl."

SIX

"WORD ON THE street is that Ramirez got religion," Ranger said, relaxed against my kitchen counter, arms crossed over his chest.

"So maybe he doesn't want to rape and mutilate me. Maybe he just wants to save me."

"Either way, you should carry a gun."

When Ranger left I listened to the single message on my phone machine. "Stephanie? This is your mother. Remember you promised to take your grandmother to the funeral parlor tomorrow night. And you can come early and have something to eat with us. I'm going to have a nice leg of lamb."

The lamb sounded good, but I would have preferred the message to have been about Fred. Like, guess what, the funniest thing just happened . . . Fred showed up.

There was another knock on the door, and I looked out the peephole at Bunchy.

"I know you're lookin' out at me," he said. "And I know you're thinking you should go get your gun and your pepper spray and your electronic torture device, so just go get them all because I'm getting tired of standing here."

I opened the door a bit, leaving the security chain in place.

"Give me a break," Bunchy said.

"What do you want?"

"How come the Rambo guy gets in and I don't?"

"I work with him."

"You work with me, too. I just did a surveillance shift for you."

"Anything happen?"

"I'm not telling you until you let me in."

"I don't need to know that bad."

"Yes, you do. You're nosy."

He was right. I was nosy. I slid the chain off and opened the door.

"So what happened?" I asked.

"Nothing happened. The grass grew an eighth of an inch." He got a beer out of the refrigerator. "You know, your aunt is a real boozer. You should get her into AA or something." He noticed the dress on the counter. "Wowy kazowy," he said. "This your dress?"

"I got it to wear to a wedding."

"You need a date? I don't look so bad when I get cleaned up."

"I have a date. I've been sort of seeing this guy—"

"Yeah? What guy?"

"His name's Morelli. Joe Morelli."

"Oh, man, I know him. I can't believe you're going with Morelli. The guy is a loser. Excuse me for saying so, but he porks everyone he meets. You shouldn't have anything to do with him. You could do better."

"How do you know Morelli?"

"We have a professional relationship, being that he's a cop and I'm a bookie."

"I asked him about you, and he said he never heard of you."

Bunchy tipped his head back and laughed. It was the first time I'd ever heard him laugh, and it wasn't bad.

"He might know me by one of my other names," Bunchy said. "Or maybe he just doesn't want to come clean because he knows I might spill the beans about him."

"What would these other names be?"

"They're secret names," he said. "If I told you, then they wouldn't be secret anymore."

"Out!" I said, pointing stiff-armed to the door.

MORELLI CALLED AT nine the next morning. "Just wanted to remind you the wedding is tomorrow," he said. "I'll pick you up at four. And don't forget you have to come in to make a report on the Sloane Street shooting."

"Sure."

"You get any leads on Fred?"

"No. Nothing worth mentioning. Good thing I don't do this for a living."

"Good thing," Morelli said, sounding like he was smiling.

I hung up, and I called my friend Larry at RGC.

"Guess what, Larry?" I said. "I found the check. It was on my uncle's desk. Payment for three months' worth of garbage pickup. And the check has been canceled and everything."

"Fine," Larry said. "Bring the check in, and I'll credit the account."

"How late are you open?"

"Five."

"I'll be there before you close."

I shoveled my gear into my shoulder bag, locked my apartment behind me, and took the stairs to the lobby. I exited the building and crossed the lot to my car. I had the key in hand, ready to unlock my door, when I felt the presence of someone behind me. I turned and found myself toe-to-toe with Benito Ramirez.

"Hello, Stephanie," he said. "Nice to see you again. The champ missed you while he was away. He thought about you a lot."

The champ. Better known as Benito Ramirez, who was too crazy to talk about himself in the first person.

"What do you want?"

He smiled his sick smile. "You know what the champ wants."

"How about you tell me."

"He wants to be your friend. He wants to help you find Jesus."

"If you continue to stalk me, I'll get a restraining order."

The smile stayed on his mouth, but his eyes were cold and hard. Steel orbs floating in empty space. "Can't restrain a man of God, Stephanie."

"Move away from my car."

"Where are you going?" Ramirez asked. "Why don't you go with the champ? The champ'll take you for a ride." He stroked my cheek with the back of his hand. "He'll take you to see Jesus."

I dug down in my shoulder bag and pulled out my gun. "Get away from me."

Ramirez laughed softly and took a step backward. "When it's your time to see God, there'll be no escape."

I unlocked the driver's side door, slid behind the wheel, and drove away with Ramirez still standing in the lot. I stopped for a light two blocks down Hamilton and realized there were tears on my cheeks. Shit. I swiped the tears away and yelled at myself. "You are *not* afraid of Benito Ramirez!"

That was a stupid, empty statement, of course. Ramirez was a monster. Anyone with a grain of sense would be afraid of him. And I was beyond afraid. I was terrified to tears.

———

BY THE TIME I reached the office I was in pretty decent condition. My hands had stopped shaking, and my nose wasn't running. I still had some nausea, but I didn't think I'd throw up. It seemed like a weakness to be so frightened, and I wasn't crazy about the feeling. Especially since I'd chosen to work in a form of law enforcement. Hard to be effective when you're blubbering in fear. My one point of pride was that I hadn't shown my fear to Ramirez.

Connie stroked vermilion nail polish onto her thumbnail. "You calling the hospitals and the morgue about Fred?"

I placed the check facedown on the copier, closed the lid, and pushed the button. "Every morning."

"What's next?" Lula wanted to know.

"I got a picture of Fred from Mabel. I thought I'd flash it around the strip mall and maybe go door-to-door on the streets behind Grand Union." Hard to believe there wasn't someone out there who saw Fred leave the parking lot.

"Don't sound like a lot of fun to me," Lula said.

I took the copy of the check and dropped it into my shoulder bag. Then I made a folder with Fred's name on it, dropped the original check into the folder, and filed it in the office file cabinet under Shutz. It would have been easier to put it in my desk . . . but I didn't have a desk.

"How about Randy Briggs?" Lula said. "Aren't we gonna visit him today?"

Short of burning the building down, I didn't know how to get Randy Briggs out of his apartment.

Vinnie stuck his head out of his office. "I hear somebody say something about Briggs?"

"Not me. I didn't say nothing," Lula said.

"You have one chickenshit case," Vinnie said to me. "Why haven't you brought this guy in?"

"I'm working on it."

"Yeah, and it's not her fault," Lula said, "on account of he's wily."

"You have until eight o'clock Monday morning," Vinnie said. "Briggs' ass isn't in the slammer by Monday morning, I'm giving the case to somebody else."

"Vinnie, you know a bookie named Bunchy?"

"No. And trust me, I know every bookie on the East Coast." He pulled his head back into his office and slammed the door shut.

"Tear gas," Lula said. "That's the way to get him. We just lob a can of tear gas through his dumb-ass window and then wait for him to come running out, gagging and choking. I know where we can get some, too. I bet we could get some from Ranger."

"No! No tear gas," I said.

"Well, what are you gonna do? You gonna let Vinnie give this to Joyce Barnhardt?"

Joyce Barnhardt! Shit. I'd eat dirt before I'd let Joyce Barnhardt bring in Randy Briggs. Joyce Barnhardt is a mutant human being and my arch enemy. Vinnie hired her on as a part-time bounty hunter a couple months ago in exchange for services I didn't want to think about. She'd tried to steal one of my cases back then, and I had no intention of letting that happen again.

I went to school with Joyce, and all through school she'd lied and snitched and was loosey-goosey with other girls' boyfriends. Not to mention, I'd been married for less than a year when I'd caught Joyce woman-superior on my dining room table with my sweating, cheating ex-husband.

"I'm going to reason with Briggs," I said.

"Oh boy," Lula said. "This is gonna be good. I gotta see this."

"No. I'm going alone. I can do this by myself."

"Sure," Lula said. "I know that. Only it'd be more fun if I was there."

"No! No, no, no."

"Boy, you sure do got an attitude these days," Lula said. "You were better when you were getting some, you know what I mean? I don't know why you gave Morelli the boot anyway. I don't usually like cops, but that man has one fine ass."

I knew what she meant about my attitude. I was feeling damn cranky. I hitched my bag onto my shoulder. "I'll call if I need help."

"Unh," Lula said.

THINGS WERE QUIET at Cloverleaf Apartments. No traffic in the lot. No traffic in the dingy foyer. I took the stairs and knocked on Briggs' door. No answer. I moved out of sight and dialed his number on my cell phone.

"Hello," Briggs said.

"It's Stephanie. *Don't hang up!* I have to talk to you."

"There's nothing to talk about. And I'm busy. I have work to do."

"Look, I know this court thing is inconvenient for you. And I know it's unfair because you were unjustly charged. But it's something you have to do."

"No."

"Then do it for me."

"Why should I do it for you?"

"I'm a nice person. And I'm just trying to do my job. And I need the money to pay for a pair of shoes I just bought. And even more, if I don't bring you in, Vinnie is going to give your case to Joyce Barnhardt. And I hate Joyce Barnhardt."

"Why do you hate Joyce Barnhardt?"

"I caught her screwing my husband, who is now my ex-husband, on my dining-room table. Can you imagine? My dining-room table."

"Jeez," Briggs said. "And she's a bounty hunter, too?"

"Well, she used to do makeovers at Macy's, but now she's working for Vinnie."

"Bummer."

"Yeah. So, how about it? Won't you let me bring you in? It won't be so bad. Honest."

"Are you kidding? I'm not letting a loser like you bring me in. How would it look?"

Click. He hung up.

Loser? Excuse me? Loser? Okay, that does it. No more Ms. Nice Person. No more reasoning. This jerk is going down. "*Open this door!*" I yelled. "*Open this goddamn door!*"

A woman popped her head out from the apartment across the hall. "If you don't stop this racket I'm going to call the police. We don't put up with this kind of goings-on here."

I turned and looked at her.

"Oh, dear," she said and slammed her door shut.

I gave Briggs' door a couple kicks with my foot and hammered on it with my fists. "Are you coming out?"

"Loser," he said through the door. "You're just a stupid loser, and you can't make me do anything I don't want to do."

I hauled my gun out of my shoulder bag and fired one off at the lock. The round glanced off the metal and lodged in the door frame. Christ. Briggs was right. I was a fucking loser. I didn't even know how to shoot off a lock.

I ran downstairs to the Buick and got a tire iron out of the trunk. I ran back upstairs and started whacking away at the door with the tire iron. I made a couple dents but that was about it. Bashing the door in with the tire iron was going to take a while. My forehead was beaded with sweat, and sweat stained the front

of my T-shirt. A small crowd of people had collected at the far
end of the hall.

"You gotta get the tire iron between the door and the jamb,"
an old man at the end of the hall said. "You gotta wedge it in."

"Shut up, Harry," a woman said. "Anyone can see she's crazy.
Don't encourage her."

"Only trying to be helpful," Harry said.

I followed his advice and wedged the iron between the door
and the jamb and leaned into it. A chunk of wood splintered off
the jamb and some metal stripping pulled away.

"See?" Harry said. "I told you."

I gouged some more chunks from the doorjamb down by the
lock. I was trying to get the tire iron back in when Briggs opened
the door a crack and looked out at me.

"What are you, nuts? You can't just destroy someone's door."

"Watch me," I said. I shoved the tire iron at Briggs and put
my weight behind it. The security chain popped off its mooring,
and the door flew open.

"Stay away from me!" he hollered. "I'm armed."

"What, are you kidding me? You're holding a fork."

"Yes, but it's a meat fork. And it's sharp. I could poke your
eye out with this fork."

"Not on your best day, Shorty."

"I hate you," Briggs said. "You're ruining my life."

I could hear sirens in the distance. Swell. Just what I needed . . .
the police. Maybe we could call in the fire department, too. And
the dogcatcher. And hell, how about a couple newspaper report-
ers.

"You're not taking me in," Briggs said. "I'm not ready." He
lunged at me with his fork. I jumped away, and the fork ripped
a hole in my Levi's.

"Hey," I said, "these were almost new pants."

He came at me again, shouting, "I hate you. I hate you." This time I smacked the fork out of his hand, and he stumbled into an end table, knocking the table over, smashing a lamp in the process. "My lamp," he shrieked. "Look what you did to my lamp." He lowered his head and charged at me bull-style. I stepped to the side, and he crashed into a bookcase. Books tumbled out, and knickknacks shattered on the polished wood floor.

"Stop it," I said. "You're wrecking your apartment. Get a grip on yourself."

"I'll get a grip on you," he snarled, lunging forward, catching me with a body tackle at knee level.

We both went down hard to the floor. I had him by about seventy pounds, but he was in a frenzy and I couldn't pin him. We rolled around, locked together, cursing and breathing heavy. He slithered away from me and ran for the door. I scrambled after him on hands and knees and grabbed him by the foot at the top of the stairs. He yelped and fell forward, and we both went head over heels tumbling down the stairs to the landing, where we tangled again. There was some scratching and hair grabbing and attempted eye-gouging. I had him by the front of his shirt when we lost balance and pitched down the second flight of stairs.

I flopped to a stop in the foyer, flat on my back, gasping for air. Briggs was squashed under me, dazed into inertia. I blinked my eyes to clear my head and two cops swam into focus. They were staring down at me, and they were smiling.

One of the cops was Carl Costanza. I'd gone to school with Carl and we'd stayed friends . . . in a remote sort of way.

"I heard you liked the top," Carl said, "but don't you think this is carrying it a little far?"

Briggs squirmed under my weight. "Get off me. I can't breathe."

"He doesn't deserve to breathe," I said. "He ripped my Levi's."

"Yeah," Carl said, lifting me off Briggs, "that's a capital offense."

I recognized the other cop as Costanza's partner. His name was Eddie Something. Everyone called him Big Dog.

"Jeez," Big Dog said, barely controlling laughter, "what did you do to this poor little guy? Looks like you beat the crap out of him."

Briggs was standing on wobbly legs. His shirt was untucked and he'd lost a shoe. His left eye was starting to bruise and swell, and his nose was bleeding.

"I didn't do anything!" I yelped. "I was trying to take him into custody and he went berserk."

"That's right," Harry said from the top of the landing. "I saw the whole thing. This runty little guy just about ruined himself. And this lady hardly put a hand to him. Except of course when they were wrestling."

Carl looked at the cuff still attached to Briggs' wrist. "Your bracelet?" he asked me.

I nodded.

"You're supposed to cuff both hands."

"Very funny."

"You got papers?"

"Upstairs in my shoulder bag."

We climbed the stairs while Big Dog baby-sat Briggs.

"Holy shit," Costanza said when he saw Briggs' door. "Did you do this?"

"He wouldn't let me in."

"Hey, Big Dog," Costanza yelled. "Lock the little guy in the car and come take a look. You gotta see this."

I gave Costanza the bond documents. "Maybe we could keep this all kind of quiet—"

"Holy shit," Big Dog said when he saw the door.

"Steph did that," Costanza told him proudly.

Big Dog clapped me on the shoulder. "I guess they don't call you the bounty hunter from hell for nothing."

"Everything seems to be in order," Costanza said to me. "Congratulations. You caught yourself a Munchkin."

Big Dog examined the doorjamb. "You know there's a slug in here?"

Costanza looked at me.

"Well, I didn't have a key—"

Costanza put his hands over his ears. "I don't want to hear this."

I limped into Briggs' apartment, found a set of keys on a hook in his kitchen, and used one to lock his door. Then I collected his shoe, which had been left on the landing, gave the shoe and the keys to Briggs, and told Carl I'd follow him in.

When I walked back to the Buick, Bunchy was waiting for me. "Cripes," he said. "You beat the bejeezus out of that little guy. Who the hell was he, the Son of Satan?"

"He's a computer operator who got picked up for carrying concealed. He really isn't such a bad guy."

"Man, I'd hate to see what you do to someone you don't like."

"How did you know where to find me? And why weren't you in my parking lot when I needed you?"

"I picked you up leaving the office. I overslept this morning, so I tried hitting your usual haunts and got lucky. What's new with Fred?"

"I haven't found him."

"You aren't giving up, are you?"

"No, I'm not giving up. Listen, I have to go. I have to get my body receipt."

"Don't drive too fast. There's something wrong with my transmission. It makes this real bad sound when I do over forty."

I watched him walk to his car. I was pretty sure I knew what he was, and he wasn't a bookie. I just didn't know why he was tagging after me.

COSTANZA AND BIG Dog brought Briggs through the back door to the docket lieutenant.

The docket lieutenant looked over his desk at Briggs. "Damn, Stephanie," he said, smiling, "what'd you do to the poor little guy? What, are you on the rag today?"

Juniak was passing through. "You're lucky," he said to Briggs. "Usually she blows people up."

Briggs didn't look like he thought that was funny. "I've been framed," he said.

I got my body receipt for Briggs, and then I went upstairs to Crimes Against Persons and gave my report on the Sloane Street shooting. I called Vinnie and told him I brought Randy Briggs in, so America could rest easier tonight. Then I drove over to RGC with Bunchy close on my bumper.

It was a little after three when I got to Water Street. Clouds had rolled in late in the day, thick and low, the color and consistency of lard. I could feel them pressing on the roof of the Buick, slowing my progress, dulling down the firing of brainy synapses. I cruised on autopilot, my thoughts sliding from Uncle Fred to Joe Morelli to Charlie Chan. Life was good for Charlie Chan. He knew freaking everything.

Two blocks from RGC I snapped out of the stupor, realizing there was something going on in the street ahead. There were cops in front of RGC. Lots of them. The medical examiner's truck was there, too, and this was not a good sign. I parked half a block from RGC and walked the rest of the way, Bunchy trailing after me like a faithful dog. I looked for a familiar face in the crowd. No luck. A small knot of uniformed RGC employees huddled on the fringe. Probably had just come in with the trucks.

"What's going on?" I asked one of the men.

"Somebody got shot."

"Do you know who?"

"Lipinski."

The shock must have shown on my face, because the man said, "Did you know him?"

I shook my head. "No. I was just coming to settle my aunt's bill. How did it happen?"

"Suicide. I was the one who found him," another of the men said. "I brought my truck in early, and I went inside to get my paycheck. And there he was with his brains blown out. He must have put the gun in his mouth. Christ, there was blood and brains all over the place. I wouldn't have thought Lipinski had that much brains."

"Are you sure it was suicide?"

"There was a note, and I read it. Lipinski said he was the one who offed Martha Deeter. Said they'd had a fight over an account, and he shot her. And then he tried to make it look like she was robbed. Said he couldn't live with what he'd done, so he was checkin' out."

Oh boy.

"That's horseshit," Bunchy said. "That smells like a load of horseshit."

I hung around for a while longer. The forensic photographer left. And most of the police left. The RGC men left one by one. And then I left, too, with Bunchy in tow. He'd gotten quiet after his horseshit pronouncement. And very serious.

"Two RGC employees are dead," I said to him. "Why?"

We locked eyes for a moment, and he shook his head and walked away.

I TOOK A fast shower, dried my hair, and dressed in a short denim skirt and red T-shirt. I took a look at my hair and decided it needed some help, so I did the hot roller thing. My hair still didn't look wonderful after the rollers, so I lined my eyes and added extra mascara. Stephanie Plum, master of diversion. If your hair is bad, shorten your skirt and add extra mascara.

Before I left the apartment, I took a minute to go through the Yellow Pages and find a new garbage company for Mabel.

Bunchy was in the lobby when I came down. He was leaning against the wall, and he was still looking serious. Or maybe he just looked tired.

"You look nice," he said to me. "Real nice, but you wear too much makeup."

GRANDMA WAS AT the door when I arrived. "Did you hear about the garbage guy? Blew his brains out. Lavern Stankowski called and said her son, Joey, was working the EMS truck. And he said he never saw anything like it. Said there was brains all over the place. Said the whole back half of the guy's head was stuck to the wall in the garbage office."

Grandma slid her uppers around some. "Lavern said the deceased was being laid out at Stiva's. Imagine the job Stiva's going to have with that one. Probably use up two pounds of putty to fill all the holes. Remember Rita Gunt?"

Rita Gunt was ninety-two when she died. She'd lost a lot of weight in the later years of her life, and her family had asked Stiva to give her a more robust look for her last public appearance. I guess Stiva had done the best he could with what he had to work with, but Rita had gone into the ground looking like Mrs. Potato Head.

"If somebody was going to kill me I wouldn't want it to be with a bullet to the head," Grandma said.

My father was in the living room in his favorite chair. And from the corner of my eye I saw him peek around the edge of his newspaper.

"I want to get poisoned," Grandma said. "That way my hair wouldn't get messed."

"Hmm," my father said thoughtfully.

My mother came out from the kitchen. She smelled like roast lamb and red cabbage, and her face glowed from stove steam. "Any word about Fred?"

"Nothing new," I said.

"I think there's something funny going on with these garbage people," Grandma said. "Somebody's killing the garbage people, and I bet they killed Fred, too."

"Larry Lipinski left a suicide note," I told her.

"It could have been forged," Grandma said. "It could have been a fake to throw everybody off guard."

"I thought it was aliens that took Fred," my father said from behind his paper.

"That would account for a lot of things," Grandma said. "Nothing to say aliens didn't off the garbage people, too."

My mother shot my father a warning glance and went back to the kitchen. "Everyone come to the table before the lamb gets cold," she said. "And I don't want to hear any more talk about aliens and killing."

"It's the change," Grandma whispered to me. "Your mother's been snarfy ever since she started the change."

"I heard that," my mother said. "And I'm *not* snarfy."

"I keep telling her she should take them hormone pills," Grandma said. "I've been thinking about taking them myself. Mary Jo Klick started taking them, and she said there were parts to her that had got all shriveled, and after a week on them hormones she was all plumped up again." Grandma looked down at herself. "I wouldn't mind getting plumped up in some of them parts."

We all went to the table and took our places. Grace was said at Christmas and Easter. Since this wasn't either of those, my father shoveled food onto his plate and dug in, head down, concentrating on the task at hand.

"What do you think happened to Uncle Fred?" I asked, catching his attention between forkfuls of lamb and potato.

He looked up surprised. No one ever asked his opinion. "Mob," he said. "When someone disappears without a trace, it's the mob. They've got ways."

"Why would the mob want to kill Uncle Fred?"

"I don't know," my father said. "All I know is it sounds like the mob."

"We better hurry," Grandma said. "I don't want to be late for the viewing. I want to get a good seat right up front, and there'll probably be a crowd, being that the deceased was shot. You know how some people are nosy about that sort of thing."

There was silence at the table, no one daring to make a comment.

"Well, I guess I might be a little nosy," Grandma finally said.

When we were done I put some lamb and potatoes and vegetables in a disposable aluminum pie plate.

"What's that for?" Grandma wanted to know.

I added a plastic knife and fork. "Stray dog down by the Kerner's."

"He eat with a knife and fork?"

"Don't ask," I said.

SEVEN

STIVA'S FUNERAL HOME was in a big white house on Hamilton. There'd been a fire in the basement, and much of the house was newly rebuilt and refurnished. New green indoor-outdoor carpet on the front porch. New ivory medallion wallpaper throughout. New industrial-strength blue-green carpeting in the lobby and viewing rooms.

I parked the Blue Bomb in the lot and helped Grandma wobble inside on the black patent-leather pumps she always wore to evening viewings.

Constantine Stiva was in the middle of the lobby, directing traffic. Mrs. Balog in slumber room three. Stanley Krienski in slumber room two. And Martha Deeter, who was clearly going to be the big draw, was laid out in room one.

Not long ago I'd had a run-in with Constantine's son, Spiro. The result had been the aforementioned fire and the mysterious disappearance of Spiro. Fortunately, Con was the consummate undertaker, his demeanor always controlled, his smile sympathetic, his voice as smooth as vanilla custard. There was never any ugly mention of the unfortunate incident. After all, I was a potential customer. And with my line of work it might be sooner rather than later. Not to mention Grandma Mazur.

"And who are you visiting tonight?" he asked. "Ah yes, Ms. Deeter is resting in room one."

Resting. Unh.

"Let's get a move on," Grandma said, taking me by the hand and pulling me forward. "Looks like there's already a crowd collecting."

I scanned the faces. Some regulars like Myra Smulinski and Harriet Farver. Some other people who probably worked for RGC and most likely wanted to make sure Martha was really dead. A knot of people dressed in black, staying close to the casket—family members. I didn't see any representatives from Big Business. I was pretty sure my father was wrong about the mob doing in Uncle Fred and the garbage people. Still, it didn't hurt to keep my eyes open. I also didn't see any aliens.

"Will you look at this," Grandma said. "Closed casket. Isn't this a fine howdy-do. I get dressed up and come out to pay my respects, and I don't even get to see anything."

Martha Deeter was shot and autopsied. They'd taken her brain out to get weighed. After she was put back together she probably looked like Frankenstein. I was personally relieved to see a closed casket.

"I'm going to check out the flowers," Grandma said. "See who sent what."

I did another crowd scan and spotted Terry Gilman. *Hello!* Maybe my father was right. It was rumored that Terry Gilman worked for her uncle Vito Grizolli. Vito was a family man who ran a dry cleaning business that laundered a lot more than dirty clothes. What I heard from Connie, who was connected in a nonparticipating sort of way, was that Terry had started out in collections and was moving up the corporate ladder.

"Terry Gilman?" I said with more statement than question, extending my hand.

Terry was slim and blond and had dated Morelli all through high school. None of which endeared her to me. She was wearing an expensive gray silk suit and matching heels. Her manicure was to die for, and the gun she carried in a slim-line shoulder holster was discreetly hidden by the line of her jacket. Only someone who had worn a similar rig would notice Terry's.

"Stephanie Plum," Terry said, "nice to see you again. Were you friends with Martha?"

"No. I'm here with my grandma. She likes to come to scope out the caskets. How about you? Were you friends with Martha?"

"Business associates," Terry said.

That hung in the air for a moment.

"I hear you're working for your uncle Vito."

"Customer relations," Terry said.

Another silence.

I rocked back on my heels. "Funny how Martha and Larry died from gunshots one day apart."

"Tragic."

I lowered my voice and leaned a little closer. "That wasn't your job, was it? I mean, you weren't the one to, uh—"

"Whack them?" Terry said. "No. Sorry to disappoint you. It wasn't me. Anything else you want to know?"

"Well, yeah, actually my uncle Fred is missing."

"I didn't whack him either," Terry said.

"I didn't think so," I said, "but it never hurts to ask."

Terry glanced at her watch. "I've got to give my respects, and then I'm out of here. I have two more viewings tonight. One at Moser and one across town."

"Boy, sounds like Vito's business is booming."

Terry shrugged. "People die."

Uh-huh.

Her eyes focused on something beyond my shoulder, and her interest shifted. "Well, well," she said, "look who's here."

I turned to see who put the purr in Terry's voice and wasn't all that surprised. It was Morelli.

He draped a proprietary arm around my shoulders and smiled at Terry. "How's it going?"

"Can't complain," Terry said.

Morelli cut his eyes to the casket at the end of the room. "You know Martha?"

"Sure," Terry said. "We go way back."

Morelli smiled some more.

"I think I'll go find Grandma," I said.

Morelli tightened his hold on me. "Not yet. I need to talk to you." He nodded at Terry. "Will you excuse us?"

"I need to be moving on anyway," Terry said. She sent Joe a smoochy air kiss and went off in search of the Deeters.

Joe dragged me out to the lobby.

"That was *very* friendly back there," I said, trying hard not to narrow my eyes and grind my teeth.

"We have a lot in common," Morelli said. "We both work in vice."

"Hmm."

"You know, you're kind of cute when you're jealous."

"I'm *not* jealous."

"Liar."

Now my eyes were definitely narrowed, but I was secretly thinking it'd be nice if he'd kiss me. "Did you want to discuss something?"

"Yeah. I want to know what the hell went on today. Did you really beat the shit out of that poor little Briggs guy?"

"No! He fell down the stairs."

"Oh boy," Morelli said.

"He *did*!"

"Honey, I say that all the time, and it's never true."

"There were witnesses."

Morelli was trying to look serious, but I could see the grin twitching at the corners of his mouth. "Costanza said you tried to shoot the lock off, and when that didn't work you took an axe to the door."

"That's totally wrong . . . it was a tire iron."

"Christ," Morelli said. "Is it that time of the month?"

I pressed my lips together.

He tucked a clump of hair behind my ear and trailed a fingertip down my cheek.

"Guess I'll find out tomorrow."

"Oh?"

"A woman's always an easy mark at a wedding," Morelli said.

I thought about the tire iron. It'd be really satisfying to clonk Morelli on the head with it. "Is that why you invited me?"

Morelli grinned.

Yep. He definitely deserved to get smacked with the tire iron. Then after I smacked him I'd kiss him. Run my hand down his chest to his flat hard stomach to his nice hard . . .

Grandma materialized at my elbow. "How nice to see you," she said to Morelli. "Hope this means you're going to start paying attention to my granddaughter again. Things are pretty dull since you got cut out of the scene."

"She broke my heart," Morelli said.

Grandma shook her head. "She don't know much."

Morelli looked pleased.

"Well, I'm ready to go," Grandma said. "Nothing to see here. They've got the lid nailed down. Besides, there's a Jackie Chan movie coming on at nine o'clock, and I don't want to miss it.

Eeeya!" she said, making a kung fu–type move. "You could come over to watch it with us," Grandma said to Morelli. "We've got some pie left from dessert, too."

"Sounds good," Morelli said, "but I'm going to have to take a rain check. I'm working tonight. I have to relieve someone on a stakeout."

BUNCHY WAS NOWHERE in sight when we came out of the funeral home. So maybe the way to get rid of him was to feed him. I dropped Grandma off and continued on to my apartment. I circled the parking lot once, looking between cars, making sure Ramirez wasn't waiting for me.

Rex was running on his wheel when I came in. He stopped and twitched his whiskers at me when I flicked the light on.

"Food!" I said to Rex, showing him the brown grocery bag that always accompanied me home from a dinner at my parents. "Lamb leftovers, mashed potatoes, vegetables, a jar of pickled beets, two bananas, a quarter pound sliced ham, half a loaf of bread, and apple pie." I broke off a chunk of pie and dropped it into Rex's food dish, and Rex almost fell off his wheel in excitement.

I would have liked a piece of pie, too, but I thought about the little black dress and had a banana instead. I was still hungry after the banana, so I made myself half a ham sandwich. After the sandwich I picked at the lamb. And finally I gave in and ate the pie. Tomorrow morning I'd get up first thing and go for a run. Maybe. No! Definitely! Okay, I knew how to do this. I'd call Ranger and see if he wanted to run with me. Then he'd be over here first thing tomorrow and make me go out and get some exercise.

"Yo," Ranger said, answering the phone. His voice was husky, and I realized it was late and I'd probably awakened him.

"It's Stephanie. I'm sorry to be calling so late."

He took a slow breath. "No problem. Last time you called me late at night you were naked and chained to your shower curtain rod. I hope this isn't going to be disappointing."

That had happened when we'd first started working together and I barely knew him. He'd broken into my apartment and released me with clinical efficiency. I suspected he'd act differently now. The thought of him coming upon me naked and chained *now* gave me a hot flash.

"Sorry," I said. "You only get one call like that in a lifetime. This call's about exercise. Um, I could use some."

"Now?"

"No! In the morning. I want to go running, and I'm looking for a partner."

"You're not looking for a partner," Ranger said. "You're looking for an enforcer. You hate to run. You must be worried about getting into that black dress. What did you eat just now? Piece of cake? Candy bar?"

"Everything," I said. "I just ate everything."

"You need some self-control, Babe."

Boy, that was the truth. "Are you going to run with me, or what?"

"Only if you're serious about getting into shape."

"I am."

"You're a terrible liar," Ranger said. "But since I don't want to have some fat chick working for me, I'll be there at six."

"I'm not a chick," I yelled. But he'd already hung up.

Damn.

I SET THE alarm for five-thirty, but was awake at five and dressed by five-fifteen. I wasn't all that enthusiastic about running anymore. And I didn't especially care about being on time as a courtesy to Ranger. My fear was that I'd oversleep, and when Ranger broke into my apartment to wake me up, I'd drag him into bed with me.

And then what would I tell Joe? We sort of had an agreement. Except neither of us knew exactly what the agreement meant. In fact, now that I thought about it, maybe we didn't have an agreement at all. Actually, it was more like we were in agreement negotiations.

Besides, I wasn't going to do anything with Ranger because getting involved with Ranger would be the equivalent to sky diving without a parachute. I was temporarily oversexed, but I wasn't any more stupid than usual.

I had a ham sandwich and the rest of the pie for breakfast. I did some stretches. I tweezed my eyebrows. I changed from shorts to sweats. And at six o'clock I was in the lobby, watching Ranger pull into the lot.

"Man," he said, "you must be serious about running. I didn't expect you to actually be *up* at this hour. Last time we ran I had to drag you out of bed."

I was wearing sweats, and I was freezing my butt off, wondering where the hell the sun was. Ranger was wearing a T-shirt with the sleeves cut out, and he didn't look cold at all. He did a couple hamstring stretches, a couple neck rolls, and began jogging in place.

"You ready?" Ranger asked.

A mile later I pulled up and bent at the waist, trying to suck in some air. My shirt was soaked in sweat and my hair was plastered to my head. "Hold it a minute," I said. "I have to throw up. Boy, I'm really out of shape." And maybe I shouldn't have had the ham and pie.

"You aren't going to throw up," Ranger said. "Keep going."

"I can't keep going."

"Do another quarter mile."

I shoved off behind him. "Boy, I'm really out of shape," I said again. Guess running once every three months wasn't enough for maximum fitness.

"Two more minutes," Ranger said. "You can make it."

"I really think I'm going to throw up."

"You're *not* going to throw up," Ranger said. "One more minute."

The sweat was dripping off my chin and running into my eyes, blurring my vision. I wanted to wipe it away, but I couldn't lift my arm that high. "We there yet?"

"Yes. Mile and a quarter," Ranger said. "See, I knew you could do it."

I was unable to speak, so I nodded my head.

Ranger was jogging in place. "Want to keep moving," he said. "You ready to go?"

I bent over and threw up.

"That's not gonna save you," Ranger said.

I gave him a stiff middle finger.

"Shit," Ranger said, looking down at the mess I'd made on the ground. "What's that pink stuff?"

"Ham sandwich."

"Maybe you want to just shoot yourself in the head."

"I like ham."

He jogged a few feet in front of me. "Come on. We'll do another mile."

"I just threw up!"

"Yeah, so?"

"So I'm not running anymore."

"No pain, no gain, Babe."

"I don't like pain," I said. "I'm going home. And I'm walking."

He pushed off. "I'll catch you on the way back."

Look on the bright side, I thought. At least I didn't have to worry about breakfast going straight to my thighs. And throwing up is so attractive that chances were real good I wouldn't have to worry about Ranger having a libido attack over me anytime in the near future.

I was walking one block from Hamilton, in a neighborhood of small single-family houses. Traffic was picking up on Hamilton, but one block over, where I walked, activity was centered in kitchens. Lights were on, coffee was brewing, cereal bowls were being set out. It was Saturday, but Trenton wasn't sleeping in. Kids had to be chauffeured to football and soccer. Laundry had to go to the cleaner. Cars needed washing. And the farmer's market was calling . . . fresh vegetables, eggs, baked goods, and sausages.

The sun was weak in a murky sky, and the air felt cold against my sweat-soaked clothes. I was three blocks from my apartment building, planning my day. Canvass the area around the strip mall, showing Uncle Fred's photo. Get home in time to pour myself into the little black dress. All the while keeping an eye out for Bunchy.

I heard a runner coming up behind me. Ranger, I thought, steeling myself not to get coerced into racing him home.

"Hello, Stephanie," the runner said.

My walking faltered. The runner was Ramirez. He was dressed in sweats and running shoes, but he wasn't sweating. And he wasn't breathing heavy. He was smiling, dancing around me on the balls of his feet, alternately shadowboxing and jogging in place.

"What do you want?" I asked.

"The champ wants to be your friend. The champ can show you things. He can take you places you've never been."

I was torn between wanting Ranger to show up and save me, and not wanting Ranger to see Ramirez at all. I suspected Ranger's solution to my stalking problem might be death. There was a good possibility that Ranger killed people on a regular basis. Only bad guys, of course, so who was I to criticize? Still, I didn't want him killing someone on my behalf. Not even if it was Ramirez. Although, if Ramirez died in his sleep or was accidentally run over by a truck, it wouldn't bother me too much.

"I'm not going anywhere with you, ever," I said. "And if you continue to harass me I'll take steps to make sure it stops."

"It's your destiny to go with the champ," Ramirez said. "You can't escape it. Your friend Lula went with me. Ask her how she liked it, Stephanie. Ask Lula what it's like to be with the champ."

I got a mental picture of Lula left naked and bloodied on my fire escape. Good thing I'd already thrown up because if there was anything in my stomach I'd be ralphing now.

I strode off, walking away from him. You don't debate with a madman. He pitty-patted after me for half a block, and then he laughed softly and called good-bye, and he was gone, jogging off toward Hamilton.

Ranger didn't reach me until I was at my parking lot. His skin was slick with sweat, and his breathing was labored. He'd been running hard, and he looked like he'd enjoyed it.

"Are you okay?" he asked. "Your face is white. I thought you'd have recovered by now."

"Think you're right about ham," I said.

"You want to try this again tomorrow?"

"I don't think I'm cut out to be this healthy."

"You still looking for work?"

I mentally cracked my knuckles. I needed money, but Ranger's jobs weren't turning out so good. "What is it this time?"

Ranger unlocked his car, reached inside, and retrieved a large yellow envelope. "I have a high-bond FTA floating around Trenton. I have someone watching his girlfriend's house and someone watching his apartment. The guy's mother lives in the Burg. I don't think it's worthwhile to put someone on the mother's house twenty-four hours, but you know a lot of people in the Burg, and

I thought you might be able to find an informant." He handed the envelope over. "The guy's name is Alphonse Ruzick."

I knew the Ruzicks. They lived on the other side of the Burg, two doors down from Carmine's Bakery, across from the Catholic school. Sandy Polan lived on that block. I'd gone to school with Sandy. She was married to Robert Scarfo now, so I guess she was Sandy Scarfo, but I still thought of her as being Sandy Polan. She had three kids, and the last one looked a lot more like the next-door neighbor than like Robert Scarfo. I peeked inside the envelope. Photo of Alphonse Ruzick, apprehension authorization, bond agreement, and personal information sheet.

"Okay," I said. "I'll see if I can find someone to rat on Alphonse."

I pushed through the glass door to the lobby and did a fast sweep to make sure Ramirez wasn't lying in wait for me. I took the stairs and felt safe when I stepped onto my floor. There was the smell of bacon cooking behind Mrs. Karwatt's door. And the television was blaring in Mr. Wolesky's apartment. A normal morning. Business as usual. Aside from the fact that I'd barfed and been scared half to death by a psychopathic maniac.

I opened my door and found Bunchy on the couch, reading the paper.

"You've got to stop breaking into my apartment," I said. "It's rude."

"I feel conspicuous sitting out in the hall. I figure it doesn't look good for you to have men loitering. What'll people think?"

"Then loiter in your car, in the lot."

"I was cold."

Someone knocked on my door. I went to the door and peeked out. It was my neighbor from across the hall, Mr. Wolesky.

"Did you take my paper again?" he asked.

I got the paper from Bunchy and returned it to Mr. Wolesky.

"Out," I told Bunchy. "Good-bye."

"What are you doing today? Just so I know."

"I'm going to the office, and then I'm putting some posters up at the Grand Union."

"The office, huh? Maybe I'll pass on the office. But you can tell Lula there's gonna be payback for making me lose you the other day."

"You should be happy she didn't use her stun gun."

He stood at the couch with his hands in his pockets. "You want to tell me about the color copies on your table?"

Damn. I hadn't put the prints away. "They're nothing special."

"Body parts in a garbage bag?"

"Do you find them interesting?"

"I don't know who it is, if that's what you're getting at." He moved to the table. "Twenty-four pictures. The whole roll. Two with the bag tied up. That's got me thinking. And they're recent, too."

"How do you know that?"

"There are newspapers stuck in the bag along with the body. I looked at them with your magnifying glass, and you see this one here with the color? I'm pretty sure this is a supplement from Kmart advertising the Mega Monster. I know because my kid made me go get him one the second he saw the ad."

"You have a kid?"

"Why is that such a big shock? He lives with my ex-wife."

"When was the first time the ad ran?"

"I called and checked. It was a week ago Thursday."

The day before Fred disappeared.

"Where'd you get these pictures?" Bunchy asked.

"Fred's desk."

Bunchy shook his head. "Fred was involved in some very bad shit."

I locked and bolted the door after Bunchy left. I showered

and dressed in Levi's and a black turtleneck. I tucked the turtle-neck in and added a belt. I stuffed Uncle Fred's picture into my shoulder bag and took off to do my pseudo–private investigator thing.

My first stop was at the office to collect my pittance on Briggs.

Lula looked up from the filing when I walked in. "Girl, we've been waiting for you. We heard how you beat the crap out of that Briggs guy. Not that he didn't deserve it, but I think if you was gonna beat the crap out of someone, you could let me in on it. You know how bad I wanted to beat the crap out of that little wiener."

"Yeah," Connie said to me, "you've got some nerve hogging all the brutality."

"I didn't do anything," I said. "He fell down the stairs."

Vinnie opened his office door and stuck his head out. "Jesus Christ," he said. "How many times have I told you not to hit people in the face? You hit them in the body where it doesn't show. Kick them in the nuts. Sucker-punch them in the kid-ney."

"He fell down the stairs!" I said again.

"Yeah, but you pushed him, right?"

"No!"

"See, that's good," Vinnie said. "Lying is good. Stick with that story. I like it." He stepped back into his office and slammed the door shut.

I gave Connie the body receipt, and Connie wrote me a check.

"I'm off to find a witness," I said.

Lula had her purse in her hand. "I'll go with you. Just in case that Bunchy guy decides to follow you some more. I'll take care of his ass."

I smiled. This should be interesting.

WE STARTED AT the copy store on Route 33. I enlarged Fred's photo and reproduced it onto a hand-printed request for information about Fred's disappearance.

After the copy store, I cruised into the Grand Union lot and was disappointed not to see Bunchy waiting for us. I parked close to the store, and Lula and I took the posters inside.

"Hold on here," Lula said. "They got Coke on sale. This is a real good price for Coke. And they got some good-lookin' lunchmeat in the deli section. What time is it? Is it lunchtime? You mind if I do some food shopping?"

"Hey," I said to Lula, "don't let me slow you down." I tacked a poster onto the bulletin board in the front of the store. Then I took the original photo and started quizzing shoppers while Lula foraged in the bakery aisle.

"Have you seen this man?" I asked.

The reply would be no. Or sometimes, "Yeah, that's Fred Shutz. What a putz."

No one could remember seeing him on the day of the disappearance. And no one had seen him since. And no one especially cared that he was missing.

"How's it going?" Lula asked, wheeling a shopping cart past me, en route to the car.

"Slow. No takers."

"I'm gonna drop these bags off. And then I'm going to look in that little video store at the end."

"Knock yourself out," I said. I showed Fred's photo to a few more people and at noon I broke for lunch. I searched my pockets and the bottom of my bag and came up with enough money to buy a small bag of nutritious, already washed and ready-to-eat baby carrots. For the same amount of money I could also buy a giant Snickers bar. Boy, what a tough decision.

Lula returned from the video store just as I was licking the last of the chocolate off my fingers. "Look at this," Lula said. "They had *Boogie Nights* on sale. I don't care much about the movie. I just like to look at the ending once in a while."

"I'm going door-to-door with Fred's photo," I told her. "Want to help?"

"Sure, you just give me one of them posters, and I'll door-to-door the hell out of you."

We divided the neighborhood in half and decided to work until two o'clock. I was done early, scoring a big zero. One woman said she saw Fred go off with Harrison Ford, but I thought that was unlikely. And another woman said she'd seen a vision of Fred floating across her television screen. I didn't put a lot of stock in that, either.

Since I had some time to kill I went back to the Grand Union to buy pantyhose for the wedding. I stepped into the glass vestibule and noticed an elderly woman was staring at the Fred poster I'd tacked up on the community bulletin board. That's good, I thought. People read these things.

I bought the pantyhose, and as I was leaving I saw the woman was still standing in front of the poster. "Have you seen him?" I asked.

"Are you Stephanie Plum?"

"Yes."

"I thought I recognized you. I remember your picture from when you blew up that funeral home."

"Do you know Fred?"

"Sure, I know Fred. He's in my seniors club. Fred and Mabel. I didn't realize he was missing."

"When did you see him last?"

"I was trying to remember that. I was sitting on the bench outside Grand Union here, waiting for my nephew to come pick me up, on account of I don't drive anymore. And I saw Fred come out of the cleaners."

"That must have been Friday."

"That's what I think, too. I think it was Friday."

"What did Fred do when he came out of the cleaners?"

"He went to his car with the clothes. And it looked like he laid them out real careful on the backseat, although it was hard to tell from here."

"What happened next?"

"A car pulled up alongside Fred and a man got out, and him and Fred talked for a while. And then Fred got in the car with the man and they drove away. I'm pretty sure that's the last time I saw Fred. Except I can't be certain of the day. My nephew would know."

Holy shit. "Did you know the man Fred was talking to?"

"No. He wasn't familiar to me. But I got the feeling Fred knew him. They seemed friendly."

"What did he look like?"

"Goodness. I don't know. He was just a man. Ordinary."

"Caucasian?"

"Yes. And about the same height as Fred. And he was dressed in a suit."

"What color hair? Was his hair long or short?"

"It wasn't like I was paying attention to remember something," she said. "I was just passing time until Carl got here. I suppose his hair was short and maybe brown. I can't actually remember, but if it was unusual, it would have stuck in my mind."

"Would you know him if you saw him again? Would you recognize him from a picture?"

"I don't think I could say for sure. He was a ways away, you know, and I didn't see his face much."

"How about the car he was driving? Do you remember the color?"

She was silent for a moment, her eyes unfocused while she searched for a mental image of the car. "I just wasn't paying attention," she said. "I'm sorry. I can't recall the car. Except that it wasn't a truck or anything. It was a car."

"Did it look like they were arguing?"

"No. They were just talking. And then the man walked around the car and got behind the wheel. And Fred got in the passenger side. And they drove away."

I gave her my card in exchange for her name, address, and phone number. She said she didn't mind if I called to ask more questions. And she said she'd keep her eyes open and call me if she saw Fred.

I was so psyched I almost didn't see Lula standing two inches from me. "Wow!" I said, bumping into her.

"Earth to Stephanie," Lula said.

"How'd you do?" I asked her.

"Lousy. There's a bunch of dummies living here. Nobody knows nothing."

"I didn't have any luck back there, either," I said. "But I found someone in the store who saw Fred get into a car with another man."

"You shitting me?"

"Swear to God. The woman's name is Irene Tully."

"So who's the man? And where's ol' Fred?" Lula asked.

I didn't know the answers to those questions. Some of the wind went out of my sails when I realized not a whole lot had changed. I had a new puzzle piece, but I still didn't know if Fred was in Fort Lauderdale or the Camden landfill.

We'd been walking back to Lula's Firebird, and I'd been lost in thought. I looked at the Firebird and thought there was something strange about it. It hit me at the same time Lula started shrieking.

"My baby," Lula yelled. "My baby, my baby."

The Firebird was up on blocks. Someone had stolen all four wheels.

"This is just like Fred," she said. "What is this, the Bermuda Triangle?"

We got closer and looked in the car window. Lula's groceries were stuffed onto the front seat, and two of the wheels were in the back. Lula popped the trunk and found her other two wheels.

"What the hell?" she said.

An old brown Dodge rolled to a stop beside us. Bunchy.

Okay, who do we know who can open doors without keys? Who has a score to settle with Lula? And who has returned to the scene of the crime?

"Not bad," I said to Bunchy. "Sort of a sadistic sense of humor . . . but not bad."

He smiled at my comment and eyed the car. "You ladies got a problem?"

"Someone took the wheels off my Firebird," Lula said, looking like she'd figured it out, too. "Don't suppose you know who could've done something like this."

"Vandals?"

"Vandals, my ass."

"I have to be getting along now," Bunchy said, smiling ear to ear. "Toodles."

Lula hauled a small cannon out of her shoulder bag and pointed it at Bunchy. "You slime-faced bag of monkey shit."

The smile was gone in a flash, and Bunchy laid rubber out of the lot.

"Good thing I got auto club," Lula said.

An hour later, I was back in my Buick. I was running short on time, but I wanted to talk to Mabel.

I almost zipped right past her house, because the '87 Pontiac station wagon wasn't parked at the curb. In its place was a new silver-gray Nissan Sentra.

"Where's the station wagon?" I asked Mabel when she answered the door.

"Traded it in," she said. "I never did like driving that big old boat." She looked at her new car and smiled. "What do you think? Isn't it zippy-looking?"

"Yeah," I said. "Zippy. I ran into someone today who said she might have seen Fred."

"Oh, dear," Mabel said. "Don't tell me you've found him."

I blinked twice because she hadn't sounded like that would be happy news. "No."

She put her hand to her heart. "Thank goodness. I don't mean to sound uncaring, but you know, I just bought the car, and Fred wouldn't understand about the car."

Okay, now we know where Fred stacks up against a Nissan Sentra. "Anyway, this woman said she might have seen Fred on the day he disappeared. She said she thought she saw Fred talking to a man in a suit. Do you have any idea who the man might be?"

"No. Do you?"

Question number two. "It's very important that I know everything Fred did the day before he disappeared."

"It was just like all the other days," Mabel said. "He didn't do anything in the morning. Puttered around the house. Then we ate lunch, and he went out to the store."

"Grand Union?"

"Yes. And he was only gone about an hour. We didn't need much. And then he worked in the yard, cleaning up the last of the leaves. That was all he did."

"Did he go out at night?"

"No . . . wait, yes, he went out with the leaves. If you have too many bags of leaves, you have to pay extra to the garbage company. So whenever Fred had more than his allotted number of bags, he'd wait until it was dark, and then he'd drive one or two bags to Giovichinni's. He said it was the least Giovichinni could do for him being that he always overcharged on his meat."

"When did Fred leave the house Friday morning?"

"Early. Around eight, I guess. When he came home he was complaining because he had to wait for RGC to open."

"And when did he come back to the house?"

"I don't remember exactly. Maybe around eleven. He was home for lunch."

"That's a long time just to go to RGC to complain about a bill."

Mabel looked thoughtful. "I didn't really pay much attention, but I guess you're right."

He didn't go to Winnie's because he was there in the afternoon.

While I was in the neighborhood I cruised over to the Ruzicks'. The bakery was on the corner, and the rest of the houses on the street were duplexes. The Ruzick house was yellow brick with a yellow-brick stoop in front and a front yard that was three feet deep. Mrs. Ruzick kept her windows clean and her porch swept. There were no cars in front of the house. The backyard was long and narrow, leading to an alley that was one lane wide. The duplexes were divided by double driveways, at the end of which sat single-car garages.

I toyed with the idea of talking to Mrs. Ruzick, but gave it up. She had a reputation for being outspoken and had always been fiercely protective of her two worthless sons. I went to Sandy Polan instead.

"Wow, Stephanie!" Sandy said when she opened the door. "I haven't seen you in a long time. What's up?"

"I need a snitch."

"Let me guess. You're looking for Alphonse Ruzick."

"Have you seen him?"

"No, but he'll be around. He always comes to eat Saturday dinner with Mama. He is *such* a loser."

"Would you mind doing lookout for me? I'd do it myself, but I have to go to a wedding this afternoon."

"Oh my God. You're going to Julie Morelli's wedding! It's true about you and Joe."

"What about me and Joe?"

"I heard you were living with him."

"I had a fire in my apartment, and I rented a room from him for a short time."

Sandy's face scrunched up in disappointment. "You mean you weren't sleeping with him?"

"Well, yeah, I guess I was sleeping with him."

"Oh my God. I knew it! I just knew it! What's he like? Is he excellent? Is he . . . you know, big? He doesn't have a little twinkie, does he? Oh, God, don't tell me if he has a little twinkie."

I looked at my watch. "Gee, look at the time. I have to be going—"

"Oh, you've got to tell me or I'll die!" Sandy said. "I had *such* a crush on him in high school. *Everyone* did. If you tell me, I swear I won't tell another soul."

"Okay, it's not a little twinkie."

Sandy looked at me expectantly.

"That's it," I said.

"Did he tie you up? He always looked like the kind of guy who liked to tie women up."

"No! He didn't tie me up!" I gave her my card. "Listen, if you see Alphonse, give me a call. Try my cell phone number first, and if that doesn't work, try my pager."

EIGHT

I WAS SUPER late when I barreled through the back door to my apartment building. I quickly crossed to the bank of mailboxes on the far side of the lobby, spun the dial on my box, and grabbed my mail. A phone bill, a wad of junk mail, and an envelope from RangeMan Enterprises. My curiosity was stronger than my desire to be punctual, so I tore the RangeMan envelope open on the spot. RangeMan Enterprises is Ricardo Carlos Manoso. Better known as Ranger. Incorporated as RangeMan.

It was a payroll check issued by Ranger's accountant, paying me for the two jobs I screwed up. I had a moment of guilt, but brushed it aside. I didn't have time to feel guilty right now.

I rushed upstairs, hurled myself into the shower, and was out in record time. I went for the big soft curly look to my hair, natural frosted polish on my nails, and an extra sweep of mascara on my lashes. I tugged the little black dress into place, checked myself out in the mirror, and thought I looked pretty darn good.

I transferred a few things to a small black beaded purse, hooked a pair of long, dangly rhinestone earrings into my ears, and slipped my faux-diamond cocktail ring onto my ring finger.

My apartment is on the parking-lot side of the building, and my bedroom window opens to an old-fashioned fire escape. More modern buildings have balconies instead of fire escapes. Those buildings charge twenty-five dollars more a month than mine for rent, so I like my fire escape just fine.

The only problem with the fire escape is that people can climb up as well as down. Now that Ramirez was back on the street, I checked my bedroom window fourteen times a day to make sure it was locked. And when I left the apartment, not only was the window locked, but the curtain was pushed open, so I could immediately see upon entering the room if the window was broken.

I went to the kitchen to say good-bye to Rex. I gave him a green bean from my cache of leftovers and told him not to worry if I came home late. He watched me for a beat and then took the bean to his soup can. "Don't look at me like that," I said to Rex. "I'm *not* going to sleep with him."

I looked down at the black dress with the low scoop neck and slinky little skirt. Who was I kidding? Morelli wouldn't waste any time getting me out of this dress. We'd be lucky if we got to the wedding at all. Is that what I wanted? Shit. I didn't know what I wanted.

I ran back to the bedroom, kicked off the heels, and shimmied out of the black dress. I tried on a tan suit, a red knit dress, an apricot cocktail dress, and a gray silk suit. I ransacked my closet some more and came up with a tea-length rayon dress. It was a soft teal color with a small pink rose print and a skirt that was soft and swirly. It wasn't hot like the little black dress, but it was sexy in an understated romantic way. I changed my pantyhose, junked the earrings, dropped the dress over my head, shoved my feet into low-heeled shoes, and dumped the contents of the black purse into a small tan bag.

I had just buttoned the last button on the dress when the

doorbell rang. I grabbed a sweater and hustled to get the door. I threw the door open and didn't see anyone.

"Down here."

It was Randy Briggs.

"Why aren't you in jail?"

"I made bail," he said. "Again. And thanks to you I don't have anyplace to live."

"You want to run that by me again?"

"You wrecked my door, and while I was in jail, thieves came in and ransacked my apartment. Stole everything and set fire to my couch. Now I don't have anyplace to live while they fix my apartment. And when your cousin wrote my bail he said I had to have an address. So here I am."

"Vinnie sent you here?"

"Yeah. Isn't that a kick in the ass? You want to help me with this stuff I've got?"

I stuck my head out the door. Briggs had a couple big suitcases propped against the wall.

"You are *not* living here," I told him. "You must be crazy to think for a single moment that I'd let you live here."

"Listen, Toots, I don't like it any more than you do. And believe me, I'll be out of here as soon as possible." He pushed past me, wheeling one of the suitcases. "Where's my bedroom?"

"You don't have a bedroom," I said. "This is a one-bedroom apartment. And that one bedroom is *mine*."

"Christ," he said, "when was the last time you got laid? You need to relax a little." He had the second suitcase by the handle.

"Halt!" I said, blocking the doorway. "You are *not* living here. You aren't even *visiting* here."

"This is what it says on my bond agreement. Call your rat-faced cousin and ask. You want to violate my bond agreement? You want to come after me again?"

I held my ground.

"It's only for a couple days. They have to put down a new rug and put in a new door. And in the meantime I have a job to do. Which, by the way, thanks to you again, I'm behind schedule."

"I don't have time to stand here and argue. I'm going out, and there's no way I'm leaving you alone in my apartment."

He put his head down and pushed past me. "Don't worry about it. I'm not interested in hocking your silverware. I just want a place to work." He flopped the suitcase on its back, unzipped it, took out a laptop computer, and set it on my coffee table.

Shit.

I dialed Vinnie at home. "What's the deal with Briggs?" I asked.

"He needed a place to stay, and I thought if he stayed with you, you could keep an eye on him."

"Are you nuts?"

"It's only for a couple days until they get a door on his apartment. Which, for your information, I took a lot of grief over. You *destroyed* that door."

"I don't baby-sit FTAs."

"He's harmless. He's just a little guy. And besides, he threatened me with a civil liberties suit. And if he goes through with it, you're not gonna come out looking like roses. You beat the shit out of him."

"I didn't!"

"Look, I gotta go. Just humor him, will you?"

Vinnie disconnected.

Briggs was on the couch, booting up his computer. He was sort of cute with his little legs sticking out. Kind of like a big, cranky doll with a bashed-in face. He had a Band-Aid across his broken nose, and a beauty of a black eye. I didn't think he could win a lawsuit, but I didn't want to put it to the test.

"This comes at a bad time for me," I said to him. "I have a date."

"Yeah, I bet that's a big event in your life. And just between you and me, that dress is a dud."

"I like this dress. It's romantic."

"Men don't like romantic, Sis. Men like sexy. Short and tight. Something you can get your hand up real easy. And I'm not saying *I'm* like that . . . I'm just telling you about men."

I heard the elevator doors open down the hall. Morelli was here. I snatched my sweater and handbag and ran for the door. "Don't touch *anything*," I said. "When I get back I'm going to inspect this apartment, and it better be exactly the way I left it."

"I go to bed early, so be quiet if you get home late. Being that you're wearing that dress, I don't guess I have to worry about you spending the night with this guy."

I met Morelli in the hall. "Hmm," Morelli said when he saw me. "Pretty, but not what I'd expected."

I couldn't say the same for him. He was *exactly* what I'd expected. He was edible. California-cut charcoal silk gabardine suit, French-blue shirt, very cool tie. Black Italian loafers.

"What did you expect?" I asked.

"Higher heels, shorter skirt, more breast."

Damn that Briggs. "I had another outfit," I told him, "but I had to use my little black beaded purse with it, and it was too small to hold my cell phone and pager."

"This is a wedding," Morelli said. "You don't need a cell phone and pager."

"You have a pager clipped to your belt."

"It's this job I'm on. We're close to wrapping it up, and I don't want to miss the takedown. I'm working with a couple Treasury guys who make me look like a Boy Scout."

"Dirty?"

"Crazy."

"I got a break today with Uncle Fred. I found a woman who

saw Fred talking to a man in a suit. And then they got in the man's car and drove away."

"You should call Arnie Mott and let him know what you've got," Morelli said. "You don't want to withhold information on a possible kidnapping and murder."

HOLY ASCENSION CHURCH had a small lot that was already filled. Morelli parked a block and a half from the church and blew out a sigh. "I don't know why I agreed to do this. I should have pulled duty."

"Weddings are fun."

"Weddings suck."

"What don't you like about weddings?"

"I have to talk to my relatives."

"Okay, I'll concede you that one. What else?"

"I haven't been to church in a year. The Monsignor's going to assign me to Hell."

"Maybe you'll see Fred there. I don't think he went to church, either."

"And I have to wear a suit and tie. I feel like my uncle Manny."

His uncle Manny was a construction expediter. Manny could expedite the completion of a building project by insuring that no unexplained fires would take place during the construction process.

"You don't look like your uncle Manny," I said. "You look very sexy." I felt the material in his trouser leg. "This is a beautiful suit."

His eyes softened. "Yeah?" His voice pitched low. "Why don't we skip the wedding. We could still go to the reception."

"The reception isn't for another hour. What would we do?"

He slid his arm along the back of my seat and twirled a curl around his finger.

"No!" I said, trying to get some conviction behind it.

"We could do it in the truck. We've never done it in the truck."

Morelli drove a four-wheel drive Toyota pickup. It was pretty nice, but it wasn't going to replace a queen-size bed. And besides, my hair would get mussed. Not to mention I was afraid Bunchy might be watching. "I don't think so," I said.

He brushed his lips across my ear and told me some of the things he wanted to do to me. A rush of heat fluttered through my stomach. Maybe I should reconsider, I thought. I liked all of those things. A lot.

A mile-long car pulled to the curb behind us.

"Damn," Morelli said. "It's my uncle Dominic and aunt Rosa."

"I didn't know you had an uncle Dominic."

"He's from New York State. And he's in retail," Morelli said, opening his door. "Don't ask him too many questions about the business."

Aunt Rosa was out of the car and running toward us. "Joey," she yelled. "Let me look at you. It's been so long. Look, Dominic, it's little Joey."

Dominic ambled up and nodded at Joe. "Long time."

Joe introduced me.

"I heard you had a girl," Rosa said, talking to Joe, beaming at me. "It's about time you settled down. Give your mother more grandchildren."

"One of these days," Joe said.

"You're not getting any younger. Pretty soon it'll be too late."

"It's never too late for a Morelli," Joe said.

Dominic made a move like he was going to smack Joe in the head. "Wise guy," he said. Then he smiled.

THERE ARE ONLY a few places big enough to handle an Italian wedding reception in the Burg. Julie Morelli held hers in the back room of Angio's. The room could hold two hundred and was reaching maximum capacity when Joe and I arrived.

"And when is *your* wedding?" Joe's Aunt Loretta wanted to know, smiling broadly, giving Joe the squinty eye. She shook her finger at him. "When are you going to make an honest woman out of this poor thing? Myra, come here," she called. "Joe's here with his girl."

"This is such a pretty dress," Myra said, examining my roses. "It's so nice to find a modest young woman."

Oh, great. I always wanted to be a modest young woman. "I need a drink," I said to Joe. "Something with cyanide."

I spied Terry Gilman across the room, and she wasn't modest at all. She was wearing a dress that was short and clingy, and shimmery gold. Leaving me to wonder where the gun was hidden. She turned and stared directly at Joe for a couple beats, then she blew him a kiss.

Joe acknowledged her with a noncommittal smile and a nod of his head. If it had been more I'd have stabbed him with one of the butter knives.

"What's Terry doing here?" I asked Joe.

"Cousin to the groom."

A hush fell over the crowd. For a moment there was total silence, and then talking resumed, first with low murmurings and finally building to a roar.

"What was that silence all about?" I asked Joe.

"Grandma Bella's arrived. That was the sound of terror spreading through the room."

I looked to the entrance and sure enough, there she was . . . Joe's grandma Bella. She was a small woman with white hair and piercing hawklike eyes. She dressed in black and looked like she belonged in Sicily, herding goats, making the lives of her daughters'-in-law a living misery. Some people believed Bella had special powers . . . some thought she was wacko. Even the non-believers were reluctant to incur her wrath.

Bella scanned the room and picked me out. "You," she said, pointing a bony finger at me. "You, come here."

"Oh, shit!" I whispered to Joe. "Now what?"

"Just don't let her smell fear, and you'll be fine," Joe said, guiding me through the crowd, his hand at the small of my back.

"I remember this one," Bella said to Joe, referring to me. "This is the one you sleep with now."

"Well, actually . . ." I said.

Joe brushed a kiss across the nape of my neck. "I'm trying."

"I see babies," Bella said. "You will give me more great-grandchildren. I know these things. I have the eye." She patted my stomach. "You're ripe tonight. Tonight would be good."

I looked at Joe.

"Don't worry," he said. "I've got it covered. Besides, there's no such thing as the eye."

"Hah!" Bella said. "I gave Ray Barkolowski the eye, and all his teeth fell out."

Joe grinned down at his grandmother. "Ray Barkolowski had periodontal disease."

Bella shook her head. "Young people," she said. "They believe in nothing." She took my hand and dragged me after her. "Come. You should meet the family."

I looked back at Joe and mouthed "Help!"

"You're on your own," Joe said. "I need a drink. A big one."

"This is Joe's cousin, Louis," Grandma Bella said. "Louis fools around on his wife."

Louis looked like a thirty-year-old loaf of fresh raised white bread. Soft and plump. Scarfing down appetizers. He stood next to a small olive-skinned woman, and from the look she gave him, I assumed they were married.

"Grandma Bella," he said, croaky-voiced, his cheeks mottled in red, mouth stuffed with crab balls. "I would never—"

"Silence," she said. "I know these things. You can't lie to me. I'll put the eye on you."

Louis sucked in some crab and clutched his throat. His face got red, then purple. He flailed his arms.

"He's choking!" I said.

Grandma Bella tapped her finger to her eye and smiled like the wicked witch in *The Wizard of Oz*.

I gave Louis a good hard *thwack* between his shoulder blades, and the crab ball flew out of his mouth.

Grandma Bella leaned close to Louis. "You cheat again, and next time I'll kill you," she said.

She moved off toward a group of women. "One thing you learn about Morelli men," she said to me. "You don't let them get away with a thing."

Joe nudged me from behind and put a drink in my hand. "How's it going?"

"Pretty good. Grandma Bella put the eye on Louis." I took a sip. "Champagne?"

"All out of cyanide," he said.

AT EIGHT O'CLOCK the waitresses were clearing the plates off the tables, the band was playing, and all the Italian ladies were on the dance floor, dancing with one another. Kids were running between the tables, squealing and shrieking. The wedding party was at the bar. And the Morelli men were out back, smoking cigars and passing gas.

Morelli had forsaken the cigar ritual and was slouched back

in his chair, studying the buttons on my dress. "We could go now," he said. "And no one would notice."

"Your grandma Bella would notice. She keeps looking over here. I think she might be getting ready to do the eye thing again."

"I'm her favorite grandson," Morelli said. "I'm safe from the eye."

"So your grandma Bella doesn't scare you?"

"You're the only one who scares me," Morelli said. "You want to dance?"

"You dance?"

"When I have to."

We were sitting close, with our knees touching. He leaned forward and took my hand and kissed the inside, and I felt my bones heat up and start to liquefy.

I heard the click of stiletto heels approaching and caught a flash of gold in my peripheral vision.

"Am I disturbing something?" Terry Gilman said, all glossy lipstick and carnivorous, perfect white teeth.

"Hello, Terry," Joe said. "What's going on?"

"Frankie Russo's taking the men's room apart. Something about his wife eating potato salad off Hector Santiago's fork."

"And you want me to talk to him?"

"Either that or shoot him. You're the only one with a legal piece. He's racking up a hell of a bill in there."

Morelli gave my hand another kiss. "Don't go anywhere."

They walked off together, and I had a moment of doubt that they might not be going to the men's room. That's dumb, I told myself. Joe isn't like that anymore.

Five minutes later he still hadn't returned, and I was having a hard time controlling my blood pressure. I was distracted by ringing, far off in the distance. I realized with a start that it wasn't far off at all—it was my cell phone, the ringing smothered in my purse.

It was Sandy. "He's here!" she said. "I was just walking the dog, and I looked in the Ruzicks' windows, and there he was, watching television. It was easy to see because the lights are all on, and Mrs. Ruzick never pulls her shades."

I thanked Sandy and dialed Ranger. No answer, so I left a message on his machine. I tried his car phone and cell phone. No answer at those numbers either. I called his pager and left my cell phone number. I tapped my finger on the table for five minutes while I waited for a call back. No call back. No Joe. Little wisps of smoke were starting to escape from my hairline.

The Ruzicks' house was three blocks away. I wanted to go over and keep my eye on things, but I didn't want to walk out on Joe. No problem, I told myself. Just go find him. He's in the men's room. Only he wasn't in the men's room. No one was in the men's room. I asked a few people if they knew where I could find Joe. Nope. No one knew where I could find Joe. Still no call from Ranger.

The steam was coming out my ears now. If this kept up I'd start whistling like a teakettle. Wouldn't that be embarrassing?

Okay, I'll leave him a note, I decided. I had a pen but no paper, so I wrote on a napkin. "Be right back," I wrote. "I have to check on an FTA for Ranger." I propped the napkin up against Joe's drink and left.

I power-walked the three blocks and pulled up across from the Ruzick house. Sure enough, Alphonse was there, big as life, watching television. I could see him crystal clear through the living room window. No one had ever accused Alphonse of being smart. You might say that about me too, because I'd remembered to take my purse, but I'd left my sweater and cell phone at Angio's. And now that I was standing still, I was freezing. No problem, I told myself. Go to Angio's, get your stuff, and come back.

It would have been a good plan, except at that moment Alphonse stood, scratched his belly, hiked up his pants, and walked out of the room. Damn. Now what?

I was across the street from the Ruzicks', crouched between two parked cars. I had good line of sight to the living room and front of the house, but all else was lost to me. I was contemplating this problem when I heard the back door open and close. Shit. He was leaving. He'd probably parked his car in the alley behind the house.

I ran across the street and hugged the shadows on the side of the house. Sure enough, I could see the hulking outline of Alphonse Ruzick making his way to the alley, carrying a bag. He was charged with armed robbery and assault with a deadly weapon. He was forty-six, and he weighed in at 230 pounds, with the bulk of his weight in his gut. He had a little pinhead and a brain to match. And he was getting away. Damn Ranger. Where the hell was he?

Alphonse was halfway down the yard when I yelled. I didn't have a weapon. I didn't have cuffs. I didn't have anything, but I yelled, anyway. It was all I could think to do.

"Stop!" I yelled. "Bail Enforcement Agent! Drop to the ground."

Alphonse didn't even turn to look. He just took off, cutting across yards, rather than going for the alley. He ran for all he was worth, handicapped by his lard butt and beer gut, hanging on to the bag in his right hand. Dogs barked, porch lights flashed, and back doors were thrown open all down the block.

"Call the police," I yelled, chasing after Alphonse, my skirt up around my neck. "Fire, fire. Help. Help."

We reached the end of the block, and I was within an arm's length when he whirled around and hit me with the bag. The impact burst the bag and knocked me off my feet. I was flat on my back, covered in garbage. Alphonse hadn't been leaving at all. He'd been taking the garbage out for his mother.

I scrambled to my feet and charged after Alphonse. He'd rounded the block and was running back to his mother's. He had half a house length on me when he pulled a set of keys from his pocket, pointed at a Ford Explorer parked at the curb, and I heard the alarm system chirp off.

"Stop!" I yelled. "You're under arrest! Stop or I'll shoot!"

It was a stupid thing to say because I didn't have a gun. And even if I had a gun I certainly wouldn't shoot him. Alphonse looked over his shoulder to check me out, and it was enough to uncoordinate the forward momentum of his blubber. The result was that he started to stumble, and I inadvertently plowed into his gelatinous body.

We both went down to the sidewalk, where I hung on for dear life. Alphonse was trying to get to his feet, and I was trying to keep him on the ground. I could hear sirens in the distance and people yelling and running toward us. And I was thinking I just had to wrestle around with him long enough for help to get to me. He was on his knees, and I had a fistful of his shirt in my hand, and he batted me away like I was a bug.

"Dumb cunt," he said, getting to his feet. "You haven't got a gun."

I get called lots of names. That's not one of my favorites. I latched onto his cuff and pulled his feet out from under him. He seemed suspended in air for a fraction of a second, and then he crash-landed with a loud *whump* that shook the ground and hit about 6.7 on the Richter scale.

"I'm gonna kill you," he said, sweating and panting, rolling on top of me, hands to my neck. "I'm gonna fuckin' kill you."

I squirmed under him and sunk my teeth into his shoulder.

"Yow!" he yelled. "Sonovabitch. What are you, a goddamn vampire?"

We rolled around for what seemed like hours, locked onto each other. Him trying to kill me, and me just hanging on like a tick on a dog's back, oblivious to my surroundings and the state of my skirt, afraid if I let go he'd beat me to death. I was exhausted, and I was thinking I was about at the end of the line when I was hit with a splash of ice-cold water.

We both instantly unlocked and flopped onto our backs, sputtering.

"What?" I said. "What?" I blinked my eyes and saw there were lots of people around us. Morelli and Ranger, a couple uniformed cops, and some people from the neighborhood. Plus Mrs. Ruzick was there, holding a big empty pot.

"Works every time," Mrs. Ruzick said. "Except usually I hose down cats. This neighborhood has too many cats."

Ranger grinned down at me. "Good bust, Tiger."

I got to my feet and took stock of myself. No broken bones. No bullet holes. No knife wounds. Ruined manicure. Soaking wet hair and dress. What looked like vegetable soup clinging to my skirt.

Morelli and Ranger were staring at my breasts and smiling at the wet dress that was plastered to my skin.

"So I have nipples," I snapped. "Get over it."

Morelli gave me his jacket. "What's with the vegetable soup on your skirt?"

"He hit me with a bag of garbage."

Morelli and Ranger were smiling again.

"Don't say anything," I told them. "And if you value your lives you'll stop grinning."

"Hey, man," Ranger said, grinning wider than ever. "I'm out of here. I've got to take Bluto for a ride."

"Show's over," Morelli said to the neighbors.

Sandy Polan was there. She gave Joe an appraising once-over, giggled, and left.

"What was that about?" Joe asked me.

I gave him a palms-up. "Go figure."

I traded his jacket for my sweater when we got to his truck. "Out of morbid curiosity, how long were you standing there watching me wrestle with Ruzick?"

"Not long. A minute or two."

"And Ranger?"

"The same."

"You could have jumped in and helped me."

"We were trying. We couldn't get hold of you the way you were tumbling around. Anyway, you looked like you were doing okay."

"How did you know where I was?"

"I talked to Ranger. He called your cell phone."

I looked down at my dress. It was probably wrecked. Good thing I hadn't worn the little black number.

"Where were you? I went to the men's room, and it was empty."

"Frankie needed some air." Morelli stopped for a light and glanced over at me. "Whatever possessed you to go after Alphonse like that? You were unarmed."

Charging after Alphonse wasn't what bothered me. Okay, so it hadn't been the bright thing to do. But it hadn't been as stupid as walking the streets, alone and unarmed, when Ramirez might have been stalking me.

Morelli parked the truck in the lot and walked me up to my apartment. He backed me against my door and kissed me lightly on the lips. "Do I get to come in?"

"I have coffee grounds in my hair." And Randy Briggs in my apartment.

"Yeah," Morelli said. "Makes you smell kind of homey."

"I don't know if I'm up to being romantic tonight."

"We don't have to be romantic," Morelli said. "We could just have some really dirty sex."

I rolled my eyes.

Morelli kissed me again. A good-night kiss this time. "Call me when you want some," he said.

"Some what?" As if I didn't know.

"Some anything."

I let myself into my apartment and tiptoed past Briggs, who was asleep on my couch.

SUNDAY MORNING I woke up to rain. It was coming down in a steady drone on my fire escape, spattering against my window. I opened the curtains and thought, ick. The world was gray. Beyond the parking lot, the world didn't exist at all. I looked at the bed. Very tempting. I could crawl into bed and stay there until the rain stopped, or the world came to an end, or until someone showed up with a bag of doughnuts.

Unfortunately, if I went back to bed I might lie there taking stock of my life. And my life had some problems. The project that was taking most of my time and mental energy wasn't going to get me lunch money. Not that it mattered, I was determined to find Fred, dead or alive. The projects Ranger gave me weren't working out. And the bounty hunter projects were a big goose egg. If I thought about my life long enough I might reach the conclusion I needed to go out and get a real job. Something that required pantyhose every day and a good attitude.

Even worse, I might get to thinking about Morelli, and that I was an idiot not to have invited him to spend the night. Or worse still, I might think about Ranger, and I didn't want to go there *at all!*

And then I remembered why I hadn't invited Morelli into my

apartment. Briggs. I closed my eyes. Let it all be a bad dream.

Bam, bam, bam, on my door. "Hey!" Briggs yelled. "You haven't got any coffee. How am I supposed to work without coffee? Do you know what time it is, Sleeping Beauty? What, do you sleep all day? No wonder you can't afford any food in this hellhole."

I got up and got dressed and stomped out to the living room. "Listen, Shorty, who the hell do you think you are, anyway?"

"I'm the guy who's gonna sue your ass. That's who I am."

"Give me a little time, and I could really learn to hate you."

"Jeez, and just when I was thinking you were my soul mate."

I gave him my best eat-dirt-and-die look, zipped myself into my rain jacket, and grabbed my shoulder bag. "How do you like your coffee?"

"Black. Lots of it."

I sprinted through the rain to the Buick and drove to Giovichinni's. The front of the store was redbrick, sandwiched between other businesses. On either side of Giovichinni's the buildings were single story. Giovichinni's was two stories, but the second floor wasn't used for much. Storage and an office. I drove to the end of the block and took the service alley that ran behind the store. The back side of Giovichinni's was redbrick, just like the front. And the back door opened to a small yard. At the end of the yard was a dirt parking area for delivery trucks. Two doors down was a real estate office. The back wall was stuccoed over and painted beige. And the back door opened to a small asphalt parking lot.

So suppose cheapskate Fred drives his leaves to Giovichinni's in the dark of night. He parks the car and turns off his lights. Doesn't want to get caught. He unloads the leaves and hears a car coming. What would he do? Hide. Then maybe he's there hiding, and he sees someone come along and deposit a garbage bag behind the real estate office.

After that I was lost. I had to think about *after that* some more.

Next stop was the 7-Eleven and then home with a large coffee for me and a Big Gulp of coffee for Briggs and a box of chocolate-covered doughnuts . . . because if I had to put up with Briggs, I needed doughnuts.

I shucked my wet jacket and settled down at the dining room table with the coffee and doughnuts and a steno pad, doing my best to ignore the fact that I had a man typing away at my coffee table. I listed out all the things I knew about Fred's disappearance. No doubt now that the photographs played a large role. When I ran out of things to write in the steno pad, I locked myself in my bedroom and watched cartoons on television. This took me to lunchtime. I didn't feel like eating lamb leftovers, so I finished off the box of doughnuts.

"Cripes," Briggs said, "do you always eat like this? Don't you know about the major food groups? No wonder you have to wear those 'romantic' dresses."

I retreated to my bedroom, and while I was retreating I took a nap. I was startled awake by the phone ringing.

"Just wanted to make sure you were going to come take me to the Lipinski viewing tonight," Grandma said.

The Lipinski viewing. Ugh. Trekking out in the rain to see some dead guy wasn't high on my list of desirable things to do. "How about Harriet Schnable?" I suggested. "Maybe Harriet could take you."

"Harriet's car's on the fritz."

"Effie Reeder?"

"Effie died."

"Oh! I didn't know that."

"Almost everybody I know has died," Grandma said. "Bunch of wimps."

157

"Okay, I'll take you."

"Good. And your mother says you should come for dinner."

I BUZZED THROUGH the living room, but before I could get to the door Briggs was on his feet.

"Hey, where are you going?" he asked.

"Out."

"Out where?"

"My parents' house."

"I bet you're going there for dinner. Man, that's the pits. You're gonna leave me here with nothing to eat, and you're going to your parents' house for dinner."

"There's some cold lamb in the refrigerator."

"I ate that for lunch. Hold on, I'll go with you."

"No! You will *not* go with me."

"What, are you ashamed of me?"

"Yes!"

"WELL, WHO'S THIS little guy?" Grandma asked when I walked in with Briggs.

"This is my . . . friend, Randy."

"Aren't you something," Grandma said. "I never saw a midget up close."

"Little person," Briggs said. "And I never saw anyone as old as you up close, either."

I gave him a smack on the top of his head. "Behave yourself," I said.

"What happened to your face?" Grandma wanted to know.

"Your granddaughter beat me up."

"No kidding?" Grandma said. "She did a pip of a job."

My father was in front of the TV. He turned in his chair and looked at us. "Oh, cripes, now what?" he said.

"This is Randy," I told him.

"He's kinda short, isn't he?"

"He's not a boyfriend."

My father went back to the television. "Thank God for that."

There were five places set at the table. "Who's the fifth person?" I asked.

"Mabel," my mother said. "Your grandmother invited her."

"I thought it would give us a chance to grill her. See if she's holding something out," Grandma said.

"There will be *no grilling*," my mother said to my grandmother. "You invited Mabel over for dinner, and that's what we're going to have . . . a nice dinner."

"Sure," Grandma said, "but it wouldn't hurt to ask her a few questions."

A car door slammed at the front of the house and everyone migrated to the foyer.

"What's that car Mabel's driving?" Grandma asked. "That's not the station wagon."

"Mabel bought a new car," I said. "She thought the old one was too big."

"Good for her," my mother said. "She should be able to make those decisions."

"Yeah," Grandma said. "But she better hope Fred's dead."

"Who's Mabel and Fred?" Briggs asked.

I gave him the condensed explanation.

"Cool," Briggs said. "I'm starting to like this family."

"I brought a coffee cake," Mabel said, handing a box to my mother, closing the door with her other hand. "It's prune. I know Frank likes prune." She craned her neck to the living room. "Hello, Frank," she called.

"Mabel," my father said.

"Nice car," Grandma said to Mabel. "Aren't you afraid Fred'll come back and have a cow?"

"He shouldn't have left," Mabel said. "And anyway, how am I to know he'll come back? I got a new bedroom set, too. It's getting delivered tomorrow. New mattress and everything."

"Maybe you were the one who bumped Fred off," Grandma said. "Maybe you did it for the money."

My mother slammed a bowl of creamed peas down on the table. "*Mother!*" she said.

"It was just a thought," Grandma said to Mabel.

We all took our seats, and my mother set a highball down for Mabel and a beer for my father and brought a kid cushion for Briggs to sit on.

"My grandchildren use these," she said.

Briggs looked over at me.

"My sister Valerie's kids," I said.

"Hah," he said. "So you're a loser in the grandchildren race, too."

"I have a hamster," I told him.

My father forked some roast chicken onto his plate and reached for the mashed potatoes.

Mabel swilled down half her highball.

"What else you gonna buy?" Grandma asked her.

"I might go on a vacation," Mabel said. "I might go to Hawaii. Or I might go on a cruise. I always wanted to go on a cruise. Of course I wouldn't do that for a while. Unless Stephanie finds that man. Then that might speed things up."

"What man?" Grandma wanted to know.

I told her about the woman at the Grand Union.

"Now we're getting somewhere," Grandma said. "This is more like it. All we have to do is find that man." She turned to me. "You have any suspects?"

"No."

"Nobody at all?"

"I'll tell you who I suspect," Mabel said. "I suspect that garbage company. They didn't like Fred."

Grandma waved a chicken leg at her. "That's just what I said the other day. There's something funny going on with that garbage company. We're going to the viewing tonight to look into it." She ate some chicken while she thought. "You met the deceased when you went to the garbage office, didn't you?" she asked me. "What did he look like? He look like the guy who took Fred for a ride?"

"I guess he could fit the description."

"Too bad it's gonna be a closed casket. If it was open we could take the Grand Union woman with us and see if she recognizes Lipinski."

"Hell," my father said, "why don't you just haul Lipinski out and put him in a lineup?"

Grandma looked at my father. "You think we could do that? I imagine he'd be stiff enough."

My mother sucked in some air.

"I don't know if you stay stiff," Mabel said. "I think you might loosen up again."

"How about passing the gravy," my father said. "Could I get some gravy down here?"

Grandma's face lit with inspiration. "There'll be lots of Lipinski's relatives there tonight. Maybe one of them will give us a picture! Then we can show the picture to the Grand Union lady."

I thought this was all a little grim, considering Mabel was at the table, but Mabel seemed unfazed.

"What do you think, Stephanie?" she asked. "Do you think I should go to Hawaii? Or do you think I should take a cruise?"

"Jesus," Briggs said to me, "you turned out pretty good considering your gene pool."

NINE

"WOW, LOOK AT this," Grandma said, peering out at the parking lot. "This place is packed tonight. That's on account of Stiva has a full house. He's got somebody in every room. I was talking to Jean Moon, and she said her cousin Dorothy died yesterday morning, and they couldn't get her into Stiva's. Had to take her to Mosel."

"What's wrong with Mosel?" Briggs asked.

"He don't know nothing about makeup," Grandma said. "Uses too much rouge. I like when the deceased looks nice and natural."

"Yeah, I like that, too," Briggs said. "Nothing worse than an unnatural corpse."

The rain had slowed to a drizzle, but it still wasn't a glorious night to be out, so I dropped Grandma and Briggs off at the door and went in search of a parking place on the street. I found one a block away, and by the time I reached Stiva's front porch my hair was more frizz than curl and my cotton knit sweater had grown two inches.

Larry Lipinski was in room number one, as was befitting a

suicidal killer. Family and friends were clustered in a knot around the casket. The rest of the room was filled with the same crowd I'd seen at the Deeter viewing. There were the professional mourners like Grandma Mazur and Sue Ann Schmatz. And there were the garbage people.

Grandma Mazur marched over to me with Briggs running after her. "I already gave my condolences," she said. "And I want to tell you they're a real standoffish group. It's a shame when people like that get to take rooms away from people like Dorothy Moon."

"I guess that means they wouldn't give you a picture."

"Zip," Grandma said. "They gave me zip."

"They gave it to her in a big way, too," Briggs said, smiling. "You should have been there."

"I don't think he's the one, anyway," I said.

"I'm not so sure," Grandma said. "These people look to me like they got something to hide. I think this is a shifty lot."

If I was related to someone who'd confessed to murder, I'd probably be feeling a little uncomfortable, too.

"Don't worry," Grandma said. "I thought this might happen, and I've got a plan."

"Yeah, the plan is we forget about it," I said.

Grandma slid her uppers around while she scanned the crowd. "Emma Getz told me the deceased in room number four is done up real nice. I thought I might take a look."

"Me too," Briggs said. "I don't want to miss anything."

I wasn't interested in how room four was done up, so I volunteered to wait in the lobby. Waiting got old after a couple minutes, so I wandered over to the tea table and helped myself to some cookies. Then the cookies got old, so I went to the ladies' room to check out my hair. Big mistake. Best not to look at my hair. I went back to the cookies and put one in my pocket for Rex.

I was counting the ceiling tiles, wondering what to do next, when the fire alarm went off. Since not that long ago Stiva's almost burned to the ground, no one was wasting any time vacating the premises. People poured from the viewing rooms into the lobby and ran for the door. I didn't see Grandma Mazur, so I struggled through the crowd to viewing room four. The room was empty when I got there, with the exception of Mrs. Kunkle, who was serene in her twelve-thousand-dollar mahogany and solid brass slumber chamber. I ran back to the lobby and was about to check outside for Grandma Mazur when I noticed the door to room one was closed. All the other doors were open, but the Lipinski door was closed.

Sirens whined in the distance, and I had a bad feeling about room one. Stiva was on the other side of the lobby, yelling to his assistant to check the back rooms. He turned and looked at me, and his face went white.

"It wasn't me!" I said. "I swear!"

He followed after the assistant, and the second he was out of sight I ran to room one and tried the door. The knob turned but the door wouldn't open, so I put my weight behind it and gave it a shove. The door flew open, and Briggs fell over backward.

"Shit," he said, "close the door, you big oaf."

"What are you doing?"

"I'm doing lookout for your grandma. What do you think I'm doing?"

At the other end of the room, Grandma had the lid up on Larry Lipinski. She was standing one foot on a folding chair, one foot on the edge of the casket, and she was taking pictures with a disposable camera.

"Grandma!"

"Boy," she said, "this guy don't look so good."

"Get down!"

"I gotta finish this roll out. I hate when there's pictures left over."

I ran down the aisle between the folding chairs. "You can't do this!"

"I can now that I got this chair. I was only getting the side of his face before. And that wasn't working good, on account of there's a lot of his head missing."

"Stop taking pictures this instant and get down!"

"Last picture!" Grandma said, climbing off the chair, dropping the camera into her purse. "I got some beauts."

"Close the lid! Close the lid!"

Crash!

"Didn't realize it was so heavy," Grandma said.

I moved the chair back against the wall. I scrutinized the casket to make sure everything looked okay. And then I took Grandma by the hand. "Let's get out of here."

The door was wrenched open before we got to it, and Stiva gave me a startled look. "What are you doing in here? I thought you were leaving the building."

"I couldn't find Grandma," I said. "And um—"

"She came in here to rescue me," Grandma said, hanging on to me, making her way to the door. "I was paying my respects when the alarm went off, and everybody stampeded out of here. And somebody knocked me over, and I couldn't get up. The midget was in here with me, but it would have taken two of them to do the job. If it wasn't for my granddaughter coming to get me I'd have burned to a cinder."

"Little person!" Randy Briggs said. "How many times do I have to tell you, I'm *not* a midget."

"Well, you sure do look like a midget," Grandma said. She sniffed the air. "Do I smell smoke?"

"No," Stiva said. "It looks like a false alarm. Are you all right?"

"I think so," Grandma said. "And it's a lucky thing, too, because I got fragile bones on account of I'm so old." Grandma glanced over at me. "Imagine that, a false alarm."

Imagine that. Unh. Mental head slap.

There were two fire trucks in the street when we left. Mourners were outside, shivering in the drizzle, kept in place by curiosity and the fact that their coats were inside. A police car was angled at the curb.

"You didn't set that alarm off, did you?" I asked Grandma Mazur.

"Who, me?"

MY MOTHER WAS waiting at the door when we got back to the house. "I heard the sirens," she said. "Are you all right?"

"Sure we're all right," Grandma said. "Can't you see we're all right?"

"Mrs. Ciak got a call from her daughter, who told her there was a fire at Stiva's."

"No fire," Grandma said. "It was one of them false alarms."

My mother's mouth had turned grim.

Grandma shook the rain off her coat and hung it in the closet. "Ordinarily I guess I might feel bad that the fire department had to go out for nothing, but I noticed Bucky Moyer was driving. And you know how Bucky loves to drive that big truck."

Actually this was true about Bucky. In fact, he'd been suspected on more than one occasion for setting off a false alarm himself just so he could take the truck out.

"I have to go," I said. "I have a lot to do tomorrow."

"Wait," my mother said, "let me give you some chicken."

———

GRANDMA CALLED AT eight. "I got a beauty parlor appointment this morning," she said. "I thought maybe you could give me a ride, and on the way we could drop the you-know-what off."

"The film?"

"Yeah."

"When is your appointment?"

"Nine."

WE STOPPED AT the photo store first. "Do that one-hour thing," Grandma said, handing me the film.

"That costs a fortune."

"I got a coupon," Grandma said. "They give them to us seniors on account of we haven't got a lot of time to waste. We have to wait too long to get our pictures back, and we could be dead."

After I deposited Grandma at the hair salon I drove to the office. Lula was on the Naugahyde couch, drinking coffee, reading her horoscope. Connie was at her desk, eating a bagel. And Vinnie was nowhere in sight.

Lula put the paper down as soon as she spied me walking through the door. "I want to know *all* about it. Everything. I want details."

"Not much to tell," I said. "I chickened out and didn't wear the dress."

"What? Say that again?"

"It's sort of complicated."

"So you're telling me you didn't get any this weekend."

"Yeah."

"Girl, that's a sad-ass state of affairs."

Tell me about it.

"You got any FTAs?" I asked Connie.

"Nothing came in on Saturday. And it's too early for today."

"Where's Vinnie?"

"At the lockup, writing bail on a shoplifter."

I left the office and stood outside, staring at the Buick. "I hate you," I said.

I heard someone laughing softly behind me and turned to find Ranger.

"You always talk to your car like that? Think you need a life, Babe."

"I've got a life. What I need is a new car."

He stared at me for a couple beats, and I was afraid to speculate on what he was thinking. His brown eyes were assessing, and his expression was mildly amused. "What would you be willing to do for a new car?"

"What did you have in mind?"

Again, the soft laugh. "Would it still have to be morally correct?"

"What kind of car are we talking about?"

"Powerful. Sexy."

I had a feeling those words might be included in the job description, too.

A light rain had started to fall. He pulled my jacket hood up and tucked my hair in. His finger traced a line at my temple, our eyes met, and for a terrifying moment I thought he might kiss me. The moment passed, and Ranger pulled back.

"Let me know when you decide," he said.

"Decide?"

He smiled. "About the car."

"Okeydokey."

Unh! I climbed into the Buick and roared off into the mist. I stopped for a light and thunked my head on the steering wheel while I waited for the green. Stupid, stupid, stupid, stupid, I thought while I thunked. Why had I said "okeydokey"? What a dopey thing to say! I did one last thunk and the light turned.

Grandma was getting coated with hairspray when I got to the salon. Her hair was steel gray, and she kept it cut short and curled in rolls that marched in side-by-side rows on her pink skull. "I'm almost done," she said. "Did you get the pictures?"

"Not yet."

She paid for her wash and set, stuffed herself into her coat, and carefully tied the plastic rain bonnet on her head. "That was some viewing last night," she said, being cautious how she walked on the wet pavement. "What a lot of excitement. You weren't even there when Margaret Burger pitched a fit over the guy in room three. You remember how Margaret's husband, Sol, died from a heart attack last year? Well, Margaret said it was all over a problem Sol was having with the cable company. Margaret said they drove Sol to high blood pressure. And she said the guy who did it was the dead guy in room three, John Curly. Margaret said she came to spit on his dead body."

"Margaret Burger came to Stiva's to spit on someone?" Margaret Burger was a sweet white-haired lady.

"That's what she told me, but I didn't actually see her spit. I guess I came in too late. Or maybe after she saw this John Curly person she decided not to do it. He looked even worse than Lipinski."

"How did he die?"

"Hit and run. And from the looks of him he must have got hit by a truck. Boy, I'm telling you these companies are something. Margaret said Sol was arguing over his bill, just like Fred, and this smart-mouth in the office, John Curly, didn't want to hear anything."

I parked in front of One-Hour Photo and got Grandma's pictures.

"These aren't so bad," she said, shuffling through the pack.

I looked over at them. Eeew.

"You think it's real obvious he's dead?" Grandma asked.

"He's in a casket."

"Well, I still think they're pretty good. I think we should see if that Grand Union lady recognizes him."

"Grandma, we can't ring some woman's doorbell and show her pictures of a dead man."

Grandma pawed through her big black patent-leather handbag. "The only other thing I got is the memorial brochure from Stiva. The picture's kind of fuzzy, though."

I took the paper from Grandma and looked at it. It was a photo of Lipinski and his wife. And below it was the Twenty-third Psalm. Lipinski was standing with his arm around a slim woman with short brown hair. It was a snapshot, taken outdoors on a summer day, and they were smiling at each other.

"Kind of funny they used that picture," Grandma said. "I overheard people talking, saying as how Lipinski's wife left him last week. Just up and went. And she didn't show up for the viewing, either. Nobody could find her to tell her about it. Was like she just disappeared off the face of the earth. Just like Fred. Except from what I heard, Laura Lipinski left on purpose. Packed her bags and said she wanted a divorce. Isn't that a shame?"

Now I know there are billions of women out there who are slim with short brown hair. But my mind made the leap anyway to the severed head with the short brown hair. Larry Lipinski was the second RGC employee to die a violent death in the space of a week. And while it seemed like a remote connection, Fred had been in contact with Lipinski. Lipinski's wife was gone. And Lipinski's wife could, in a very vague way, fit the body in the bag.

"Okay," I said, "let's show the pictures to Irene Tully." What the hell. If she freaked out I'd write it off as an average day. I dug her address out of my bag. Apartment 117, Brookside Gardens. Brookside Gardens was an apartment complex about a quarter mile from the strip mall.

"Irene Tully," Grandma said. "The name sounds familiar, but I can't place her."

"She said she knew Fred from the seniors' club."

"I guess that's where I heard of her. There's lots of people in that seniors' club, and I don't go to the meetings all the time. I can only take so much of old people. If I want to see loose skin I can look in the mirror."

I turned into Brookside Gardens and started searching for numbers. There were six buildings arranged around a large parking area. The buildings were two-story brick, done up in colonial modern, which meant the trim was white and the windows were framed by shutters. Each apartment had its own outside entrance.

"Here it is," Grandma said, unbuckling her seat belt. "The one with the Halloween decoration on the door."

We walked up the short sidewalk and rang the bell.

Irene looked out at us. "Yes?"

"We need to ask you about the disappearance of Fred Shutz," Grandma said. "And we got a picture to show you."

"Oh," Irene said. "Is it a picture of Fred?"

"Nope," Grandma said. "It's a picture of the kidnapper."

"Well, actually, we aren't really sure Fred was kidnapped," I said. "What Grandma meant was—"

"Take a look at this," Grandma said, handing Irene one of the photos. "Of course, the suit might be different."

Irene studied the photo. "Why is he in a casket?"

"He's sort of dead now," Grandma said.

Irene shook her head. "This isn't the man."

"Maybe you're just thinking that because his eyes are closed, and he don't look so shifty," Grandma said. "And his nose looks a little smushed. I think he might have fallen on his face after he blew his brains out."

Irene studied the picture. "No. It's definitely not him."

"Bummer," Grandma said. "I was sure he was the one."

"Sorry," Irene said.

"Well, they're still pretty good pictures," Grandma said, when we got back to the car. "They would have been better if I could have got his eyes to open."

I took Grandma home and bummed lunch off my mom. All the while I was looking for Bunchy. Last I saw him was Saturday, and I was beginning to worry. Figure that one out. Me worrying about Bunchy. Stephanie Plum, mother hen.

I left my parents and took Chambers to Hamilton. Bunchy picked me up on Hamilton. I saw him in my rearview mirror, pulled to the curb, and got out to talk to him.

"Where've you been?" I asked. "Take Sunday off?"

"I had some work to catch up on. Bookies gotta work sometimes too, you know."

"Yeah, only you're not a bookie."

"We gonna start that again?"

"How'd you find me just now?"

"I was riding around, and I got lucky. How about you? You get lucky?"

"That's none of your damn business!"

His eyes crinkled with laughter. "I was talking about Fred."

"Oh. One step forward, two steps backward," I said. "I get things that seem like leads and then they go nowhere."

"Like what?"

"I found a woman who saw Fred get into a car with another man the day he disappeared. Problem is, she can't describe the man or the car. And then something weird happened at the funeral home, and it feels to me like it might tie in, but I can't find any logical reason why."

"What was the weird thing?"

"There was a woman at one of the viewings who seemed to

have a similar problem to the one Fred was having with the garbage company. Only this woman had problems with her cable company."

Bunchy looked interested. "What kind of problems?"

"I don't know exactly. Grandma told me about it. She just said they were similar to Fred's."

"I think we should talk to this woman."

"We? There's no we."

"I thought we were working together. You brought me lamb and everything."

"I felt sorry for you. You were pathetic, sitting out there in your car."

He wagged his finger at me. "I don't think so. I think you're getting to like me."

Like a stray dog. Maybe not that much. But he was right about talking to Margaret Burger. What was the harm? I had no idea where Margaret Burger lived, so I went back to my parents' house and asked Grandma.

"I can show you," she said.

"Not necessary. Just tell me."

"And miss all the action? No way!"

Why not? I had Bunchy tagging along. Maybe I should ask Mrs. Ciak and Mary Lou and my sister, Valerie. I took a deep breath. Sarcasm always made me feel better. "Get in the car," I said to Grandma.

I took Chambers to Liberty and turned onto Rusling.

"It's one of these houses," Grandma said. "I'll know it when I see it. I went to a get-together there once." She looked over her shoulder. "I think someone's following us. I bet it's one of them garbage people."

"It's Bunchy," I said. "I'm sort of working with him."

"No kidding? I didn't realize this had turned into such a big investigation. We've got a whole team here."

I stopped at the house Grandma had described, and we all got out and collected together on the sidewalk. It had stopped raining, and the temperature had risen to pleasant.

"My granddaughter tells me you're working together," Grandma said to Bunchy, looking him over. "Are you a bounty hunter, too?"

"No, ma'am," he said. "I'm a bookie."

"A bookie!" Grandma said. "Isn't that something. I always wanted to meet a bookie."

I knocked on Margaret Burger's door, and before I could introduce myself Grandma stepped forward.

"Hope we aren't disturbing you," Grandma said. "But we're conducting an important investigation. Stephanie and me and Mr. Bunchy."

Bunchy elbowed me. "*Mr.* Bunchy," he said.

"Not at all," Margaret Burger said. "I guess this is about poor Fred."

"We can't find him no-how," Grandma said. "And my granddaughter thought your problem with that cable company sounded real similar. Except, of course, they gave Sol a heart attack instead of making him disappear."

"They were awful people," Margaret said. "We paid our bills on time. We never missed a payment. And then when we had trouble with the cable box, they said they never heard of us. Can you imagine?"

"Just like Fred," Grandma said. "Isn't that right, Stephanie?"

"Uh, yeah, it sounds—"

"So then what?" Bunchy said. "Did Sol complain?"

"He went down there in person and raised a big fuss. And that's when he had his heart attack."

"What a shame," Grandma said. "Sol was only in his seventies, too."

"Do you have any canceled checks from the cable company?"

Bunchy asked Margaret. "Something from before you had the problem?"

"I could look in my file," Margaret said. "I keep all my checks for a couple years. But I don't think I have any of the cable checks. After Sol died, that awful cable person, John Curly, came and tried to look like he was being helpful about solving the mix-up. I didn't buy that for a minute. He was just trying to cover his tracks because he messed up the computer records. He even said as much, but it was too late for Sol. He'd already been given the heart attack."

Bunchy looked resigned to what he was hearing. "John Curly took the canceled checks," Bunchy said, more statement than question.

"He said he needed them for his records."

"And he never brought them back?"

"Never. And next thing I know I get a statement from them welcoming me like I was a brand-new customer. I'm telling you, that cable company is a mess."

"Anything else you want to know?" I asked Bunchy.

"No. That's about it."

"How about you, Grandma?"

"I can't think of anything more."

"Well then," I said to Margaret, "I guess there isn't anything else. Thanks for talking to us."

"I hope Fred turns up," Margaret said. "Mabel must be be-side herself."

"She's holding up pretty good," Grandma said. "I guess Fred wasn't one of those husbands you really mind losing."

Margaret nodded, like she understood completely what Grandma was saying.

I dropped Grandma off and continued on home to my apart-ment. Bunchy followed me the whole way and parked behind me.

"Now what?" Bunchy said. "What are you going to do now?"

"I don't know. You have any ideas?"

"I'm thinking there's something going on with the garbage company."

I considered telling him about Laura Lipinski but decided against it.

"Why did you want to see Margaret's canceled checks?" I asked.

"No special reason. Just thought they'd be interesting."

"Uh-huh."

Bunchy rocked back on his heels with his hands in his pockets. "How about the checks from the garbage company? You ever get any of them?"

"Why? You think they'd be interesting, too?"

"Might be. You never know about stuff." His eyes focused on something behind me, and his face changed expression. Wariness, maybe.

I felt a body move so close it was skimming my own, and a warm hand protectively settled at the base of my neck. Without turning I knew it was Ranger.

"This is Bunchy," I said to Ranger, by way of introduction. "Bunchy the bookie."

Ranger didn't move. Bunchy didn't move. And I wasn't moving, held in a kind of suspended animation by Ranger's force field.

Finally Bunchy took a couple steps backward. It was the sort of maneuver a man might make when confronted with a grizzly. "I'll be in touch," Bunchy said, pivoting on his heel, walking to his car.

We watched Bunchy drive out of the lot.

"He's not a bookie," Ranger said, his hand still holding me captive.

I stepped away and turned to face him, putting space between us.

"What was with the intimidation routine you just did?"

Ranger smiled. "You think I intimidated him?"

"Not a whole lot."

"I don't think so, either. He's got a few face-offs behind him."

"Am I right in assuming you didn't like him?"

"Just being cautious. He was carrying and he was lying. And he's a cop."

I already knew all those things. "He's been following me for days. So far he's been harmless."

"What's he after?"

"I don't know. Something to do with Fred. Right now he knows more than I do. So I figure it's worthwhile to play along with him. He's probably a Fed. I think he has a tracking device on my car. Jersey cops can't usually afford to do stuff like that. And I think he must be working with a partner to be able to pick me up, but I haven't spotted the partner yet."

"Does he know you've made him?"

"Yeah, but he doesn't want to talk about it."

"I can help with the tracking problem," Ranger said, handing me a set of keys.

"What's this?"

TEN

"THIS IS TEMPTATION," Ranger said, leaning against a new midnight-black Porsche Boxster.

"Could you be more specific about the temptation? Like, what kind of temptation were you thinking about?"

"Temptation to broaden your horizons."

I had a lot of unease over Ranger's definition of "broad horizons." I suspected his horizons were a teensy bit closer to hell than I might want to travel. For starters, there was the car and the slight possibility that it wasn't entirely legitimate.

"Where do you get these cars?" I asked him. "You seem to have a never-ending supply of new, expensive black cars."

"I have a source."

"This Porsche isn't stolen, is it?"

"Do you care?"

"Of course I care!"

"Then it isn't stolen," Ranger said.

I shook my head. "It's a really cool car. And I appreciate your offer, but I can't afford a car like this."

"You don't know the price yet," Ranger said.

"Is it more than five dollars?"

"The car isn't for sale. It's a company car. You get the car if you continue to work with me. You're ruining my image in that Buick. Everyone who works with me drives black."

"Well, hell," I said, "I wouldn't want to ruin your image."

Ranger just kept looking at me.

"Is this charity?" I asked him.

"Guess again."

"I'm not selling my soul, am I?"

"I'm not in the soul-buying business," Ranger said. "The car's an investment. Part of the working relationship."

"So what do I have to do in this working relationship?"

Ranger uncrossed his arms and pushed off from the car. "Jobs come up. Don't accept any that make you uncomfortable."

"You aren't doing this just to amuse yourself, are you? To see what I'd be willing to do for an expensive car?"

"That would be somewhere in the middle of the list," Ranger said. He looked at his watch. "I have a meeting. Drive the car. Think it over."

He had his Mercedes parked next to the Porsche. He slid behind the wheel and drove away without looking back.

I almost collapsed on the spot. I put a hand to the Porsche to steady myself, and then immediately yanked my hand away, afraid I'd left prints. Dang!

I ran inside and looked around for Randy Briggs. His laptop was on the coffee table, but his jacket was gone. I toyed with the idea of packing all his things into the two suitcases, moving them into the hall, and locking my door, but gave it up as futile.

I cracked open a beer and called Mary Lou. "Help!" I said.

"What help?"

"He gave me a car. And he touched me twice!" I looked at

my neck in the hall mirror to see if I was branded where his hand had rested.

"Who? What are you talking about?"

"Ranger!"

"Omigod. He gave you a car?"

"He said it was an investment in our working relationship. What does that mean?"

"What kind of car is it?"

"A new Porsche."

"That's at least oral sex."

"Be serious!" I said.

"Okay, the truth is . . . it's beyond oral sex. It could be, you know, butt stuff."

"I'll return the car."

"Stephanie, this is a Porsche!"

"And I think he's flirting with me, but I'm not sure."

"What does he do?"

"He's gotten sort of physical."

"How physical?"

"Touchy."

"Omigod, what did he touch?"

"My neck."

"Is that all?"

"My hair."

"Hmmm," Mary Lou said. "Was it sexy touching?"

"It felt sexy to me."

"And he gave you a Porsche," Mary Lou said. "A Porsche!"

"It isn't like it's a gift. It's a company car."

"Yeah, right. When do I get to ride in it? You want to go to the mall tonight?"

"I don't know if I should be driving it for personal stuff." In fact, I didn't know if I should be driving it *at all* until I made sure about the butt thing.

"You really think this is a company car?" Mary Lou asked.

"So far as I can see, everyone who works for Ranger drives a new black car."

"A Porsche?"

"Usually an SUV, but maybe a Porsche happened to fall off the back of the truck yesterday." I could hear screaming in the background. "What's happening?"

"The kids are having a conflicting opinion. I suppose I should go mediate."

Mary Lou had started taking parenting classes because she couldn't get the two-year-old to stop eating the dog's food. Now she said things like "the kids are having a conflicting opinion" instead of "the kids are trying to kill each other." I think it sounds much more civilized, but when you come right down to it . . . the kids were trying to kill each other.

I hung up and took the check Fred had written to RGC out of my shoulder bag and studied it. Nothing unusual that I could see. A plain old check.

The phone rang, and I put the check back in my bag.

"Are you alone?" Bunchy asked.

"Yes, I'm alone."

"Something going on between you and that Ranger guy?"

"Yes." I just didn't know what it was.

"We didn't get much chance to talk," Bunchy said. "I was wondering what you were gonna do next."

"Look, why don't you just tell me what it is you want me to do."

"Hey, I'm following *you* around, remember?"

"Okay, I'll play the game. I thought I'd go back to the bank tomorrow and talk to a friend of mine. What do you think of that?"

"Good idea."

It was close to five. Joe would most likely be home now, watching the news on television, fixing himself something to eat, getting ready for *Monday Night Football*. If I invited myself to his house for *Monday Night Football*, I could show him the check and see what he thinks. And I could ask him to check into Laura Lipinski. If things went well, maybe I could also make up for opportunities missed on Saturday night.

I dialed his number.

"Hey," I said. "I thought maybe you wanted company for *Monday Night Football*."

"You don't like football."

"I sort of like football. I like when they all jump on each other. That's pretty interesting. So do you want me to come over?"

"Sorry. I have to work tonight."

"All night?"

There was a moment of silence while Morelli processed the hidden message. "You want me bad," he said.

"I was just being friendly."

"Will you still be feeling friendly tomorrow? I don't think I'll be working tomorrow."

"Order a pizza."

After I hung up I looked guiltily at the hamster cage. "Hey, I'm just being friendly," I said to Rex. "I'm not going to sleep with him."

Rex still didn't come out of his can, but I could see the pine shavings moving. I think he was laughing.

The phone rang around nine.

"I have a job for you tomorrow," Ranger said. "Are you interested?"

"Maybe."

"It's of high moral quality."

"And the legal quality?"

"Could be worse. I need a decoy. I have a deadbeat who needs to be separated from his Jaguar."

"Are you stealing it or repossessing it?"

"Repossessing. All you have to do is sit in a bar and talk to this guy while we load his car onto a flatbed."

"That sounds okay."

"I'll pick you up at six. Wear something that'll hold his attention."

"What bar is this?"

"Mike's Place on Center."

Thirty minutes later, Briggs came home. "So what do you do on Monday nights?" he asked. "You watch football?"

I went to bed at eleven, and two hours later I was still thrashing around, unable to sleep. I had Larry Lipinski's missing wife, Laura, on my mind. The back of her head, severed at the neck, stuffed in a garbage bag. Her husband dead from a self-inflicted gunshot wound. Hacked up his wife. Shot his coworker. I really didn't know if it was Laura Lipinski. What were the chances? Probably not good. Then who was in that bag? The more I thought about it, the more convinced I became that it was Laura Lipinski.

I looked at the clock for the hundredth time.

Laura Lipinski wasn't the only thing keeping me awake. I was having a hormone attack. Damn Morelli. Whispering all those things in my ear. Looking sexy in his Italian suit. Surely Morelli would be home by now. I could call him, I thought, and tell him I was coming to visit. After all, it was his fault I was in this hellish state.

But what if I call, and he *isn't* home, and I get recorded on his caller ID? Major embarrassment. Best not to call. Think of something else, I ordered myself.

Ranger flashed into my mind. No! Not Ranger!

"Damn." I kicked the covers off and went out to the kitchen to get some orange juice. Only there wasn't any orange juice. There wasn't *any* kind of juice, because I never went food shopping. There were still some leftovers from my mother, but no juice.

I really needed juice. And a Snickers bar. If I had juice and a Snickers bar, I probably could forget about sex. In fact, I didn't even need the juice anymore. Just the Snickers bar.

I stuffed myself into a pair of old gray sweats, shoved my feet into unlaced boots, and pulled a jacket over my plaid flannel nightshirt. I grabbed my purse and my keys, and because I was trying not to be stupid, I also grabbed my gun.

"I don't know what the hell you're going after," Briggs said from the couch, "but bring one back for me, too."

I clomped off, out of my apartment, down the hall, into the elevator.

When I got to the lot, as fate would have it, I realized I'd taken the Porsche key. Hah! Who am I to dispute fate? Guess I just had to drive the Porsche.

I started out for the 7-Eleven, but I was there in no time at all, and it seemed a shame not to at least work the kinks out of the car. Especially since I hadn't yet *found* any kinks. I continued on down Hamilton, turned into the Burg, wound around some, left the Burg, and sonovagun, before I knew it, I was in front of Morelli's townhouse. His truck was parked at the curb, and the house was dark. I idled in front of the house for a minute, thinking about Morelli, wishing I was comfy in bed with him. Well, what the hell, I thought, maybe I should ring his doorbell and tell him I was in the neighborhood, so I thought I'd stop by. No harm in that. Just being friendly. I caught a glimpse of myself in the rearview mirror. Eek. Should have done something with my hair. And my legs might need shaving now that I thought about it. Rats.

Okay, maybe it's not such a good idea to visit Morelli right now. Maybe I should go home first and shave and scrounge up some sexy underwear. Or maybe I should just wait until tomorrow. Twenty-four hours, give or take a couple. I wasn't sure I could hold out for twenty-four hours. He was right. I wanted him bad.

Get a grip! I told myself. We're talking about a simple sex act here. This isn't a medical emergency like having a heart attack. This can wait twenty-four hours.

I took a deep breath. Twenty-four hours. I was feeling better. I was in control. I was a rational woman. I put the Porsche into gear and cruised down the street.

Piece of cake. I can last it.

I got to the corner and noticed lights in my rearview mirror.

Not many people out in this neighborhood, at this hour, on a work night. I turned the corner, parked, cut my lights, and watched the car stop in front of Morelli's house. After a couple minutes Morelli got out and walked to his door, and the car began to roll down the street toward me.

I gripped the wheel tight, so the Porsche wouldn't be tempted to go into reverse and zoom back to Morelli's. Less than twenty-four hours, I repeated, and my legs would be smooth as silk and my hair would be clean. But wait a minute! Morelli has a shower and a razor. This is all baloney. There's no need to wait.

I shifted into reverse just as the other car came into the intersection. I caught a glimpse of the driver and felt my heart go dead in my chest. It was Terry Gilman.

Say what? Terry Gilman!

There was an explosion of red behind my eyeballs. Shit. I was such a sap. I hadn't suspected. I'd thought he'd changed. I'd believed he was different from the other Morellis. Here I was worrying over leg hair, when Morelli was out doing God knows what with Terry Gilman. Unh! Major mental smack in the head.

I squinted at the car as it cleared the intersection and motored on. Terry was oblivious to my presence. Probably planning out the rest of her night. Probably going off to whack someone's grandmother.

Well, who cares about Morelli, anyway. Not me. I could care less. There was only one thing I cared about. Chocolate.

I put my foot to the pedal and careened away from the curb. Clear the streets. Stephanie's got a Porsche and needs a Snickers bar.

I reached the 7-Eleven in record time, blasted through the store, and left with a full bag. Hey, Morelli, orgasm this.

I entered my lot at warp speed, screeched to a stop, stomped up the stairs, down the hall, and kicked my door open. *"Shit!"*

Rex stopped running on his wheel and looked at me.

"You heard me," I said. "Shit, shit, shit."

Briggs sat up. "What the hell's going on? I'm trying to get some sleep here."

"Don't push your luck. Don't speak to me."

He squinted at me. "What are you wearing? Is that some new form of birth control?"

I grabbed the hamster cage and bag of candy, carted everything off to my bedroom, and slammed my door shut. I ate the 100 Grand bar first, and then the Kit Kat, and then the Snickers. I was starting to feel sick, but I ate the Baby Ruth and the Almond Joy and the Reese's Peanut Butter Cup.

"Okay, I'm feeling much better now," I said to Rex.

Then I burst into tears.

When I was done crying I told Rex it was only hormones reacting with a prediabetic surge of insulin from eating all those candy bars . . . so he shouldn't worry. I went to bed and immediately fell asleep. Crying is fucking exhausting.

I awoke the next morning with my eyes crusty and puffed from crying and my spirit lower than slug slime. I lay there for about ten minutes wallowing in my misery, thinking of ways to kill myself, deciding on smoking. But then I didn't have any cigarettes, and I wasn't in a mood to traipse back to the 7-Eleven. Anyway, I was working with Ranger now, so probably I could just let nature take its course.

I dragged myself out of bed and into the bathroom where I stared at myself in the mirror. "Get a grip, Stephanie," I said. "You have a Porsche and a SEALs hat, and you're broadening your horizons."

I was afraid after all those candy bars I was also broadening my ass, and I should get some exercise. I was still dressed in my sweats, so I wriggled into a sports bra and laced up my running shoes.

Briggs was already at work at his computer when I came out of my bedroom. "Look who's here . . . Mary Sunshine," he said. "Christ, you look like shit."

"This is nothing," I told him. "Wait until you see what I look like when I'm *done* running."

I returned drenched in sweat and feeling very pleased with myself. Stephanie Plum, woman in charge. Screw Morelli. Screw Terry Gilman. Screw the world.

I had a chicken sandwich for breakfast and took a shower. Just to be mean I put the beer on the top shelf in the refrigerator, told Briggs to have a rotten day, and zoomed off in my Porsche to the Grand Union. Dual-purpose trip. Talk to Leona and Allen and shop for real food. I parked about a half mile away from the store so no one would park next to me and ding my door. I got out and looked at the Porsche. It was perfect. It was a totally kick-ass car. When you had a car like this you didn't mind so much that your boyfriend was boinking a skank.

I did the shopping first, and by the time I was done and had the groceries tucked away in the trunk, the bank was open. Business was slow first thing on a Tuesday morning. No one in the lobby. There were two tellers counting out money. Probably practicing. I didn't see Leona.

Allen Shempsky was in the lobby drinking coffee, talking to a bank guard. He saw me and waved. "How's the Uncle Fred hunt going?" he asked.

"Not that good. I was looking for Leona."

"It's her day off. Maybe I can be of help."

I rooted around in my bag, located the check, and handed it over to Allen. "Anything you can tell me about this?"

He examined it front and back. "It's a canceled check."

"Anything weird about it?"

He looked at it some more. "Not that I can see. What's so special about this check?"

"I don't know. Fred was having billing problems with RGC. He was supposed to bring this check to the office the day he disappeared. I guess he didn't want to take the original, so he left it home on his desk."

"Sorry I can't be more helpful," Shempsky said. "If you want to leave it with me I can ask around. Sometimes different people pick up different things."

I dropped the check back into my bag. "Think I'll hang on to it. I have a feeling people have died because of this check."

"That's serious," Shempsky said.

I walked back to the car feeling spooky and not knowing why. Nothing alarming had happened at the bank. And no one was parked or standing by the Porsche. I checked the lot. No Bunchy. No Ramirez that I could see. Still, there was that uncomfortable feeling. Something forgotten, maybe. Or someone watching. I unlocked the car and looked back at the bank. It was Shempsky I'd sensed. He was standing to the side of the bank building, smoking a cigarette, watching me. Oh man, now I was getting the creeps from Shempsky. I blew out a breath. My imagination was in overdrive. The man was just sneaking a smoke, for Pete's sake.

The only oddity in the act was that Allen Shempsky actually

had a bad habit. A bad habit seemed like an excess of personality for Allen Shempsky. Shempsky was a nice guy who never offended anyone and was totally forgettable. He'd been like that for as long as I could remember. When we were in school he was the kid in the back of the room who never got called on. Quiet smile, never a conflicting opinion, always neat and clean. He was like a chameleon whose clothes matched the wall behind him. After knowing Allen all my life, I'd be hard-pressed to name his hair color. Maybe mouse brown. Not that he was rodentlike. He was a reasonably attractive man with an average nose and average teeth and average eyes. He was average height, of average build, and I assumed of average intelligence, although there was no way of knowing for sure.

He'd married Maureen Blum a month after they both graduated from Rider College. He had two young children and a house in Hamilton Township. I'd never driven past his house, but I was willing to bet it was forgettable. Maybe that wasn't so bad. Maybe it was a good thing to be unmemorable. I bet Maureen Blum Shempsky didn't have to worry about being stalked by Benito Ramirez.

Bunchy was waiting when I got back to my apartment building. He was in the lot, sitting in his car, looking grumpy.

"What's with the Porsche?" he wanted to know, coming over.

"It's on loan from Ranger. And if you put a tracking device on it he won't be happy."

"Do you know how much a car like this costs?"

"A lot?"

"Maybe more than you want to pay," Bunchy said.

"I hope that's not the case."

He took one of the grocery bags and followed me upstairs. "You go to the bank like you said?"

"Yep. I talked to Allen Shempsky, but I didn't learn anything new."

"What did you talk to him about?"

"The weather. Politics. Managed health care." I balanced my bag on my hip while I unlocked the door.

"Boy, you're a beaut. You don't trust anybody, do you?"

"I don't trust *you*."

"I wouldn't trust him, either," Briggs said from the living room. "He looks like he's got a social disease."

"Who's that?" Bunchy wanted to know.

"That's Randy," I said.

"Want to see him disappear?"

I looked over at Briggs. It was a tempting offer. "Some other time," I said to Bunchy.

Bunchy unpacked his bag and set everything out on the kitchen counter. "You've got some strange friends."

And they hardly counted at all compared to my relatives. "I'll make you lunch if you tell me who you're working for and why you're interested in Fred," I said.

"No can do. Besides, I think you'll make me lunch anyway."

I made canned tomato soup and grilled cheese sandwiches. I made grilled cheese because that's what I felt like eating. And I made the soup because I like to keep a clean can in reserve for Rex.

Halfway through lunch I looked at Bunchy, and Morelli's words echoed in my ear. I'm working with a couple Treasury guys who make me look like a Boy Scout, he'd said. The Hallelujah Chorus rang out in my head, and I had an epiphany. "Holy cow," I said. "You're working with Morelli."

"I don't work with anyone," Bunchy said. "I work alone."

"That's a load of pig pucky."

This wasn't the first time Morelli had been involved in one of my cases and had kept it from me, but it was the first time he'd sent someone to spy on me. This was a new all-time low for Morelli.

Bunchy sighed and pushed his dish away. "Does this mean I'm not getting dessert?"

I gave him one of the leftover candy bars. "I'm depressed."

"Now what?"

"Morelli is scum."

He looked down at the candy bar. "I told you I work alone."

"Yeah, and you told me you were a bookie."

He glanced up. "You don't know for sure that I'm not."

The phone rang, and I snatched it up before the machine could take over.

"Hey, Cupcake," Morelli said. "What do you want on your pizza tonight?"

"I want nothing. There is no pizza. There is no you, no me, no us, no pizza. And don't ever call me again, you scummy, slimy fungus-ridden dog turd, piece of fly crud." And I slammed the phone down.

Bunchy was laughing. "Let me guess," he said. "That was Morelli."

"And you!" I yelled, pointing my finger, teeth clenched. "You are *no better*."

"I gotta go," Bunchy said, still doing his Mr. Chuckles impersonation.

"So, have you always had a problem with men?" Briggs asked. "Or is this something recent?"

I WAS IN the lobby, waiting for Ranger at six o'clock. I was all showered and perfumed and hair freshly done up to look sexily unkempt. Mike's Place is a sports bar frequented by businessmen. At six o'clock it would be filled with suits catching ESPN and having a drink to unwind before going home, so I chose to look suity, too. I was wearing my Wonderbra, which worked wonders, a white silk shirt unbuttoned clear to the front clasp on the magical bra, and a black silk suit with the skirt rolled at the waist to show a lot of leg. I covered the mess at the waist with a wide fake leopard skin belt, and I stuffed my stocking-clad feet into four-inch fuck-me pumps.

Mr. Morganthal shuffled out of the elevator and winked at me. "Hey, hootchie-mamma," he said. "Want a hot date?" He was ninety-two and lived on the third floor, next to Mrs. Delgado.

"You're too late," I told him. "I've already made plans."

"That's just as well. You'd probably kill me," Mr. Morganthal said.

Ranger pulled up in the Mercedes, and idled at the door. I gave Mr. Morganthal a tweak on the cheek and sashayed out, swinging my hips, wetting my lips. I poured myself into the Mercedes and crossed my legs.

Ranger looked at me and smiled. "I told you to get his attention . . . not start a riot. Maybe you should button one more button."

I batted my eyelashes at him, in fake-flirt, which actually wasn't totally fake. "You don't like it?" I said. Hah! Take that, Morelli. Who needs you!

Ranger reached over and flipped the next two buttons open, exposing me to mid-belly. "That's the way *I* like it," he said, the smile still in place.

Shit! I quickly rebuttoned the buttons. "Wise guy," I said. Okay, so he called my bluff. No reason to panic. Just file it away for future reference. *Not ready for Ranger!*

Mr. Morganthal came out and shook his finger at us.

"I think I just sullied your reputation," Ranger said, putting the car in gear.

"Probably more like you helped me live up to expectations."

We cruised across town and parked half a block from the bar on the opposite side of the street.

Ranger took a photo from behind the sun visor. "This is Ryan

Perin. He's a regular here. Comes every day after work. Has two drinks. Goes home. Never parks his car more than half a block away on the street. He knows the dealer's trying to get it back, and he's nervous. Comes out to check on it every few minutes. Your job is to make sure he keeps his eyes on you—not the car. Keep him in the building."

"Why are you taking it here?"

"When he's home the car's in a locked garage, and the regular repo people can't get at it. When he's at work he parks it in a garage with an attendant who takes his Christmas bonus seriously." Ranger made a gun sign with his hand, finger and thumb extended. "For that matter, Perin carries too and isn't slow on the draw. That's why we need to finesse the car. Nobody wants bloodshed."

"What does this guy do for a living?"

"Lawyer. Sending all his money up his nose these days."

A dark green Jaguar rolled past us. There were no spaces open on the street. Just as he got to the end of the block a car pulled out, and the Jag slid in place.

"Wow," I said, "that was lucky."

"No," Ranger said. "That was Tank. We have cars parked all along this street, so Perin has to park down there."

Perin angled out of the car, beeped the alarm on, and headed for Mike's.

I looked at Ranger. "Will the alarm be a problem?"

"None at all."

Perin disappeared into the building.

"Okay," Ranger said. "Go get 'em, Slick. I'll give you a five-minute lead, and then I'll call the truck in." He gave me a buzzer. "If something goes wrong, hit the panic button. I'll come get you when the car's cleared the street."

Perin was dressed in a blue pinstripe. He was in his early forties, with thinning sandy blond hair and an athletic build gone soft. I stepped just to the side of the door and waited while my eyes adjusted to the change in light. There were mostly men in the room, but there were a few women, too. The women were in clusters. The men tended to be alone, eyes turned to the TV. Perin was easy to spot. He was at the far end of the polished mahogany bar. The bartender set a drink in front of him. Something clear on the rocks.

There were chairs open on either side of Perin, but I didn't want to sit down and start a conversation. I didn't want him to feel singled out. If he was nervous the direct approach might be too obvious. So I walked toward him, rummaging in my bag, looking absorbed in finding whatever. And just as I reached his stool I faked a stumble. Not enough to go down to the ground, but enough to knock into him, clutching at his sleeve for support.

"Omigod," I said. "I'm so sorry. This is so embarrassing. I wasn't watching where I was going and . . ." I looked down. "It's these shoes! I'm just not a high-heel person."

"What kind of a person are you?" Perin asked.

I gave him the million-dollar smile. "I think maybe I'm a barefoot person." I slid onto the stool next to him and signaled the bartender. "Boy, I really need a drink. It's been one of those days."

"Tell me about it," he said. "What do you do?"

"I'm a lingerie buyer." Used to be, anyway, before I started bounty-hunting.

His eyes dropped to my cleavage. "No shit?"

I hoped they loaded that car on fast. This guy had a head start on the drinky poos, and was going to be on me like white on rice. I could feel it coming.

"My name's Ryan Perin," he said, extending his hand.

"Stephanie."

He kept hold of my hand. "Stephanie the lingerie buyer. That's very sexy."

Yuk. I hate holding hands with strange men. Damn Ranger and his horizons. "Well, you know . . . it's a job."

"I bet you have a lot of great lingerie."

"Sure. I have everything. You name it, I've got it."

The bartender looked at me expectantly.

"I'll have one of those," I said, pointing to Perin's drink. "And could you hurry?"

"So tell me about your lingerie," Perin said. "You have any garter belts?"

"Oh, yeah. I wear garter belts all the time—red, black, purple."

"How about thong panties?"

"Yeah, thong panties." Every time I feel like flossing my ass.

The alarm went off on his watch.

"What's that?" I asked.

"It's a reminder to check on my car."

Damn! Don't panic. Don't panic. "What's wrong with your car?"

"This isn't such a great neighborhood at this time of night. I had a radio ripped off last week. So once in a while I just look out and make sure no one's messing with anything."

"Don't you have an alarm system?"

"Well, yeah."

"Then you don't have to worry."

"I guess you're right. Still . . ." He looked toward the door. "Maybe I should check just to be safe."

"You're not one of those obsessive-compulsive types, are you?" I asked. "I don't like those types. They're always so uptight. They never want to try anything new like, um . . . group sex."

That got his attention back.

Some spittle collected at the corner of his mouth. "You like group sex?"

"Well, I don't like to do it with too many men, but I have a

196

couple girlfriends . . ." My drink came. I knocked it back and went into a coughing fit. When I stopped coughing, my eyeballs got hot and watery. "What *is* this?"

"Bombay Sapphire."

"I'm not much of a drinker."

Perin slid a hand up my leg to just inside my skirt hem. "Tell me more about the group sex."

Stick a fork in me, I thought. Because I'm done. If Ranger didn't get here soon I was gonna be in big trouble. I was unloading everything I had, and I didn't know where to go from here. I didn't have a whole lot of experience at this sort of thing. And what I knew about group sex was zero. Which was already more than I *wanted* to know. "Thursday is my group sex night," I said. "We do it every Thursday. Unless we can't find a man . . . then we just watch television."

"How about another drink?" Perin asked.

No sooner had he gotten the words out of his mouth than he was off his bar stool, flying through the air. He crash-landed on a table, the table collapsed, and Perin lay still as a stone, spread-eagled on the floor, eyes wide, mouth open, like a big, dead beached fish.

I gasped and turned and was nose-to-nose with Benito Ramirez. "You shouldn't be whoring like this, Stephanie," Ramirez said, soft-voiced and crazy-eyed. "The champ don't like when he sees you with other men. Sees them handling you. You need to save yourself for the champ." He managed a small, sick smile. "The champ's gonna do things to you, Stephanie. Things you've never had done to you before. Did you ask Lula about the things the champ can do?"

"What are you doing here?" I shrieked. I had one eye on Perin, afraid he was going to get to his feet and run for his car. And I had one eye on Ramirez, afraid he was going to draw a knife and carve me up like a Christmas turkey.

"You can't get away from the champ," Ramirez whispered. "The champ sees everything. He sees when you go out for candy bars late at night. What's the matter, Stephanie, having trouble sleeping? The champ could fix that. He knows how to make women sleep."

My stomach clenched, and I broke into an instant cold sweat. I never saw him. He'd been lying in wait for me, following my every move, watching me. And I never saw him. Probably the only reason I was alive was because Ramirez loved the cat-and-mouse game. He loved the smell of another person's fear. Loved to torture, to prolong the pain and terror.

There'd been a black hole in the time continuum when Perin had gone airborne. Everyone in the bar, with the exception of me and Ramirez, had sat frozen in dumbfounded shock. Now everyone in the bar was on their feet.

"What the hell?" the bartender yelled, coming at Ramirez.

Ramirez turned his eyes to the bartender, and the bartender backed off.

"Hey, man," the bartender said. "You gotta take your problems outside."

Perin was standing wobble-legged, glaring at Ramirez. "What are you, nuts? Are you freaking nuts?"

"The champ don't like remarks like that," Ramirez said, his eyes shrinking in his head.

A big, no-neck guy came to Perin's rescue. "Hey, leave the little guy alone," he said to Ramirez.

Ramirez turned on him. "No one tells the champ what to do."

Bam! Ramirez sucker-punched no-neck, and no-neck went down like a house of cards.

Perin pulled his gun and fired one off. The shot went wide of Ramirez, and sent everyone in the bar running for the door. Everyone but Perin and Ramirez and me. The bartender was shouting into the phone for the police to get their asses in gear. And through the open door I caught a glimpse of the flatbed moving down the street with the green Jaguar on board.

"I don't like the police," Ramirez said to the bartender. "You shouldn't have called the police." Ramirez gave me one last look with his nobody's-home eyes and went out the back door.

I hopped off the bar stool. "Nice meeting you," I said to Perin. "I have to go now."

Ranger strolled in, looked around, shook his head, and smiled at me. "You never disappoint," he said.

ELEVEN

RANGER HAD THE Mercedes double-parked outside Mike's Place. I got in, and we took off before Perin made it through the door to the sidewalk.

Ranger glanced over at me. "Are you okay?"

"Never been better."

This brought another appraising look from Ranger.

"Well, maybe I'm a little buzzed," I said. "Think I shouldn't have drunk that whole drink." I leaned closer to Ranger, as he was looking very fine, and I was finding him superior to that rat-fink Morelli.

Ranger downshifted at a light. "Want to tell me about the gunfire?"

"Perin got one off. It didn't hit anybody, though." I smiled at him. Ranger wasn't nearly so scary when I was tanked on Bombay.

"Perin was shooting at you?"

"Well, no. There was this other guy who sort of didn't like Perin talking to me. And there was an altercation." I touched Ranger's diamond stud earring. "Pretty," I said.

Ranger grinned. "How many drinks did you have?"

"One. But it was a big one. And I'm not much of a drinker."

"Something to remember," Ranger said.

I wasn't sure exactly what he meant by that, but I hoped it had to do with sex and taking advantage of me.

He turned into my lot and rolled to a stop at the door. Major disappointment, because it meant he was dropping me off, as opposed to parking and coming in for a nightcap . . . or something.

"You have a visitor," he said.

"*Moi?*"

"That's Morelli's bike."

I swiveled to look. Sure enough, Morelli's Ducati was parked next to Mr. Feinstein's Cadillac. Damn. I stuck my hand in my shoulder bag and fished around.

"What are you looking for?" Ranger asked.

"My gun."

"Probably it's not a good idea to shoot Morelli," Ranger said. "Cops are real touchy about that sort of thing."

I wrenched myself out of the car, straightened my skirt, and huffed into the building.

Morelli was sitting in the hall when I got upstairs. He was dressed in black jeans, black motorcycle boots, a black T-shirt, and a black leather motorcycle jacket. He had a two-day beard and his hair was long, even by Morelli standards. If I hadn't been mad at him I'd have had my clothes off before I got to my door. Now, I realize I'd just had the same thought about Ranger, but there it was. What can I say? Pretty soon Bunchy and Briggs would be looking good to me.

"Boy, you have a lot of nerve coming here," I said to Morelli, fumbling for my key.

He took his key ring from his pocket and opened my door.

"Since when do you have a key to my apartment?" I asked him.

"Since you gave it to me back when we were friendlier." He looked down at me and amusement softened the set of his mouth. "Have you been drinking?"

"Occupational hazard. I had this job to do for Ranger, and drinking seemed like the right thing to do at the time."

"You want some coffee?"

"No way, that would ruin everything. Anyway, I wouldn't drink your coffee. And you can leave now, thank you."

"I don't think so." Morelli opened the refrigerator, searched around and discovered the bag of Mocha Java I'd bought at Grand Union. He measured out water and coffee and tripped the switch on my coffeemaker. "Let me take a winger here. You're mad at me, right?"

I rolled my eyes so far into the back of my head I saw myself thinking. And while my eyes were all the way back there, I looked for Briggs. Where was the little devil?

"You want to give me a clue?" Morelli said.

"You don't deserve a clue."

"That's probably true, but how about giving me one anyway."

"Terry Gilman."

"Yeah?"

"That's it. That's your entire clue, you creep."

Morelli got two mugs from the over-the-counter cabinet and filled the mugs with coffee. He added milk and handed one of the mugs to me. "I need more to go on than a name."

"No you don't. You know exactly what I'm talking about."

His pager went off, and he did some creative swearing. He looked at the read-out and made a call on my phone. "I have to leave," he said. "I'd like to stay and settle this, but something's come up."

He got to the door and turned and came back. "I almost forgot. Have you seen Ramirez?"

"Yes. And I want to get a restraining order and have his parole revoked."

"His parole has already been revoked. He picked up a hooker on Stark Street last night and almost killed her. Brutalized her and left her for dead in a Dumpster. Somehow she managed to climb out, and two kids found her this morning."

"Is she going to be okay?"

"Looks like it. She's still on critical, but she's holding her own. When did you see him?"

"About a half hour ago."

I told him about the repo and the incident with Ramirez.

I could see emotion bubbling inside Morelli. Frustration, mostly. And some anger. "I don't suppose you'd consider moving back in with me?" he asked. "Just until Ramirez is found."

Be a little crowded what with Terry there, too. "Don't suppose I would," I said.

"How about if I marry you?"

"Now you want to marry me? What happens after they catch Ramirez? We get a divorce?"

"There's no divorce in my family. Grandma Bella wouldn't hear of it. You have to die to get out of a marriage in my family."

"Gosh, that's cheery." And true. I understood some of Joe's attitude about marriage. The Morelli men had a bad track record. They drank too much. They cheated on their wives. They beat their kids. And the misery lasts 'til death do them part. Fortunately for many of the Morelli wives, death visited the Morelli men early. They were shot in bar brawls, killed themselves in DUI car crashes, and exploded their livers. "We'll talk some other time," I said. "You'd better get moving. And don't worry, I'll be careful. I've been keeping my doors and windows locked, and I'm carrying a gun."

"You have a permit to carry concealed?"

"Got it yesterday."

"I didn't hear any of this," Morelli said. He bent his head and kissed me lightly on the lips. "Make sure the gun's loaded."

He was actually a very nice guy. Some of the less desirable Morelli genes had passed him by. He had the Morelli good looks and charm and none of the abusive qualities. The womanizing part was in question.

I smiled and said thanks. Although I'm not sure what I was thanking him for. For being a decent person about the gun, I guess. Or maybe for caring about my safety. At any rate, the smile and the thanks were encouragement enough for Morelli. He pulled me to him and kissed me again, hot and serious this time. Not a kiss I'd easily forget, nor want to end.

When he broke from the kiss, still holding me close, the grin returned. "That's better," he said. "I'll call when I can."

And he was gone.

Damn! I locked the door behind him and thunked myself on the forehead with the heel of my hand. I was such a dope. I'd just kissed Morelli like there was no tomorrow. Not the message I'd wanted to give him at all. What about Terry? What about Bunchy? What about Ranger? Never mind Ranger, I thought. Ranger wasn't part of this problem. Ranger was a different problem.

Briggs stuck his head out from my bathroom doorway. "Is it safe to come out?"

"What are you doing in there?"

"I heard you in the hall and didn't want to screw it up for you. Sounded like you finally had a live one."

"Thanks, but he wasn't all that live."

"So I see."

AT ONE O'CLOCK I was still awake. It was the kiss. I couldn't stop thinking about the kiss, and the way I'd felt when Morelli had taken me in his arms. And then I got to thinking about the way I'd have felt if he'd ripped my clothes off and kissed me in *other* places. And then there was Morelli naked. And Morelli naked and aroused. And Morelli doing something about being naked and aroused. And that's why I couldn't sleep. Again.

At two o'clock I was no closer to sleep. Damn Morelli. I rolled out of bed and padded barefoot into the kitchen. I went through the cupboards and fridge, but I couldn't find exactly the right thing to satisfy my hunger. Morelli was what I wanted, of course, but if I couldn't have Morelli, what I wanted was an Oreo. *Lots* of Oreos. I should have thought to get Oreos when I was at the store.

Grand Union was open twenty-four hours. Tempting, but a bad idea. Ramirez could be out there. Bad enough to worry about him during the day when there are people around and visibility is good. Going out at night seemed foolishly risky.

I went back to bed and instead of thinking about Joe Morelli, I found myself thinking about Ramirez, wondering if he was out there, parked in the lot or on one of the side streets. I knew all the cars that belonged in the lot. If an odd car was there, I'd spot it.

Curiosity had me now. And the excitement of a possible capture. If Ramirez was sitting in my lot, I could have him picked up. I slipped from under the covers and crept to the window. The lot was well-lit. Not a place where a car could be hidden in shadow. I grabbed hold of the curtain and drew it open. I expected to look down at the lot. Instead I looked into the obsidian eyes of Benito Ramirez. He was on my fire escape, leering in at me, his face illuminated in ambient light, his massive body shadowed and threatening against the night sky, his arms outspread, and his hands flat to the window frame.

I jumped back and yelped, and terror filled every part of me. I couldn't breath. I couldn't move. I couldn't think.

"Stephanie," he sang, his voice muffled through the black glass. He laughed softly and sang my name out again. "Stephan-ieeeee."

I wheeled around and flew out of the room and into the kitchen, where I fumbled in my bag for my gun. I found the gun and ran back to the bedroom, but Ramirez was gone. My window was still closed and locked, the curtains half open. The fire escape was empty. No sign of him in the lot. No strange car that I could see. For a moment I thought I'd imagined the whole thing. And then I saw the paper taped to the outside of my window. There was a hand-printed message on the paper.

God is waiting. Soon it will be your time to see Him.

I ran back to the kitchen to dial police dispatch. My hand was shaking, and my fingers wouldn't go to the right buttons on the phone. I took a calming breath and tried again. Another breath and I was telling the answering officer about Ramirez. I hung up and dialed Morelli. Halfway through the dial I cut the connection. Suppose Terry answered. Stupid thought, I told myself. She'd dropped him off. Don't make more of it than it is. There could be an explanation. And even if Joe wasn't the world's best boyfriend, he was still a damn good cop.

I redialed and waited while the phone rang seven times. Finally Morelli's machine picked up. Morelli wasn't home. Morelli was working. Ninety percent certainty, 10 percent doubt. It was the 10 percent that kept me from calling his cell phone or pager.

I suddenly realized Briggs was standing next to me.

The usual sarcasm was gone from his voice. "I don't think I've ever seen anyone that scared," he said. "You didn't hear anything I was saying to you."

"There was a man on my fire escape."

"Ramirez."

"Yeah. You know who he is?"

"Boxer."

"More than that. He's a very terrible person."

"Let's make some tea," Briggs said. "You don't look too good."

I brought my pillow and quilt into the living room and settled on the couch with Briggs. Every light in my apartment was on, and I had my gun within reach on the coffee table. I sat like that until daylight, dozing occasionally. When the sun was up, I went back to bed and slept until the phone woke me at eleven.

It was Margaret Burger.

"I found a check," she said. "It was misfiled. It's from that time when Sol was arguing with the cable company. I know Mr. Bunchy was interested in seeing it, but I don't know how to get in touch with him."

"I can get it to him," I told her. "I have a few things to do, and then I'll stop around."

"I'll be here all day," Margaret said.

I didn't know what I was going to get out of the check, but I thought it couldn't hurt to take a look. I made fresh coffee and chugged a glass of orange juice. I took a fast shower, dressed in my usual uniform of Levi's and a long-sleeve T-shirt, drank my coffee, ate a Pop-Tart, and called Morelli. Still no answer, but I left a message this time. The message was that Morelli should page me immediately if Ramirez was caught.

I took the pepper spray out of my shoulder bag and clipped it onto the waistband of my Levi's.

Briggs was in the kitchen when I left. "Be careful," he said.

My stomach knotted when I got to the elevator, and again when I stepped out of the lobby, into the lot. I quickly crossed to the car, powered up the Porsche, and watched my rearview mirror as I drove.

It occurred to me that I was no longer looking around every

corner for Uncle Fred. Somehow the Uncle Fred search had morphed into a mystery about a butchered woman and dead office workers and an uncooperative garbage company. I told myself it was all the same. That somehow it all tied to Fred's disappearance. But I wasn't completely convinced. It was still possible that Fred was in Fort Lauderdale, and I was spinning my wheels while Bunchy laughed his ass off. Maybe Bunchy was actually Allen Funt in disguise, and I was on funniest bounty hunter bloopers.

Margaret opened the door on the first knock. She had the canceled check ready and waiting for me. I scrutinized it, but didn't see anything out of the ordinary.

"You can take it if you want," Margaret said. "It's no good to me. Maybe that nice Mr. Bunchy would want to see it too."

I dropped the check in my bag and thanked Margaret. I was still spooked from finding Ramirez on my fire escape, so I drove to the office to see if Lula wanted to ride shotgun for the rest of the day.

"I don't know," Lula said. "You aren't doing anything with that Bunchy guy, are you? He has a sick sense of humor."

We'll take my car, I told her. Nothing to worry about.

"I guess that would be okay," Lula said. "I could wear a hat to disguise myself, so no one recognizes me."

"No need," I said. "I have a new car."

Connie looked up from her computer screen. "What kind of car?"

"Black."

"That's better than powder blue," Lula said. "What is it? Another one of them little Jeeps?"

"Nope. It's not a Jeep."

Both Connie and Lula looked at me expectantly. "Well?" Lula said.

"It's . . . a Porsche."

"Say what?" Lula said.

"Porsche."

They were both at the door.

"Damned if it doesn't look like a Porsche," Lula said. "What'd you do, rob a bank?"

"It's a company car."

Lula and Connie did some more of the expectant looking at me with their eyebrows up at the top of their heads.

"Well, you know how I've been working with Ranger . . ."

Lula peered into the car's interior. "You mean like getting that guy to blow hisself up? And like the time you lost the sheik? Hold on here," Lula said. "Are you telling me Ranger gave you this car because you're working with him?"

I cleared my throat and polished a thumbprint off the right-rear quarter panel with the hem of my flannel shirt.

Lula and Connie started smiling.

"Dang," Lula said, punching me in the arm. "You go, girl."

"It's not that kind of work," I said.

The smile on Lula had stretched ear to ear. "I didn't say anything about what kind of work. Connie, did you hear me say anything about this kind of work or that kind of work?"

"I know what you were thinking," I said.

Connie jumped in. "Let's see . . . there's oral sex. And then there's regular sex. And then there's—"

"Getting close now," Lula said.

"All the men who work with Ranger drive black cars," I told them.

"He give them SUVs," Lula said. "He don't give them no Porsche."

I bit into my lower lip. "So you think he wants something?"

"Ranger don't do stuff for nothing," Lula said. "Sooner or later he gets his price. You telling me you don't know the price?"

"Guess I was hoping I was one of the guys, and the car was part of my job."

"I've seen the way he looks at you," Lula said. "And I know he don't look at any of the guys like that. Think what you need is a job description. Not that it would matter if it was me. If I could get my hands on that man's body, I'd buy *him* a Porsche."

We drove to the Grand Union strip mall, and I parked in front of First Trenton.

"What we doing here?" Lula wanted to know.

Good question. The answer was a little vague to me. "I have a couple canceled checks I want to show my cousin. She's a teller here."

"Something special about these checks?"

"Yeah. Only I don't know what." I gave them to Lula. "What do you think?"

"Looks like a couple plain-ass checks to me."

The bank was busy at lunchtime, so we got in line to see Leona. I looked over at Shempsky's office while I waited my turn. The door was open, and I could see Shempsky at his desk, on the phone.

"Hey," Leona said when I got to her window. "What's up?"

"I wanted to ask you about a check." I passed Margaret's check to her. "You see anything unusual here?"

She looked at it front and back. "No."

I gave her Fred's check to RGC. "How about this one?"

"Nope."

"Anything strange about the accounts?"

"Not that I can see." She typed some information into her computer and scanned the screen. "Money comes in and goes out pretty fast on this RGC account. My guess is this is a small liquid account RGC keeps at the local level."

"Why do you say that?"

"RGC is the biggest waste hauler in the area, and I don't see enough transactions here. Besides, I use RGC, and my checks to RGC are canceled through Citibank. When you work at a bank, you notice things like that."

"How about the cable check?"

Leona looked at it again. "Yep. Same thing. My checks are canceled someplace else."

"Is it unusual to assign customers to two different banks?"

She shrugged. "I don't know. I guess not, since both these companies are doing it."

I thanked Leona, and dropped the checks back into my bag. I almost collided with Shempsky when I turned to leave.

"Oops," he said, jumping back. "Didn't mean to bumper-ride you. Just thought I'd come over and see how things are going."

"Things are going okay." I introduced Lula and thought it was to Shempsky's credit that he didn't seem to notice Lula's neon-orange hair or the fact that she'd poured over two hundred pounds of woman into a pair of size-nine tights and topped it off with a Cherry Garcia T-shirt and faux-fur jacket that was trimmed in what looked like pink lion mane.

"What ever happened to that check?" Shempsky asked. "Did you solve your mystery?"

"Not yet, but I'm making progress. I found a similar check from another business. And the curious thing is that both checks were canceled here."

"Why is that curious?"

I decided to fib. I didn't want to involve Leona or Margaret Burger. "The checks *I* write to those companies are canceled elsewhere. Don't you think that's weird?"

Shempsky smiled. "No. Not at all. Businesses often keep small, liquid local accounts, but deposit the bulk of their money somewhere else."

"Heard that before," Lula said.

"Do you have the other check with you?" Shempsky asked. "Would you like me to look at it?"

"No, but thanks for offering."

"Boy," Shempsky said. "You're really tenacious. I'm impressed. I assume you think this all ties in with Fred's disappearance?"

"I think it's possible."

"Where do you go from here?"

"RGC. I still need to get the account straightened out. I was going to do it last Friday, but I got there after Lipinski killed himself."

"Not a good time to take care of business," Shempsky said.

"No."

He gave me a friendly banker smile. "Well, good luck."

"She don't need luck," Lula said. "She's excellent. She always gets her man, you see what I'm saying? She's so good she drives a Porsche. How many bounty hunters you know got a Porsche?"

"It's actually a company car," I told Shempsky.

"It's a great car," he said. "I saw you drive off in it yesterday."

Finally I felt like I was on to something. I had an idea how a lot of stuff might tie together. It was still pretty half-baked, but it was something to think about. I took Klockner to Hamilton and crossed South Broad. I pulled into the industrial area and was relieved at the absence of flashing lights and police cruisers. No human disasters today. The RGC lot was empty of trucks and didn't smell bad. Clearly midday is the preferred time to visit a garbage company.

"They might be a little sensitive in here," I said to Lula.

"I can sensitive your ass off," Lula said. "I just hope they got their wall painted."

The office didn't look freshly painted, but it didn't look bloody either. A man was behind the counter, working at one of the desks. He was somewhere in his forties, brown hair, slim build. He looked up when we approached.

"I'd like to settle an account," I said. "I spoke to Larry about it, but it was never resolved. Are you new here?"

He extended his hand. "Mark Stemper. I'm from the Camden office. I'm filling in temporarily."

"Is that the wall where the brains were splattered?" Lula asked. "It don't look fresh painted. How'd you get it so clean? I never have any luck getting blood off walls like that."

"We had a cleaning crew come in," Stemper said. "I don't know exactly what they used."

"Boy, too bad, because I could use some of that."

He looked at her warily. "You get blood on your walls a lot?"

"Well, not usually on *my* walls."

"About this account," I said.

"Name?"

"Fred Shutz."

He tapped into the computer and shook his head. "Nobody here by that name."

"Exactly." I explained the problem and showed him the canceled check.

"We don't use this bank," he said.

"Maybe you have a second account there."

"Yeah," Lula said, "a local liquid account."

"No. All the offices are the same. Everything goes through Citibank."

"Then how do you explain this check?"

"I don't know how to explain it."

"Were Martha Deeter and Larry Lapinski the only office workers here?"

"In this office, yes."

"When someone mails in their quarterly payment, what happens to it?"

"It goes through here. It's logged into the system and deposited in the Citibank account."

"You've been very helpful," I said. "Thanks."

Lula followed me out. "Personally, I didn't think he was all that helpful. He didn't know nothing."

"He knew it was the wrong bank," I told her.

"I could tell that turns you on."

"I sort of had a brainstorm while I was talking to Allen Shempsky."

"You want to share that brainstorm?"

"Suppose Larry Lipinski didn't enter all the accounts. Suppose he held out ten percent for himself and deposited them someplace else?"

"Skimming," Lula said. "You think he was skimming RGC money. And then Uncle Fred come along and started making a stink. And so Lipinsky had to get rid of Uncle Fred."

"Maybe."

"You're the shit," Lula said. "Girlfriend, you are *smart*."

Lula and I did a high five and then a down low and then she tried to do some elaborate hand thing with me, but I got lost halfway through.

Actually, I thought it was more complicated than Fred getting disposed of because he made some noise over his account. It seemed more likely Fred's disappearance was related to the dismembered woman. And I still thought that woman might be Laura Lipinski. So it did sort of tie in together. I could construct a possible scenario up to the point of Fred seeing Lipinski dump the garbage bag at the real estate office. After that, I was lost.

We were about to get in the car when the side door to the building opened, and Stemper stuck his head out and waved at us. "Hey," he yelled. "Hold up a minute. That check is bothering me. Would you mind letting me make a copy?"

I didn't see where that would do any harm, so Lula and I

returned to the office with him and waited while he fiddled with the copier.

"Damn thing never works," he said. "Hold on while I change the paper."

Half an hour later, I got my check back with an apology.

"I'm sorry that took so long," he said. "But maybe it'll be worthwhile. I'll send it to Camden and see what they make of it. I think it's pretty strange. I've never run across anything like this."

We got back to the Porsche and sunk into the leather seats.

"I love this car," Lula said. "I feel like the shit in this car."

I knew exactly what she meant. It was a fantasy car. No matter if it was true, when you drove the car you felt prettier, sexier, braver, and smarter. Ranger was on to something with this broader horizon business. When I drove the Porsche I could see myself with broader horizons.

I put the car in gear and headed for the driveway out of the lot. The lot itself was surrounded by a high chain-link fence. Out-of-use trucks parked to the rear in the lot, and office workers and drivers parked in the front. Double gates opened to the street. Probably at night they closed and locked the gates. During the day the gates were open, and it was wide enough for two trucks to pass.

I rolled to a stop at the open gate, looked left and saw the first garbage truck of the day rumble home. It was a colossus of a truck. A green and white behemoth that shook the earth as it thundered closer, its bulk preceded by the stench of rotting everything, its arrival heralded by descending seagulls.

The truck swung wide to enter the lot, and Lula jumped in her seat. "Holy cats, that guy don't see us. He's taking this turn like he owns the road."

I went into reverse, but it was too late. The truck sideswiped the Porsche, shearing fiberglass off half the car. I leaned on the horn, and the truck driver stopped and looked down at us in amazement.

Lula jumped out of the car in full rant, and I followed after her, climbing over the seat because my side was smushed into the monster garbage truck.

"Jeez, lady," the driver said. "I don't know what happened. I didn't see you until you started blowing your horn."

"That don't cut it," Lula yelled. "This here's a Porsche. You know what she had to do to get this Porsche? Well, actually she hasn't done nothing yet, but I think if she gets lucky, she's gonna have to do plenty. This company better be insured." Lula turned to me. "You need to exchange insurance information. That's always the first thing you do. You got your card?"

"I don't know. I guess all that stuff is in the glove compartment," I said.

"I'll get it," Lula told me. "I can't believe this happened to a Porsche. People should be more careful when they see a Porsche on the road." She leaned into the car, rooted around in the glove compartment, and was back in a heartbeat. "This looks like it," she said, handing the card over to me. "And here's your purse. You might need your license."

"Maybe we should get the guy in the office," the driver said. "He fills out the forms for this kind of thing."

I thought that was a good idea. And while we were at it how about if I just slip away unnoticed and get a one-way ticket to Rio. I didn't want to have to explain this to Ranger.

"Yeah, we should get that office guy," Lula said. "Because I might have whiplash or something. I can feel it coming on. Maybe I need to go in and sit down."

I would have rolled my eyes, but I thought I should save my energy in case Lula suddenly got paralyzed from the half-mile-per-hour impact she'd just sustained.

We all went into the building and had just gotten through the door when there was a loud explosion. We stopped in our tracks and looked at each other. There was a moment of stunned immobility, and then we all scrambled to see what had happened.

We burst out the door and faltered when a second explosion went off and flames shot from the Porsche and licked along the undercarriage of the garbage truck.

"Oh shit," the driver said. "Take cover! I've got a full tank of gas."

"Say what?" Lula said.

And then it blew. *Barrrooooom!* Liftoff. The garbage truck jumped off the pavement. Tires and doors flew off like Frisbees, the truck bounced down with a jolt, listed to one side, and rolled over onto the furiously burning Porsche, turning it into a Porsche pancake.

We flattened ourselves against the building while pieces of scrap metal and shreds of rubber rained down around us.

"Uh-oh," Lula said. "All the king's horses and all the king's men aren't gonna put that Porsche back together again."

"I don't get it," the driver said. "It was only a scratch. I hardly scraped against your car. Why would it explode like that?"

"That's what her cars do," Lula said. "They explode. But I gotta tell you this was the best. This here's the first time she exploded a garbage truck. One time her truck got hit with an antitank missile. That wasn't bad either, but it couldn't compare to this."

I hauled the cell phone out of my bag and dialed Morelli.

TWELVE

ONLY ONE FIRE truck was left on the scene, and the remaining firemen were directing the cleanup. A crane had been brought in to move the RGC truck. When they got the truck up and off the Porsche, I'd be able to put the Porsche in my pocket. Connie had picked Lula up and taken her back to work, and most of the returning truck drivers had lost interest and dispersed.

Morelli had arrived seconds after the first fire truck and was now standing threateningly close to me, fist on hip, eyes narrowed, giving me the third degree.

"Tell me again," Morelli said, "why Ranger gave you a Porsche."

"It's a company car. Everyone who works with Ranger drives a black car, and since my car is blue—"

"He gave you a Porsche."

I narrowed my eyes back at him. "Just what is the problem here?"

"I want to know what's going on with you and Ranger is the problem."

"I *told* you. I'm working with him." And I supposed I was

flirting with him, but I didn't think it was necessary to report flirting. Anyway, talk about the pot calling the kettle black.

Morelli didn't look satisfied, and he definitely didn't look happy. "I don't suppose you bothered to check the registration number on your Porsche."

"Don't suppose I did." And it was unlikely anyone was going to check it now, being that the Porsche was blown up, and its remnants were only three inches thick.

"You weren't worried that you might be driving a hot car?"

"Ranger wouldn't give me a hot car."

"Ranger would give his mother a hot car," Morelli said. "Where do you think he gets all those cars he gives away? You think he gets them from the car fairy?"

"I'm sure there's an explanation."

"Such as?"

"Such as, I don't know. And anyway there are other things that are more important to me right now. Like why did my car explode?"

"Good question. I think it's unlikely the garbage truck side-swiping you caused the explosion. If you were a normal person I'd be hard-pressed to find an explanation. Since you're who you are . . . my guess is someone planted a bomb."

"Why did it take so long? Why didn't it go off when I started the car?"

"I asked Murphy. He's the demo expert. He thinks it might have been set on a timer, so it would go off when you were on the street, not in the lot."

"So maybe the bomber is someone from the garbage company, and he didn't want the explosion so close to home."

"We looked for Stemper, but he's nowhere."

"Did you check for his car?"

"It's still here."

"Are you kidding me? He's just disappeared?"

Morelli shrugged. "Doesn't mean much. He could have gone out for a drink with a friend. Or he could have gotten fed up with waiting for the lot to get cleared enough to get the cars out and found some other way to go home."

"But you guys are going to look for him, right?"

"Right."

"And he isn't home yet?"

"Not yet."

"I have a theory," I said.

Morelli smiled. "I love this part."

"I think Lipinski was skimming. And maybe Martha Deeter was in on it, or maybe she found out about it, or maybe she was just a pain in the ass. Anyway, I think Lipinski might have been keeping some accounts for himself." I showed Morelli the checks and told him about the banks.

"And you think this other guy who worked for the cable company, John Curly, was skimming, too?"

"There are some similarities."

"And Fred might have disappeared because he was making too much noise?"

"More than that." I told him about the Mega Monster flyer in the garbage bag, and about Laura Lipinski, and finally about Fred and the leaves.

"I'm not liking this picture," Morelli said. "I wish I'd known about these things sooner."

"I just put it together."

"Two steps in front of me. I've been really stupid on this one. Tell me about the fake bookie."

"Bunchy."

"Yeah. Whoever."

I raised an eyebrow. "I figured you two were working together."

"What's Bunchy look like?"

"A fireplug with eyebrows. About my height. Brown hair. Needs a cut. Receding hairline. Looks like a street person. Walks and talks like a cop. Drinks Corona."

"I know him, but I'd be hard-pressed to say I was working with him. He doesn't work *with* anybody."

"I don't suppose you want to share what you know with me?"

"Can't."

Wrong answer. "Okay, let me get this straight," I said. "Some Fed has been following me around for days, camping out on my doorstep, breaking into my apartment, and you think that's okay?"

"No, I don't think it's okay. I think it's grounds for beating the shit out of him. I didn't know he was doing it, and I intend to make sure it stops. I just can't tell you what it's all about right now. What I *can* tell you is that you should back off and let us take it from here. Obviously we're both going down the same road."

"Why should I be the one to back off?"

"Because you're the one who's getting bombed. You notice *my* car exploding?"

"The day isn't over."

Morelli's pager went off. Morelli looked at the read-out and sighed. "I have to go. You want a ride home?"

"Thanks, but I need to stay. I have a call in to Ranger. I'm not sure what he wants to do with the Porsche."

"Some time soon we need to talk about Ranger," Morelli said.

Oh boy. I'll look forward to that conversation.

Morelli skirted the crane and got into the dusty maroon Fairlane that was *his* company car. He cranked the engine over and pulled out of the lot.

My attention swung back to the crane operator. He was maneuvering the boom over the truck. A cable was attached, and the truck was slowly hauled upright, exposing what was left of the Porsche.

I caught a flash of black beyond the crane. It was Ranger's Mercedes.

"Just in time," I said when he strolled over.

He looked down at the flattened, charred piece of scrap metal pressed into the macadam.

"That's the Porsche," I said. "It exploded and caught fire and then the garbage truck fell over on it."

"I especially like the part about the garbage truck."

"I was afraid you might be mad."

"Cars are easy to come by, Babe. People are harder to replace. Are you okay?"

"Yeah. I was lucky. I was just waiting to see what you wanted to do with the Porsche."

"Not much anybody's going to do with that dead soldier," Ranger said. "Think we'll walk away from this one."

"It was a great car."

Ranger took one last look at it. "You might be more the Humvee type," he said, steering me toward the Mercedes.

Streetlights were on when we crossed Broad and the twilight was deepening. Ranger rolled down Roebling and stopped in front of Rossini's. "I have to meet a guy here in a few minutes. Come in and have a drink, and we can have an early dinner when I'm done. This shouldn't take long."

"Is this bounty hunter business?"

"Real estate," Ranger said. "I'm meeting my lawyer. He has papers for me to sign."

"You're buying a house?"

He opened the door for me. "Office building in Boston."

Rossini's is an excellent Burg restaurant. A pleasant mix of cozy but elegant with linen tablecloths and napkins and gourmet food. Several men in suits stood at the small oak bar at the far end of the room. A few of the tables were already occupied, and in a half-hour the room would be filled.

Ranger guided me to the bar and introduced me to his lawyer.

"Stephanie Plum," the lawyer said. "You look familiar."

"I didn't intend to burn down the funeral home," I said. "It was an accident."

He shook his head. "No, that's not it." He smiled. "I've got it. You were married to Dickie Orr. He was briefly with our firm."

"Everything Dickie did was brief," I said. Especially our marriage. The pig.

Twenty minutes later, Ranger had his business concluded, his lawyer finished his drink and left, and we moved to a table. Ranger was black today. Black T-shirt, black cargo pants, black boots, and black Gortex squall jacket. He left his jacket on, and everyone in the room knew why. Ranger wasn't the sort to leave his gun in the glove compartment.

We ordered, and Ranger slouched back in his chair. "You never say much about your marriage."

"You never say much about *anything*."

He smiled. "Low profile."

"Have you ever been married?"

"Long time ago."

I hadn't expected him to say that. "Any kids?"

He stared at me for a full minute before answering. "I have a daughter. She's nine. Lives with her mother in Florida."

"Do you ever see her?"

"When I'm in the area."

Who *was* this man? He owned office buildings in Boston. And he was the father of a nine-year-old. I was having a hard time merging this new knowledge into my mental Ranger-the-gunrunner/bounty-hunter file.

"Tell me about the bomb," Ranger said. "I get the feeling I'm not up to speed on your life."

I told him my theory.

He was still slouched back, but the line of his mouth had tightened. "Bombs aren't good, Babe. They're real messy. Give you a real bad hair day."

"You have any ideas?"

"Yeah, you ever think about taking a vacation?"

I wrinkled my nose. "I can't afford a vacation."

"I'll give you an advance on services performed."

I felt my face flush. "About those services—"

He lowered his voice. "I don't pay for the kind of service you're worried about."

Yeeesh.

I dug into my pasta. "I wouldn't go anyway. I'm not giving up on Uncle Fred. And where would I leave Rex? And Halloween is coming up. I love Halloween. I couldn't miss Halloween."

Halloween is one of my favorite holidays. I love the crisp air and the pumpkins and spooky decorations. I never cared about the candy I collected when I was a kid. I got psyched over the dress-up part. Maybe this says something about my personality, but put me behind a mask, and I'm a happy person. Not one of those ugly, sweaty rubber things that fit over your whole head. I like the kind that just fits around the eyes and makes you look like the Lone Ranger. And face paint is very cool, too.

"Of course, I don't go out trick-or-treating anymore," I said, stabbing a piece of sausage. "I go over to my parents' house now and give out candy. Grandma Mazur and I always get dressed up for when the kids come around. Last year I was Zorro, and Grandma was Lily Munster. I think this year she's going to be a Spice Girl."

"I could see you as Zorro," Ranger said.

Zorro is actually one of my favorite people. Zorro is the shit.

I had tiramisù for dessert because Ranger was paying, and because Rossini's made orgasmic tiramisù. Ranger skipped dessert, of course, not wanting to pollute his body with sugar, not desiring an extra ripple in his washboard stomach. I scarfed up the last smidgens of cake and custard and reached under the tablecloth to discreetly pop the top snap on my jeans.

I'm not a fanatic about weight. Truth is, I don't even own a scale. I judge my weight by the way my jeans fit. And unpleasant as it is to admit, these jeans weren't fitting at all. I needed a better diet. And I needed an exercise program. Tomorrow. Starting tomorrow, no more taking the elevator to the second floor, no more doughnuts for breakfast.

I studied Ranger as he drove me home, details seen in the flash of oncoming headlights and overhead streetlights. He wore no rings. A watch on his left wrist. Wide nylon band. No studs in his ears today. He had a network of fine lines around his eyes. The lines were from sun, not age. My best guess was that Ranger was somewhere between twenty-five and thirty-five. No one knew for sure. And no one knew much of his background. He moved easily through the underbelly of Trenton, speaking the language, walking the walk of the projects and minority neighborhoods. There'd been no trace of that Ranger tonight. Tonight he'd sounded more Wall Street than Stark Street.

The ride back to my building was quiet. Ranger pulled into my lot, and I did a quick scan for creepy people. Finding none, I had my door open before the car came to a complete stop. No sense lingering in the dark, alone with Ranger, tempting fate. I'd made enough of an ass of myself last time when I was half snockered.

"You in a hurry?" Ranger said, looking amused.

"Things to do."

I moved to get out of the car, and he grabbed me by the scruff of my neck. "You're going to be careful," he said.

"Y-y-yes."

"And you're going to carry your gun."

"Yes."

"Loaded."

"Okay, loaded."

He released my neck. "Sweet dreams."

I ran into the building and up the stairs, rushed into my apartment, and dialed Mary Lou.

"I need help with a stakeout tonight," I told Mary Lou. "Can Lenny sit with the kids?"

Lenny is Mary Lou's husband. He's a nice guy, but he hasn't got much upstairs. That's fine with Mary Lou because she's more interested in what's *downstairs*, anyway.

"Who are we staking out?"

"Morelli."

"Oh, honey, you heard!"

"I heard what?"

"Uh-oh. You didn't hear?"

"What? *What?*"

"Terry Gilman."

Argh. Direct shot to the heart. "What about Terry?"

"The rumor is she's been seen with Joe late at night."

Man, you can't get away with anything in the Burg. "I know about the late-night stuff. Anything else?"

"That's it."

"Besides seeing Terry, he's also involved in a project that ties in with Uncle Fred's disappearance, and he won't tell me anything."

"Asshole."

"Yeah. And after I gave him some of the best weeks of my life. Anyway, it seems like he works nights, so I thought I'd see what he was up to."

"You going to pick me up in the Porsche?"

"The Porsche is out of commission. I was hoping you could drive," I said. "I'm afraid Morelli might recognize the Buick."

"No problemo."

"And wear sneakers and something dark."

Last time we went snooping together Mary Lou wore ankle boots with spike heels and gold earrings the size of dinner plates. Not exactly the invisible snooper.

Briggs was standing behind me. "You're going to spy on Morelli? This should be good."

"He's leaving me no choice."

"I bet you five dollars he spots you."

"Deal."

"THERE COULD BE a perfectly good explanation for the Terry thing," I said to Mary Lou.

"Yeah, like he's a prick?"

That's one of the things I like about Mary Lou. She's willing to believe the worst about anyone. Of course it's easy to believe the worst about Morelli. He's never cared a whole lot about public opinion and has never made much of an attempt to improve his rogue reputation. And in the past, his reputation was well deserved.

We were in Mary Lou's Dodge minivan. It smelled like Gummi Bears and grape lollipops and McDonald's cheeseburgers. And when I turned to look out the back window I was confronted with two kiddie car seats that made me feel sort of left out of things. We were idling in front of Morelli's house, staring into his front windows, seeing nothing. The lights were on, but the curtains were drawn. His truck was parked at the curb, so probably he was home, but there was no guarantee. He lived in a rowhouse and that made surveillance difficult because we couldn't creep around the entire house and easily do our Peeping Tom thing.

"We can't see anything like this, " I said. "Let's park on the cross street and go on foot."

Mary Lou had followed my instructions and was dressed in black. Black leather jacket with fringe running down the sleeves, tight black leather slacks—and as a compromise between my suggestion of sneakers and her preferred four-inch heels, she was wearing black cowboy boots.

Morelli's house was halfway down the block, his narrow yard backed up to a one-lane service road, and the side borders of his yard were delineated by bedraggled hedgerows. Morelli hadn't yet discovered gardening.

The sky was overcast. No moon. No streetlights lining the back alley. This was all fine by me. The darker the better. I was wearing a utility belt that held pepper spray, a flashlight, a Smith and Wesson .38, a stun gun, and a cell phone. I'd constantly watched our tail for signs of Ramirez and had seen nothing. That didn't fill me with security, since spotting Ramirez clearly wasn't one of my talents.

We walked the alley and paused when we reached Morelli's yard. Lights were on in the kitchen. Shades were up at the single kitchen window and at the back door. Morelli passed in front of the window, and Mary Lou and I took a step back, further into shadow. He returned and worked at the counter, probably fixing something to eat.

The sound of the phone ringing carried out to us. Morelli answered the phone and paced in the kitchen while he talked.

"Not someone he's happy to hear from," Mary Lou said. "He hasn't cracked a smile."

Morelli hung up and ate a sandwich, still standing at the counter. He washed it down with a Coke. I thought the Coke was a good sign. If he was in for the night he probably would have had a beer. He flipped the light off and left the kitchen.

Now I had a problem. If I chose to watch the wrong half of the house I might miss Morelli leaving. And by the time I ran to the car and took off after him, it could be too late. Mary Lou and I could split up, but that would negate my reason for inviting Mary Lou along. I'd wanted another set of eyes looking for Ramirez.

"Come on," I said, creeping toward the house. "We need to get closer."

I pressed my nose to the windowpane on Morelli's back door. I could see clear to the front, looking through the kitchen and dining room. I could hear the television, but I couldn't see it. And I couldn't see any sign of Morelli.

"Do you see him?" Mary Lou wanted to know.

"No.

She peered through the back door window with me. "Too bad we can't see the front door from here. How will we know if Morelli goes out?"

"He shuts his lights off when he goes out."

Blink. The lights went out, and the sound of the front door opening and shutting carried back to us.

"Shit!" I sprang away from the door and took off for the car.

Mary Lou ran after me, doing pretty good considering the tight pants and cowboy boots and the fact that she had legs several inches shorter than mine.

We piled into the car. Mary Lou rammed the key into the ignition, and the mom car jumped into chase mode. We whipped around the corner and saw Morelli's taillights disappear as he made a right-hand turn two blocks down.

"Perfect," I said. "We don't want to be so close that he sees us."

"Do you think he's going to see Terry?"

"It's possible. Or maybe he's relieving someone on stakeout."

Now that the first rush of emotion was behind me, I found it hard to believe Joe was romantically or sexually involved with Terry. It had nothing to do with Joe the man. It had to do with Joe the cop. Joe wouldn't get himself entangled with the Grizollis.

He'd told me he had something in common with Terry—that they were both in vice. And I suspected that was the connection. I thought it possible that Joe and Terry were working together, although I couldn't imagine in what capacity. And since the Feds were in town, I guessed Vito Grizolli was involved. Maybe Joe and Terry were acting as intermediaries between Vito and the Feds. And Bunchy's interest in the checks might support my skimming theory. Although I didn't know why the government would be interested in skimming.

Joe turned onto Hamilton, drove a quarter mile, and pulled into the 7-Eleven. Mary Lou zipped past him, circled a block, and waited at the side of the road with her lights off. Joe came out of the store carrying a bag and got back into his car.

"Oh, man, I'm dying to know what's in the bag," Mary Lou said. "Do they sell condoms at the 7-Eleven? I never noticed."

"He's got dessert in that bag," I said. "My money's on ice cream. Chocolate."

"And I bet he's taking the ice cream to Terry!"

His engine caught, and he retraced his route down Hamilton.

"He's not going to Terry's," I said. "He's going home."

"What a rip. I thought I was going to see some action."

I didn't actually want to see a whole lot of action. I just wanted to find Uncle Fred and get on with my life. Unfortunately, I wasn't going to learn anything new if Morelli sat in front of his television eating ice cream all night.

Mary Lou dropped a block behind Morelli, keeping him in sight. He parked in front of his house, and Mary Lou and I parked on the cross street again. We got out of the mom car, skulked back down the alley, and stopped short at the edge of Morelli's yard. The light was on in his kitchen, and Morelli was moving in front of the window.

"What's he doing?" Mary Lou asked. "What's he doing?"

"Getting a spoon. I was right—he went out to buy ice cream."

The light blinked out, and Morelli disappeared. Mary Lou and I scuttled across Morelli's backyard and squinted into his window.

"Do you see him?" Mary Lou asked.

"No. He's disappeared."

"I didn't hear the front door open."

"No, and he's got the television on. He's just out of sight somewhere."

Mary Lou crept closer. "Too bad he's got the shades pulled on his front windows."

"I'll try to be more considerate next time," Morelli said, standing inches behind us.

Mary Lou and I yelped and instinctively sprang away, but Morelli had both of us by the back of our jackets.

"Look who we have here," Morelli said. "Lucy and Ethel. Is this the girls' night out?"

"We were looking for my cat," Mary Lou said. "It's been lost, and we thought we saw it run through your yard."

Morelli grinned at Mary Lou. "Nice to see you, Mary Lou. It's been a while."

"The kids keep me busy," Mary Lou said. "Soccer and pre-school and Kenny keeps getting these ear infections—"

"How's Lenny doing?"

"He's great. He's thinking about hiring someone else. His father's going to retire, you know."

Lenny had graduated from high school and had gone directly into the family business, Stankovik and Sons, Plumbing and Heat-ing. He made a good living at it, but he frequently smelled like stagnant water and metal piping.

"I need to talk to Stephanie," Morelli said.

Mary Lou started backing up. "Hey, don't let me get in the way. I was just leaving. I've got my car parked around the corner."

Morelli opened his back door. "You," he said, releasing my jacket. "Go in the house. I'll be right back. I'm going to walk Mary Lou to her car."

"Not necessary," Mary Lou said, looking nervous, like she was going to run like hell at any moment. "I can find my own way."

"It's dark back here," Morelli said to Mary Lou. "And you've just been contaminated by Calamity Jane. You're not getting out of my sight until you're safely locked in your car."

I did as I was told. I scurried into the house while Morelli walked Mary Lou to her car. And as soon as they cleared his yard I scrolled back through his caller ID. I scribbled the numbers on a pad by the phone, ripped the page off, and stuffed it into my pocket. The last number to come in had an identification block on it. No number available. If I'd known the number hadn't registered I might not have been so fast to jump to Morelli's command.

The ice cream was still sitting on the counter. And it was melting. Probably I should eat it, so it didn't get *totally* melted and have to get thrown away.

I was savoring the last spoonful when Morelli returned. He closed and locked the door behind him and pulled the shades.

I raised my eyebrows.

"Nothing personal," Morelli said, "but you've got bad people following you around. I don't want someone sniping at you through my kitchen window."

"You think it's that serious?"

"Honey, your car was bombed."

I was starting to get used to it. "How did you spot Mary Lou and me?"

"Rule number one, when you've got your nose pressed to someone's window . . . don't talk. Rule number two, when doing surveillance don't use a car with vanity plates that have your best friend's name on them. Rule three, never underestimate nosy neighbors. Mrs. Rupp called and wanted to know why you were standing in the alley, looking into her windows, and she was wondering if she should call the police. I explained it was most likely *my* windows you were looking in and reminded her that *I* was the police, so she needn't bother with another phone call."

"Well, it's all your fault because you won't tell me anything," I said.

"If I told you what was going on, you'd tell Mary Lou, and she'd tell Lenny, and Lenny would tell the guys down at the plumbing supply house, and the next day it'd be in the newspaper."

"Mary Lou doesn't tell Lenny anything," I said.

"What the hell was she wearing? She looked like the friendly neighborhood dominatrix. The only things missing were a whip and a pimp."

"She was making a fashion statement."

Morelli looked down at my utility belt.

"What kind of a statement is this?"

"Fear."

He gave his head a disbelieving shake. "You know what my biggest fear is? I worry that someday you might be the mother of my children."

I wasn't sure if I should be pleased or annoyed, so I changed the subject. "I deserve to know about this investigation," I said. "I'm sitting right in the middle of it." He was just implacably staring at me, so I hit him with the heavy stuff. "And I know about your late-night meetings with Terry. And not only that, but I am *not* going away. And I will continue to harass and follow you until I figure this out." So there.

"I'd tie you up and wrap you in a rug and drive you to the landfill," Morelli said, "but Mary Lou would probably finger me."

"Okay, so how about sex? Maybe we can make a deal?"

Morelli grinned. "You've got my attention."

"Start talking."

"Not so fast. I want to know what I'm going to get for this information."

"What do you want?"

"Everything."

"Not working tonight?"

He looked at his watch. "Shit. Yeah, I'm working. In fact I'm late. I need to relieve *Bunchy* on a surveillance watch."

"Who are you watching?"

He stared at me for a moment. "Okay, I'm going to tell you, because I don't want you riding all over Trenton looking for me. But if I find out you leaked this to anyone I swear I'll come get you."

I held my hand up. "Scout's honor. My lips are sealed."

THIRTEEN

MORELLI LEANED BACK against the counter and folded his arms. "Somehow it came to light that there was a discrepancy between how much money Vito Grizolli's cleaning business was taking in and how much was reported for income tax purposes."

"Gee, what a surprise."

"Yeah. Well, the Feds decided they wanted to nail him on it, so they started to do their thing, and it soon became pretty obvious that Vito, in fact, is losing money he has no knowledge of."

"Someone is skimming Vito?"

Morelli started to laugh. "Can you believe it?"

"Man, there's a lot of that going on."

"Enough to make it worthwhile for Treasury to deal with Vito so they can maybe get a bigger fish."

"Like what kind of a bigger fish?"

Morelli shrugged. "Don't know. The two brain surgeons I'm working with think it's some new crime organization."

"What do you think?"

"Until you showed me the checks, I thought it was just some guy with a death wish trying to pay off his mortgage. Now I'm not sure what I think, but a new crime organization feels far out there. I don't see any other signs of a new organization."

"Maybe it's just coincidence."

"I don't think so. There are too many things adding up. Three companies involved so far. Three accounts-receivable clerks have died. Another is missing. Fred is missing. Someone set a bomb to your car."

"How about the bank? Were Vito's missing accounts processed through First Trenton?"

"Yes. It'd be helpful to pull some records, but we'd run the risk of alerting whoever is involved that there's an investigation going on.

"It turns out, RGC had also been flagged for possible tax evasion. The RGC stands for Ruben, Grizolli, and Cotell. I knew Grizolli was part owner, but I didn't know there'd been any irregularities. My Treasury contacts didn't tell me that part."

"You're working as a team, and they didn't tell you about RGC?"

"You don't know these guys. Real hot dogs. And they don't like being coupled with local law enforcement."

I smiled at him.

"Yeah, I know," he said. "Sounds like I'm describing myself. Anyway, Bronfman, the guy you know as Bunchy, was doing surveillance at RGC, looking to see who went in and out. He was sitting in the café across the street the Friday that Fred disappeared. I guess Fred had wanted to get an early start, but he got to RGC before the office opened, so he went across the street for coffee. Bronfman and Fred got to talking and Bronfman realized Fred was one of the nonrecorded accounts. The following Tuesday, Bronfman got to thinking it might be helpful to get a canceled check from Fred, one way or another, went to talk to Fred, and discovered Fred was missing.

"When Mabel told him you were on the case, Bronfman decided he could use you to front for him. You could poke around and ask questions, and it wasn't as likely anyone would run for the hills. Didn't turn out exactly as he'd planned, because he hadn't counted on your ornery, suspicious nature."

"I didn't tell him much."

"No. His efforts got him zero. That's the good part." Morelli locked eyes with me. "Now that you know what's going on, you're going to tell me what you have, though, right?"

"Sure." Maybe.

"Christ," Morelli said.

"Hey, I might tell you something."

"I'm sorry, I didn't have enough pieces to put this together sooner."

"Part my fault," I said.

"Yeah, part your fault. You're not talking to me enough. Part my fault, too."

"What's your role with Treasury?"

"Vito wouldn't talk to them directly. Said he'd only deal with someone he knew. And I guess he feels protected when information goes through a couple of sources. Makes it easier to deny. So Vito talks to Terry, and Terry talks to me, and I talk to Frick and Frack."

"Who are you watching?"

Morelli flipped the kitchen light off. "Vito's accounts-receivable person. Harvey Tipp."

"You better be watching him close. Harvey's life expectancy might not be too good."

MORELLI DROPPED ME off on his way to relieve Bronfman.

"Thanks for the ride," I told Morelli.

He snagged my collar as I turned to leave. "We have an agreement," he said. "And you owe me."

"Now?"

"Later."

"How much later?"

"To be determined," Morelli said. "I just don't want you to forget."

Not much chance of that.

Briggs was working when I got upstairs. "You keep long hours," I said.

"I've got to get this project done. I lost a lot of ground when my apartment got burglarized. I was lucky I had my laptop in the closet in the bedroom, and they missed it. I had most of my work backed up on the laptop, so it wasn't a total disaster."

I WOKE UP at four and couldn't get back to sleep. I lay there for an hour, listening for sounds on my fire escape, planning my escape should someone toss a fire bomb through my bedroom window. Finally I gave up and tiptoed into the kitchen for a snack. I had so many things to worry about I could barely sort through them. Fred was last on the list. Morelli collecting on what was owed was closer to the top.

Briggs padded in after me. "Spooked again?"

"Yeah. Too much on my mind. I can't sleep." I looked down at him. He was wearing Winnie-the-Pooh pajamas. "Nice jammies," I said.

"I have a hard time finding things that fit. When I want to really impress the ladies I wear Spider-Man."

"Is it hard being a little person?"

"Has its ups and downs. I get a lot of perks because people think I'm cute. And I try to take advantage of my minority status."

"I noticed."

"Hey," Briggs said, "you gotta use what God gave you."

"True."

"So, you want to do something? You want to play Monopoly?"

"Okay, but I want to be the shoe."

We were still playing at seven o'clock, when the phone rang.

"I'm in your parking lot," Ranger said. "Do you want to come down, or do you want me to come up?"

"Why are you calling? You always just break in."

"I didn't want to take a chance on scaring the hell out of you and getting shot."

"Good thinking. What's the occasion?"

"Wheels, Babe."

I went to the window, pulled the curtain aside, and looked down at Ranger. He was standing alongside a black BMW.

"I'll be right down," I said to Ranger. "Give me a minute to get dressed."

I pulled on a pair of jeans, shoved my feet into ratty sneakers, and covered my flannel nightshirt with an oversized gray sweatshirt. I grabbed my keys and took off for the stairs.

"Looking a little scary, Babe," Ranger said when he saw me.

"A friend of mine suggested this look could be a new concept in birth control."

"It's not *that* scary."

I smoothed an imaginary wrinkle from my sweatshirt and closely examined a speck of lint on my sleeve. I looked up and found Ranger smiling.

"The ball's in your court," Ranger said. "Let me know when you're ready."

"For the car?"

He smiled.

"Are you sure you want to give me another car?"

"This one's equipped with sensors on the undercarriage." He held a small remote. "Push the green button to set the sensors. If there's motion under the car the alarm sounds and the red light on the dash stays lit. Unfortunately, the car doesn't know the difference between a cat, a baseball, and a bomb, so if the light is flashing you have to do some investigating. Not perfect, but better than stepping on the accelerator and being turned into confetti. Probably it's not necessary. It's unlikely someone would try to blow you up twice." He handed the remote over to me and explained the rest of the security system.

"Just like James Bond," I said.

"You have plans for the day?"

"I need to call Morelli and see if the guy who delayed me at RGC, Mark Stemper, turned up. Then I suppose I'll do my rounds. Visit Mabel. Check in at the office. Harass the garbage people." Keep my eyes peeled for Ramirez. Have my head examined.

"Somebody out there's feeling real cranky because you're not dead. You might want to wear your vest."

I watched him drive away, and before I went into the building I armed the car. I finished up the game with Briggs, took a shower, shook my head with the hopes it would style my hair, and applied mascara so people would notice my eyes and not pay too close attention to the rest of me.

I scrambled an egg and ate it with a glass of orange juice and a multivitamin. A healthy breakfast to start the day off right— just in case I lived through the morning.

I decided Ranger might have a good idea about the vest. It made me sort of flat-chested, but then, what didn't? I was wearing jeans and boots and a T-shirt with the vest Velcroed tight to my body. I buttoned a navy flannel shirt over the vest and thought it didn't look too bad.

There were no bomb alert lights flashing when I got to the car, so I slid behind the wheel feeling secure. My parents' house was first on the visitation list. I thought it wouldn't hurt to have a cup of coffee and catch up on the latest rumors.

Grandma appeared at the door the minute I swerved in to the curb. "Boy, that's a pip of a car," she said, watching me angle out and set the security system. "What kind of car is it?"

"It's a BMW."

"We just read in the paper where you had a Porsche, and it got blown up. Your mother's in the bathroom taking an aspirin."

I ran up the porch stairs two at a time. "It was in the paper?"

"Yeah, only they didn't have a picture of you, like usual. They just had a picture of the car. Boy, it looked flat as a pancake."

Great. "Did they say anything else?"

"They called you the Bombshell Bounty Hunter."

Maybe I needed an aspirin too. I dropped my shoulder bag on a kitchen chair and reached for the paper on the table. Oh, God, it was on the front page.

"The paper said the police were pretty sure it was a bomb," Grandma said. "Only after the garbage truck fell on the car I guess they had a hard time figuring out what was what."

My mother came into the kitchen. "Whose car is that parked in front of our house?"

"That's Stephanie's new car," Grandma said. "Isn't it a pip?"

One of my mother's eyebrows raised in question. "Two new cars? Where are these cars coming from?"

"Company cars," I said.

"Oh?"

"Anal sex is *not* involved," I told her.

My mother and grandmother both gasped.

"Sorry," I said. "It just slipped out."

"I thought only homosexual men did anal sex," Grandma said.

"Anybody with an anus can do it," I told her.

"Hmm," she said. "I got one of them."

I poured a cup of coffee and sat at the table. "So what's new?"

Grandma got coffee and sat across from me. "Harriet Mullen

had a baby boy. They had to do a C-section on her at the last minute, but everything turned out okay. And Mickey Szajak died. Guess it was about time."

"Are you hearing anything these days about Vito Grizolli?"

"I saw him at the meat market last week, and I thought he'd put on some weight."

"How's he doing financially?"

"I hear he's making big money on that cleaning business. And I saw Vivien driving a new Buick."

Vivien was Vito's wife. She was sixty-five, wore fake eyelashes, and dyed her hair bright red because that's the way Vito liked it. Anyone who voiced a critical opinion got fitted with cement booties and accidentally took a dive into the Delaware River.

"I don't suppose there are any rumors going around about First Trenton."

My mother and grandmother both looked up from their coffee.

"The bank?" my mother asked. "Why do you want to know about the bank?"

"I don't know. Fred had an account there. I was just fishing."

Grandma stared at my chest. "You look different. Are you wearing one of them sports brassieres?" She looked more closely. "Hot dog. I know what it is. You're wearing a bulletproof vest. Ellen, look at this," she said to my mother. "Stephanie's wearing a bulletproof vest. Isn't that something?"

My mother's face had turned white. "Why me?" she said.

NEXT STOP WAS Mabel's house.

Mabel opened the door and smiled. "Stephanie, how nice to see you, dear. Would you like tea?"

"I can't stay," I said. "I just wanted to stop around and see how you were doing."

"Isn't that sweet of you. I'm doing peachy. I think I've decided on a trip to Bermuda."

I picked a brochure off the coffee table. "Singles cruises for seniors?"

"They have some very good rates."

"Anything happen that I should know about? Like, have you heard from Fred?"

"I haven't heard a word from Fred. I suppose he's dead."

Boy, don't get all broken up over it. "It's only been two weeks," I said. "He could still turn up."

Mabel slid a longing look at the brochures. "I suppose that's true."

Ten minutes later I was at the office.

"Hey, girlfriend," Lula said. "Did you see the paper this morning? You got a big spread. And not that I'm bummed or anything, but I didn't even get a mention. And I didn't get a cool name like Bombshell Bounty Hunter either. Hell, I could bombshell your ass off."

"I know that," I said. "And that's why I was wondering if you wanted to ride along with me again today?"

"I don't know. What kind of car are you driving? You back to driving that Buick?"

"Actually, I have a Beemer."

Lula rushed to the front window and looked out. "Damn skippy. Way to go."

Vinnie stuck his head out of his office doorway. "What's going on?"

"Stephanie got a new car," Lula said. "That's it at the curb."

"Anybody hear about anything funny going on at First Trenton?" I asked. "Anybody shady work there?"

"You should ask the little guy we talked to yesterday," Lula said. "I can't remember his name, but he seemed like a nice guy. You don't think he's shady, do you?"

"Hard to tell who's shady," I said to Lula. Actually, I thought shady would be a step up for Shempsky.

"Where'd you get the car?" Vinnie asked.

"It's a company car. I'm working with Ranger."

Vinnie's face creased into a big, oily smile. "Ranger gave you a car? Hah! What kind of work you doing? Gotta be good to get a car like that."

"Maybe you should ask Ranger," I said.

"Yeah, sure, when I don't want to live anymore."

"Any new FTAs come in?" I asked Connie.

"We got two in yesterday, but they're chump change. I wasn't sure you wanted to be bothered with them. Seems like you've got a lot on your plate right now."

"What's the profile?"

"A shoplifter and a wife beater."

"We'll take the wife beater," Lula said. "We don't allow no wife beaters to just walk away. We like to give the wife beaters personal attention."

I took the file from Connie and sifted through it. Kenyon Lally. Age twenty-eight. Unemployed. Long history of spousal abuse. Two DUI convictions. Living in the projects. No mention of Kenyon shooting any previous bounty hunters.

"Okay," I said, "we'll take this one."

"Oh boy," Lula said. "I'm gonna squash this guy like a roach."

"No. No, no, no, no, no roach squashing. No unnecessary force."

"Sure," Lula said. "I know that. But we could use *necessary* force, right?"

"Necessary force won't be necessary."

"Just don't beat the crap out of him like you did with the computer nerd," Vinnie said. "I keep telling you, kick them in the kidney where it don't show."

"Must be scary being related to him," Lula said, looking over at Vinnie.

Connie filled in my authorization to apprehend and gave the file back to me. I dropped it into my bag and hiked my bag higher on my shoulder. "Later."

"Later," Connie said. "And watch out for garbage trucks."

I beeped the alarm off, and Lula and I got in the Beemer.

"This is cushy," Lula said. "Big woman like me needs a car like this. I sure would like to know where Ranger gets all these cars. See that little silver strip with the numbers on it. That's your registration number. So theoretically this car isn't even stolen."

"Theoretically." Ranger probably had those strips made by the gross. I punched Morelli's number into the car phone and after six rings I got his answering machine. I left a message and tried his pager.

"Not that it's any of my business," Lula said, "but what's going on with you and Morelli? I thought that was over with you two when you moved out."

"It's complicated."

"Your problem is you keep getting involved with men who have lots of potential in bed and no potential at the altar."

"I'm thinking of giving men up altogether," I said. "Celibacy isn't so bad. You don't have to worry about shaving your legs."

The phone rang, and I answered it on the speakerphone.

"What number is this?" Morelli wanted to know.

"It's my new car phone number."

"In the Buick?"

"No. Ranger gave me another car."

Silence.

"What kind of car is it this time?" he finally asked.

"Beemer."

"Has it got a registration number on it?"

"Yes."

"Is it fake?"

I shrugged. "It doesn't look fake."

"That'll go far in court."

"Have you heard anything about Mark Stemper?"

"No. I think he's probably playing rummy with your uncle Fred."

"How about Laura Lipinski?"

"Disappeared off the face of the earth. Left home the Thursday before your uncle disappeared."

Perfect timing to get stuffed into a garbage bag. "Thanks. That's all I wanted. Over and out."

I pulled into the Grand Union parking lot and drove to the end of the mall where the bank was located. I parked at a safe distance from other cars, exited the BMW, and set the alarm.

"You want me to stay with the car in case someone's riding around with a bomb in his backseat looking for a place to put it?" Lula asked.

"Not necessary. Ranger says the car has sensors."

"Ranger give you a car with bomb sensors? The head of the CIA don't even have a car with bomb sensors. I hear they give him a stick with a mirror on the end of it."

"I don't think it's anything space-age. Sounds to me like they're just motion detectors mounted on the undercarriage."

"Boy, I'd like to know where he got the motion detectors. This would probably be a good night to rob the governor's mansion."

I was starting to feel like a regular customer at the bank. I said hello to the guard at the door, and I waved to Leona. I looked for Shempsky, but he wasn't visible, and his office was empty.

"He's out to lunch," the guard said. "Took it earlier than usual today."

No problem. Leona was giving me the *come here!* gesture, anyway.

"I read about you in the paper," she said. "They said your car was bombed!"

"Yeah. And then a garbage truck fell on it."

"It was excellent," Lula said. "It was the shit."

"Boy, nothing fun ever happens to me," Leona said. "I've never had a car bombed or anything."

"But you work at a bank," I told her. "That's pretty cool. And you have kids. Kids are the best." Okay, so I fibbed a little about the kids. I didn't want her to feel bad. I mean we can't all be lucky enough to have a hamster.

"We came to see if you had any suspicious characters working here," Lula said.

Leona looked startled by that. "In the bank?"

"Well, maybe 'suspicious' is the wrong word," I told her. "Is there anyone here who might have connections with people who might not be totally law-abiding?"

Leona rolled her eyes. "Almost everybody. Marion Beddle was a Grizolli before she was married. You know about Vito Grizolli? And then Phil Zuck in mortgages lives next door to Sy Bernstein, the lawyer who was just disbarred for illegal practices. The guard has a brother in Rahway, doing time for burglary. You want me to go on?"

"Let's take this from a different direction. Is there anyone here who looks too successful for his job? You know, has too much money? Or is there anyone here who desperately needs money? Anyone who likes to gamble? Anyone doing expensive drugs?"

"Hmm. That's a harder question. Annie Shuman has a sick kid. Some kind of bone disease. Lots of doctor bills. Couple of people who play the numbers. I'm one of them. Rose White likes to go to Atlantic City and play the slots."

"I don't get what you want to know this for anyway," Lula said to me.

"We know of three companies with extra accounts in this bank. We think there's a possibility those accounts were opened to hold illegal money. So maybe there's a good reason the accounts were opened here."

"Like someone here in the bank is involved," Lula said.

"I see where you're going," Leona said. "You're suggesting we're laundering money. The money comes into those accounts you asked me about and almost immediately goes out."

"I don't know if it's exactly laundering," I said. "Where does the money go?"

"I don't have that information," Leona said. "You'd need a bank officer for that. And probably they wouldn't tell you. I'm sure that would be confidential. You should talk to Shempsky."

We hung around for another fifteen minutes, but Shempsky didn't materialize.

"Maybe we should go get that wife beater," Lula said. "I bet he's sitting in his living room, drinking beer, being a jerk."

I looked at my watch. Noon. Chances were good that Kenyon Lally was just getting up. Unemployed drunks were usually slow risers. Might be a good time to snag him.

"Okay," I said, "we'll take a ride over."

"Gonna fit right in with the BMW," Lula said. "Everybody in the projects gonna think you're a drug dealer."

Oh, great.

"I know about the bomb sensors and all," Lula said after we'd gone about a half mile, "but I still got the heebie-jeebies sitting next to you."

I knew exactly where she was coming from. I felt like that, too. "I could take you back to the office if you're uncomfortable."

"Hell, no. I'm not that freaked out. It just makes you wonder, you know? Anyway, I felt like that when I was a 'ho, too. You never knew when you were gonna get in the car with some maniac."

"It must have been a tough job."

"Most of my customers were repeaters, so that wasn't too bad. The worst part was standing around on the corner. Don't matter if it's hot or cold or raining, you still gotta stand there. Most people think the hard part's being on your back, but the hard part is being on your feet all day and night. I got varicose veins from standing too many hours on my feet. I guess if I'd been a better 'ho I'd have been on my back more and my feet less."

I took Nottingham to Greenwood, turned right off Greenwood, and crossed the railroad tracks. Trenton subsidized housing always reminded me of a POW camp, and in many ways, that's exactly what it was. Although, in all fairness, I have to say they aren't the worst I've ever seen. And they were preferable to living on Stark Street. I suppose the original vision was of garden apartments, but the reality is cement and brick bunkers squatting on hard-packed dirt. If I had to find a single word to describe the neighborhood, I'd have to choose *bleak*.

"We want the next building," Lula said. "Apartment 4B."

I parked around the corner, a block away, so Lally wouldn't see us coming, got out, and studied Lally's photo.

"Nice touch with the vest," Lula said. "It'll come in handy when the Welcome Wagon shows up."

The sky was gray and the wind whipped across yards. A few cars were parked on the street, but there was no activity. No dogs, no kids, no stoop sitters. It looked like a ghost town with Hitler as architect.

Lula and I walked to 4B and rang the bell.

Kenyon Lally answered the door. He was my height and rangy, wearing low-slung jeans and a thermal T-shirt. His hair was uncombed, and his face was unshaven. And he looked like a man who smacked women around.

"Hunh," Lula said when she saw him.

"We don't need no Girl Scout cookies," Lally said. And he slammed the door shut.

"I hate when people do that," Lula said.

I rang the bell again, but there was no response.

"Hey!" Lula yelled. "Bail Enforcement Agents. Open this door!"

"Go fuck yourself," Lally yelled back.

"The hell with this bullshit," Lula said. She gave the door a kick with her foot, and the door banged open.

We were both so surprised we just stood there. Neither of us had expected the door to open.

"Government housing," Lula finally said with a shake of her head. "It makes you wonder, don't it?"

"You're gonna pay for that," Lally said.

Lula was standing with her hands in her jacket pockets. "How about you make me? Why don't you come get me, Mr. Tough Guy?"

Lally charged Lula. Lula stuck out her hand, made contact with Lally's chest, and Lally went down like a sack of sand.

"Fastest stun gun in the East," Lula said. "Oops, look at that . . . damn, I accidentally kicked the wife beater."

I cuffed Lally and checked to make sure he was breathing.

"Shoot," Lula said. "I'm so careless, I accidentally kicked him again." She bent over Lally with the stun gun still in her hand. "Want me to make him jump?"

"No!" I said. "No jumping!"

FOURTEEN

AFTER FIFTEEN MINUTES, Lally's eyes were open and his
fingers were twitching, but I could see that it might take awhile
longer before he was up to walking any kind of distance.

"You should join a gym," Lula told Lally. "And you should
lay off the beer. You're out of shape. I only buzzed you once,
and look at you. I never saw anybody so pathetic from one measly
jolt."

I gave Lula the car keys. "Bring the car over so he doesn't
have to walk so far."

"You might never see me again," Lula said.

"Ranger would find you."

"Yeah," Lula said, "that'd be the best part."

Five minutes later, Lula was back.

"It's gone," she said.

"What's gone?"

"The car. The car's gone."

"What do you mean, it's gone?"

"What part of 'gone' don't you understand?" Lula asked.

"You don't mean it's been stolen?"

"Yep. That's just what I mean. The car's been stolen."

My heart did a nosedive. I didn't want to believe what I was hearing. "How could someone steal the car? We didn't hear the alarm go off."

"Must have gone off when we were inside here. It's a distance, and the wind's blowing away from us. Anyway, the brothers know how to take care of that kind of stuff. I'm real surprised, though. I figured you see a nice car in this kind of neighborhood and you think dealer. And messing with a dealer's car don't do a whole lot for your quality of life. Guess these guys were low on their daily quota. I got there just as the flatbed was turning the corner two blocks away. They must have been in the area."

"What am I going to tell Ranger?"

"Tell him the good news is they left him his plates." Lula handed me two license plates. "And guess they didn't want the registration number. They left that, too. Looks like they took it off with an acetylene torch." She dropped a small piece of scorched dashboard with the metal tag still attached into the palm of my hand.

"That's it?"

"Yep. That's what they left at the side of the road for you."

Lally was flopping around on the floor, trying to get to his feet, but his coordination was off and his hands were cuffed behind his back. He was drooling and cussing and slurring his words.

"Fruckin' bish," he said to me. "Fruckin' peesh a shit."

I searched in my bag for the cell phone, found it, and called Vinnie. I explained I had Kenyon Lally in custody, but there was a small problem with my car, and would he please come collect Lally and Lula and me.

"What's the problem?" Vinnie wanted to know.

"It's nothing. It's trivial. Don't worry about it."

"I'm not coming until you tell me. I bet this is something good."

I blew out a sigh. "The car's been stolen."

"That's it?"

"Yeah."

"Jeez, I expected something better . . . like it got hit by a train or sat on by an elephant."

"Are you going to come get us, or what?"

"I'm on my way. Hold your bladder."

We sat down to wait for Vinnie, and my cell phone rang. Lula and I exchanged glances.

"You expecting a call?" Lula asked.

Both of us thinking it might be Ranger.

"Well, answer it," Lally said. "Stoopid fruck."

"It could be Vinnie," Lula said. "He might have found a goat walking down the middle of the road and decided to do a nooner."

I searched through my bag, found the phone, crossed all my fingers and my eyes, and answered.

It was Joe. "We found Mark Stemper," he said.

"And?"

"He doesn't look good."

Damn. "How bad does he look?"

"He looks dead. Shot in the head. Someone tried to make it look like a suicide, but among other things they put the gun in the wrong hand. Stemper was left-handed."

"Oops."

"Yeah. Not very professional."

"Where'd it happen?"

"In an abandoned building a couple blocks from RGC. A watchman found him."

"You ever wonder why Harvey Tipp is still alive?"

255

"I guess he must pose no threat," Morelli said. "Or maybe he's related to Mr. Big. Or maybe he's not involved. We really have nothing on him, other than the fact that he's the logical person."

"I think it's time you talked to him."

"I think you're right." There was a moment of silence. "One more thing. Are you still driving the BMW?"

"Nope. Not me. Gave up on that puppy."

"What happened to it?"

"Stolen."

I could hear Morelli laughing over the phone.

"It's not funny!" I yelled. "Do you think I should file a police report?"

"I think you should talk to Ranger first. Do you need a ride?"

"No. Vinnie's on his way."

"Later, Hotstuff."

I disconnected and told Lula about Stemper.

"Somebody don't like leaving loose ends," Lula said.

I took a deep breath and dialed Ranger's home phone. No answer. Car phone. No answer. I could try his cell phone, but I didn't want to press my luck, so I left my number on his pager. The condemned woman gets a few extra minutes.

I'd been watching the window, and I saw Vinnie pull up in his Cadillac. I thought it might be satisfying to delay Vinnie for a half hour and see if his car disappeared, but dismissed it as being not practical. I'd only have to call yet another person to come collect us. And even worse, I'd have to spend time with Vinnie.

Lula and I dragged Lally out to the curb and waited while Vinnie popped his door locks.

"Scumbags sit in the backseat," Vinnie said.

"Hunh," Lula said, hand on hip, "who you callin' a scumbag?"

"If the shoe fits," Vinnie said.

"If the shoe fits, you'd have your pervert ass in the backseat," Lula said.

"Why me?" I asked. I realized I sounded like my mother and had a brief panic attack. I liked my mother, but I didn't want to *be* her. I didn't want to ever cook a pot roast. I didn't want to live in a house with three adults and only one bathroom. And I didn't want to marry my father. I wanted to marry Indiana Jones. I figured Indiana Jones was the middle ground between my father and Ranger. Morelli fit in there, too. In fact, Morelli wasn't too far off the Indiana Jones mark. Not that it mattered, since Morelli didn't want to get married.

Vinnie dropped Lula and me at the office and took Lally to the police station on North Clinton.

"Well, that was fun," Lula said. "Too bad about the car. I can't wait to see what you get next."

"I'm getting nothing next. I'm not taking any more cars. From now on, I'm driving the Buick. Nothing ever happens to the Buick."

"Yeah," Lula said, "but that isn't necessarily a good thing."

I dialed First Trenton, asked for Shempsky, and was told he'd gone home early with an upset stomach. I got his home number out of the directory and tried to reach him there. No answer. Just for the hell of it, I ran a fast credit check. Nothing unusual. Mortgage, credit cards all in good standing.

"Why are you checking on Shempsky?" Lula asked. "You think he's involved?"

"I keep thinking about the bomb in the Porsche. Shempsky knew I was driving a Porsche."

"Yeah, but he could have told people. He could have mentioned to someone you were going to the garbage company in your brand-new Porsche."

"True."

"Do you want a ride someplace?" Lula asked.

I shook my head no. "I could use some air and exercise," I said. "I'm going to walk home."

"That's a long walk."

"It's not so long."

I stepped outside and turned my jacket collar up against the wind. The temperature had dropped and the sky was gray. It was midafternoon, but houses had lights on to fight the gloom. Furnaces were running. Cars rolled by on Hamilton, drivers intent on getting somewhere. There were few people on the sidewalks. It was a good day to be indoors, cleaning out closets, making hot chocolate, organizing a fresh start for winter. And it was a good day to be outdoors, scuffing through the few remaining leaves, feeling flushed from the cold air. It was my favorite time of the year. And if it wasn't for the fact that people were dying left and right, and I couldn't find Uncle Fred, and someone wanted to kill me, and Ramirez wanted to send me to Jesus—it would be a *very* good day.

In an hour I was back at my building, in the lobby, and I was feeling fine. My head was clear and my circulation was in top form. The Buick was sitting in the parking lot, looking solid as a rock and just as serene. I had the keys in my pocket, and I was still wondering about Shempsky. Maybe I should ride by and see him, I thought. Surely he'll be home by now.

The elevator doors opened and Mrs. Bestler leaned out. "Going up?"

"No," I said. "I changed my mind. I have more errands to run."

"All ladies' accessories are twenty percent off on the second floor," she said. She pulled her head back and the doors closed.

I recrossed the lot and gingerly unlocked the Buick. Nothing went *boom*, so I slid behind the wheel. I started the car and jumped out. I stood a good distance away and timed ten minutes. Still no explosion. Whew. Big relief. I got back in the car, put it into gear, and drove out of the lot. Shempsky lived in Hamilton Township, off Klockner, behind the high school. Typical suburban development of single-family houses. Two cars, two incomes, two kids per family. It was easy to find his street and his house. It was all clearly marked. His house was a split-entry frame. White with black shutters. Very tidy.

I parked at the curb, walked to the door, and rang the bell. I was about to ring again when a woman answered. She was nicely dressed in a brown sweater, matching slacks, and rubber-soled loafers. Her hair was cut in a short bob. Her makeup was Martha Stewart. And her smile was genuine. She was the perfect match for Allen. I suspected I would immediately forget anything she told me, and a half hour from now I wouldn't recall what she looked like.

"Maureen?" I asked.

"Yes?"

"It's Stephanie Plum . . . we went to school together."

She slapped herself on the forehead. "Of course! I should have remembered. Allen mentioned you the other night. He said you'd stopped by the bank." The smile faded. "I heard about Fred. I'm so sorry."

"You haven't seen him, have you?" Just in case she had him in her basement.

"No!"

"I always ask," I explained, since she looked taken aback.

"And it's a good idea. I might have seen him walking down the street."

"Exactly."

So far, I hadn't seen any sign of Allen. Of course, if he was really sick he might be upstairs in bed. "Is Allen here?" I asked Maureen. "I tried to catch him at the bank, but he'd gone out to lunch, and then I got busy with another matter. I thought maybe he'd be home by now."

"No. He always comes home at five." The smile popped back in place. "Would you like to come in and wait? I could make some herb tea."

The nosy part of me would have liked to snoop through the Shempsky's house. The part of me that wanted to live to see another day thought it wise not to leave the Buick unguarded.

"Thanks, maybe some other time," I said to Maureen. "I need to keep my eye on the Buick."

"Mom," a kid yelled from the kitchen, "Timmy's got an M&M's stuck up his nose."

Maureen shook her head and smiled. "Children," she said. "You know how it is."

"Actually, I have a hamster," I said. "Hard to get an M&M's up his nose."

"I'll be right back," Maureen said. "This will only take a minute."

I stepped into the foyer and looked around while Maureen hustled off to the kitchen. The living room opened off to the right. It was a large, pleasant room done in tones of tan. An upright piano stood against the near wall. Family photos covered the top of the piano. Allen and Maureen and the kids at the beach, at Disney World, at Christmas.

Lots of pictures. Probably one wouldn't be missed if it happened to jump into my purse.

I heard a kid yelp, and Maureen chirped that everything was hunky-dory and the bad M&M's was bye-bye. "I'll be right back," Maureen said. The kitchen television was clicked on, and in the blink of an eye, I snatched the nearest photo, dropped it into my bag, and stepped back into the foyer.

"Sorry about that," Maureen said, returning. "Never a dull moment."

I handed Maureen a business card. "Maybe you could have Allen give me a call when he gets in."

"Sure."

"By the way, what kind of car does Allen drive?"

"A tan Taurus. And then there's the Lotus."

"Allen has a Lotus?"

"It's his toy."

Expensive toy.

It was necessary to pass by the strip mall on my way home, so I did a short detour into the lot and checked out the bank. The lobby was closed, but the drive-through window was open. That didn't do me any good. Allen wasn't going to be doing drive-through duty. I rode around the lot looking for a tan Taurus, but had no luck.

"Allen," I said, "where *are* you?"

And then, since I was in the neighborhood, I thought it wouldn't hurt to stop by and say hello to Irene Tully. And, what the hell, I might as well show her the picture of Allen Shempsky. You never know what could jog a person's memory.

"For goodness' sake," Irene said when she opened the door. "Are you still looking for Fred?" She gave an apprehensive glance to the Buick. "Is your grandmother with you?"

"Grandma's at home. I was hoping you wouldn't mind looking at another picture."

"Is this that dead man again?"

"No. This guy's alive." I gave her the photo of the Shempsky family.

"Isn't this nice," Irene said. "What a lovely family."

"Do you recognize any of these people?"

"Not offhand. I might have seen the man somewhere, but I can't place him."

"Could he have been the man Uncle Fred talked to in the parking lot?"

"I guess it's possible. If it wasn't this man, it was someone very much like him. He was just an ordinary man. I suppose that's why I can't remember him so good. There wasn't anything special to remember. Of course, he wasn't wearing a Mickey Mouse hat and Bermuda shorts."

I retrieved the photo. "Thanks. You've been very helpful."

"Anytime," she said. "You always have such interesting pictures."

I bypassed the street that led to my apartment building and continued down Hamilton to the Burg. I'd been thinking about the bombing, and I had a plan. Since I wasn't going anywhere tonight, I'd lock the Buick up in my parents' garage and bum a ride home from my dad. Not only would it keep the car safe, but it had the added advantage of getting me dinner.

I didn't have to worry about the garage being in use, because my father never put his car in the garage. The garage was used to store jugs of motor oil and old tires. My father had a workbench in there along one wall. He had a vise attached to the workbench, and little jars filled with nails and things lined the back of the workbench. I never saw him work at the workbench, but when he got really fed up with my grandmother, my father would hide in the garage and smoke a cigar.

"Uh-oh," Grandma said when she saw me at the door. "This don't look good. Where's the black car?"

"It got stolen."

"Already? You didn't even have it a whole day."

I went into the kitchen and got the garage keys. "I'm going to put the Buick in the garage overnight," I said to my mother. "Is that okay?"

My mother put her hand to her heart. "My God, you're going to get our garage blown up."

"Nobody's going to blow up the garage." Not unless they were sure I was in it.

"I have a ham," my mother said. "Are you staying for supper?"

"Sure."

I put the Buick in the garage, locked everything up nice and tight, and went into the house to have ham.

"It's gonna be two weeks tomorrow since Fred's been missing," Grandma said at dinner. "I thought for sure he'd have turned up by now—one way or another. Even aliens don't keep people that long. Usually they just probe your insides and let you go."

My father hunkered down over his plate.

"Of course, maybe they started probing Fred and he croaked. What do you think they'd do then? You think they'd just pitch him out? Maybe their spaceship was over Afghanistan when they tossed Fred, and we'll never find him. Good thing he isn't a woman, what with landing in Afghanistan and all. I hear they don't treat women so good over there."

My mother paused with her fork halfway to her mouth, and her eyes darted to the side window. She listened like that for a moment and then resumed eating.

"Nobody's going to bomb the garage," I said to her. "I'm almost sure of it."

"Boy, wouldn't it be something if someone *did* bomb our garage," Grandma said. "That'd be a good story to tell at the beauty parlor."

I was starting to wonder why I hadn't received a call from Ranger. It wasn't like him not to get back to me right away. I set my shoulder bag on my lap and pawed through the clutter, looking for my cell phone.

"What are you looking for?" Grandma asked.

"My cell phone. I've got so much junk in my bag I can never find anything." I started pulling stuff out and setting it on the table. Can of hairspray, hairbrush, zippered makeup pouch, flashlight, mini-binoculars, Ranger's license plates, bottle of nail polish, stun gun . . .

Grandma leaned over the table to take a better look. "What's that thing?"

"Stun gun," I said.

"What's it do?"

"It emits an electrical charge."

My father forked in more ham, focusing his concentration on his plate.

Grandma got out of her seat and came around to examine the stun gun. "What do you do with this?" she wanted to know, picking it up and studying it. "How does it work?"

I was still rooting through my bag. "You press the metal prongs against someone and push the button," I said.

"Stephanie," my mother said, "take that away from your grandmother before she electrocutes herself."

"Aha!" I said, finding my cell phone. I pulled it out and looked at it. Dead battery. No wonder Ranger hadn't called.

"Look, Frank," my grandmother said to my father, "did you ever see anything like this? Stephanie says you just stick it against someone and push the button . . ."

My mother and I both jumped out of our seats. "No!"

Too late. Grandma had the prongs pressed against my father's arm. *Zzzzzt.*

My father's eyes glazed over, a piece of ham fell out of his mouth, and he crashed to the floor.

"He must have had a heart attack," Grandma said, looking down at my father. "I told him and told him, he uses too much gravy."

"It's the stun gun!" I yelled at her. "That's what happens when you use a stun gun on someone!"

Grandma bent down for a closer look. "Did I kill him?"

My mother was on her knees alongside my grandmother. "Frank?" she shouted. "Can you hear me, Frank?"

I took his pulse. "He's okay," I said. "Grandma just scrambled some brain cells. It's not permanent. He'll be good as new in a couple minutes."

My father opened an eye and farted.

"Oops," Grandma said. "Someone must have stepped on a duck."

We all backed away and fanned the air.

"I have a nice chocolate cake for dessert," my mother said.

I used my parents' phone in the kitchen and left a new message on Ranger's machine. "Sorry about my cell phone. The battery conked out. I'll be home in about a half-hour. I need to talk to you." Then I called Mary Lou and asked her to give me a lift home. I didn't think it was such a good idea to ask my dad to drive so soon after getting zapped. And I didn't want my mom to take me and leave my grandmother and father alone in the house together. And first and foremost, I didn't want to be there when my father went nuts at Grandma Mazur.

"I've been *dying* to hear from you," Mary Lou said when she picked me up. "What happened with Morelli last night?"

"Not a lot. We talked about the case he's working on, and then he took me home."

"That's it?"

"Pretty much."

"No fooling around?"

"Nope."

"So let me get this straight. Last night you were with the two sexiest men in the entire world, and you didn't score with either one of them?"

"There are other things in this life besides scoring with men," I said.

"Like what?"

"I could score with myself."

"You could go blind doing that."

"No! I mean, I could feel good about myself. You know, like

when you do a job and it turns out excellent. Or when you set a moral standard for yourself and stick to it."

Mary Lou gave me the open-mouth, wrinkled-nose, this-is-a-load-of-bullshit look. "What?"

"Well, okay, so I've never had any of those things happen, but they could!"

"And pigs could fly," Mary Lou said, "but personally, I'd rather have an orgasm."

Mary Lou swung into the lot and stopped short, jerking both of us against the shoulder harness. "Omigod," she said. "Do you see what I think I see?"

Ranger's Mercedes was parked in shadow just beyond the door.

"Damn," Mary Lou said, "if he was waiting for me, I'd need Depends."

Ranger was leaning against the car, arms folded across his chest, not moving. Very foreboding in the dark. Definitely Depends material.

"Thanks for the ride," I said to Mary Lou, my eyes on Ranger, wondering about his mood.

"You going to be okay? He looks so . . . dangerous."

"It's the hair."

"It's more than the hair."

It was the hair, the eyes, the mouth, the body, the gun on his hip . . .

"I'll call you tomorrow," I told Mary Lou. "Don't worry about Ranger. He's not as bad as he looks." Okay, so I fib now and then, but it's always for a good cause. No point Mary Lou spending the night in a state.

Mary Lou gave Ranger one last look and whipped out of the lot. I took a deep breath and ambled over.

"Where's the BMW?" Ranger asked.

I pulled the plates and the piece of dashboard out of my bag and gave them to him. "I sort of had a problem . . ."

His eyebrows raised, and a smile started to twitch at the corners of his mouth. "This is what's left of the car?"

I nodded my head and swallowed. "It got stolen."

The smile widened. "And they left you the plates and registration tag. Nice touch."

I didn't think it was a nice touch. I thought it was very crappy. In fact, I was thinking my *life* was crappy. The bomb, Ramirez, Uncle Fred—and just when I thought I'd succeeded at something and made a capture, someone stole my car. The whole crappy world was thumbing its nose at me. "Life sucks," I said to Ranger. A tear popped out of my eye and slid down my cheek. Damn.

Ranger studied me for a moment, turned, and dropped the plates in his backseat. "It was a car, Babe. It wasn't important."

"It's not just the car. It's *everything*." Another tear squeezed out. "I have all these problems."

He was very close. I could feel the heat from his body. And I could see that his eyes were dilated black in the dark parking lot.

"Here's something else to worry about," he said. And he kissed me—his hand at the nape of my neck and his mouth on mine, soft at first, then serious and demanding. He drew me closer and kissed me again and desire washed over me, hot and liquid and scary.

"Oh boy," I whispered.

"Yeah," he said. "Think about it."

"What I think . . . is that it's a bad idea."

"Of course it's a bad idea," Ranger said. "If it was a good idea I'd have been in your bed a long time ago." He took a notecard from his jacket pocket. "I have a job for you tomorrow. The young sheik is going home and needs a ride to the airport."

"No! No way am I driving that little jerk."

"Look at it this way, Steph. He deserves you."

He had a point. "Okay," I said. "I haven't got anything else to do."

"Instructions are on the card. Tank will bring the car around for you."

And he was gone.

"Omigod," I said. "What did I just do?"

I rushed into the lobby and pushed the elevator button, still talking to myself. "He kissed me and I kissed him," I said. "What was I thinking?" I rolled my eyes. "I was thinking . . . *yes!*"

The elevator door opened and Ramirez stepped out at me. "Hello, Stephanie," he said. "The champ's been waiting for you."

I shrieked and jumped away, but I'd had my mind on Ranger and not Ramirez, and I didn't move fast enough. Ramirez grabbed a handful of hair and yanked me toward the door. "It's time," he said. "Time to see what it's like to be with a real man. And then when the champ is done with you, you'll be ready for God."

I stumbled and went down to one knee, and he dragged me forward. I had my hand in my bag, but I couldn't find my gun or the stun gun. Too much junk. I swung the bag as hard as I could and caught him in the face. He paused, but he didn't go down.

"That wasn't nice, Stephanie," he said. "You're gonna have to pay for that. You're gonna have to get punished before you go to God."

I dug my heels in and screamed as loud as I could.

Two doors opened on the first floor.

"What's going on here?" Mr. Sanders said.

Mrs. Keene stuck her head out. "Yeah, what's the racket?"

"Call the police," I yelled. "Help! Call the police."

"Don't worry, dear," Mrs. Keene said, "I've got my gun." She fired two off and took out an overhead light. "Did I get him?" she asked. "Would you like me to shoot again?"

Mrs. Keene had cataracts and wore glasses as thick as the bottom of a beer glass.

Ramirez had bolted for the door at the first shot.

"You missed him, Mrs. Keene, but that's okay. You scared him off."

"Do you still want us to call the police?"

"I'll take care of it," I told them. "Thanks."

Everyone thought I was a big professional bounty hunter, and I didn't want to ruin that image, so I calmly walked to the stairs. I climbed one step at a time, and I told myself to stay focused. Get yourself into your apartment, I thought. Lock the door, call the police. I should have found my gun and gone into the lot after Ramirez. But the truth is, I was too scared. And if I was being really honest here, I wasn't such a good shot. Better to leave it to the police.

By the time I got to my door, I had my key in my hand. I took a deep breath and got the key in on the first try. The apartment was dark and quiet. Too early for Briggs to be asleep. He must have gone out. Rex was silently running on his wheel. The red light was lit on my answering machine. Two messages. I suspected one was from Ranger, left early afternoon. I flipped the light on, dropped my bag on the kitchen counter, and played the messages.

The first was from Ranger, just as I'd thought, telling me to page him again.

The second was from Morelli. "This is important," he said. "I have to talk to you."

I dialed Morelli at home. "Come on," I said. "Pick up the phone." No answer, so I started working my way down the speed dial. Next on the list was Morelli's car phone. No answer there either. Try his cell phone. I took the phone into my bedroom, but only got as far as the bedroom door.

Allen Shempsky was sitting on my bed. The window behind him was broken. No secret how he got into my bedroom. He was holding a gun. And he looked terrible.

"Hang up," he said. "Or I'll kill you."

FIFTEEN

"WHAT ARE YOU doing?" I asked Shempsky.

"Good question. I thought I knew. I thought I had it all figured out." He shook his head. "It's all gone to heck in a handbasket."

"You look awful." His face was flushed, his eyes were bloodshot and glassy, and his hair was a mess. He was in a suit, but his shirt was hanging out, and his tie was twisted to one side. His slacks and jacket were wrinkled. "Have you been drinking?"

"I feel sick," he said.

"Maybe you should put the gun down."

"Can't. I have to kill you. What *is* it with you anyway? Anyone else would know when to quit. I mean, no one even liked Fred."

"Where is he?"

"Hah! Another good question."

I heard muffled noise coming from my closet.

"It's the dwarf," Shempsky said. "He scared the hell out of me. I thought no one was in here. And all of a sudden this little Munchkin came running in."

I was at the closet in two strides. I opened the door and

looked down. Briggs was trussed up like a Christmas goose, his hands tied behind his back with my bathroom clothesline, mailing tape across his mouth. He seemed okay. Very scared and boiling mad.

"Shut the door," Shempsky said. "He's quieter if you shut the door. I guess I have to kill him, too, but I've been procrastinating. It's like killing Doc or Sneezy or Grumpy. And I have to tell you I feel real bad about killing Sneezy. I really like Sneezy."

If you've never had a gun pointed at you, you can't imagine the terror. And the regret that life was too short, too unappreciated. "You don't really want to kill Sneezy and me," I said, working hard to keep my voice from shaking.

"Sure I do. Hell, why not. I've killed everybody else." He sniffed and wiped his nose on his jacket sleeve. "I'm getting a cold. Boy, I tell you, when things start going bad . . ." He ran his hand through his hair. "It was such a good idea. Take a few customers and keep them for yourself. Real clean. Except I didn't count on people like Fred stirring things up. We were all making money. Nobody was getting hurt. And then things started to go wrong and people started to panic. First Lipinski and then John Curly."

"So you killed them?"

"What else could I do? It's the only way to really keep someone quiet, you know."

"What about Martha Deeter?"

"Martha Deeter," he said on a sigh. "One of my many regrets is that she's dead, and I can't kill her again. If it wasn't for Martha Deeter . . ." He shook his head. "Excuse my language, but she had a real stick up her ass about the accounts. Everything strictly by the books. Wouldn't budge on the Shutz thing. Even though it was none of her business. She was a stupid receptionist, but she wouldn't keep her nose out of anything. After you left the office she decided she was going to make an example out of you and your aunt. Sent a fax off to the home office suggesting they look into the matter and prosecute you for making fraudulent claims. Can you imagine what that could lead to? Even if they just called to pacify you, it could start an investigation."

"So you killed her?"

"It seemed like the prudent thing to do. Looking back it might have been a little extreme, but like I said before, it's really the only way you can be sure of keeping someone quiet. Human nature, such as it is, is *not* dependable. And you know, I discovered this amazing thing. It's not that hard to kill someone."

"Where did you learn about bombs?"

"The library. Actually, I'd built the bomb for Curly, but by chance I happened to see him crossing the street to get to his car. It was late at night, and he was coming out of a bar. Nobody around. Couldn't believe how lucky I was. So I ran him over a bunch of times. I had to make sure he was dead, you know. Didn't want him to suffer. He wasn't such a bad guy. It was just he was a loose end."

I gave an involuntary shiver.

"Yeah," he said, "it was kind of creepy the first time I ran over him. I tried to pretend it was a bump in the road. So anyway, I had this bomb all ready to go, and then I found out you were going over to RGC again. I called Stemper and gave him some baloney about delaying you for a half hour so the bank could run the check through the system."

"Then you had to kill Stemper."

"Stemper was *your* fault. Stemper'd still be alive if you hadn't been so compulsive about that check. Two dollars," Shempsky said, sniffling. "All these people are dead, and my life is unraveling because of two fucking dollars."

"Seems to me it started with Laura Lipinski."

"You figured that out?" He slumped a little. "She was giving Larry a hard time. He'd made the mistake of telling her about the money, and she wanted it. She was leaving him, and she wanted the money. Said if she didn't get it, she'd go to the police."

"So you killed her?"

"The mistake we made was in getting rid of the body. I'd never done anything like that before, so I figured chop it up, stuff it in a couple garbage bags, leave them spread out over town the night before garbage pickup. First off, let me tell you, it isn't easy to chop up a body. And second, cheapskate Fred was out, trying to save a buck on his leaves, and saw Larry and me with the bag. I mean, what are the chances?"

"I don't get Fred's part in this."

"He saw us dump the bag and didn't think anything of it. I mean he was out there doing the same thing. The next morning Fred goes to RGC, and Martha pisses him off and sends him packing. Fred gets a block away and thinks to himself that he knows Martha's office partner. He thinks about it for another block and realizes he's the guy who dumped the bag. So Fred goes to the real estate office alongside the deli with a camera and starts taking pictures. I guess he was going to wave them in Larry's face, trying to embarrass him enough to give him his money. Only after a couple pictures Fred thinks the bag looks too lumpy and smells pretty bad. And Fred opens the bag."

"Why didn't Fred report this to the police?"

"Why do you think? Money."

"He was going to blackmail you." That's why Fred left the canceled check on his desk. He didn't need it. He had the pictures.

"Fred said he didn't have any retirement account. Worked at the button factory for fifty years and had hardly any retirement account. Said he read where you needed ninety thousand to get into a decent nursing home. That's what he wanted. Ninety thousand."

"What about Mabel? Didn't he want nursing home money for her, too?"

Shempsky shrugged. "He didn't say anything about Mabel."

Cheap bastard.

"Why did you kill Larry?" Not that I actually cared at this point. What I cared about was time. I wanted more of it. I didn't want him to pull the trigger. If it meant I had to talk to him then that's what I was going to do.

"Lipinski got cold feet. He wanted out. Wanted to take his money and run. I tried to talk to him, but he was really freaked out. So I went over to see if I could calm him down."

"You succeeded. You can't get much calmer than dead."

"He wouldn't listen, so what could I do? I thought I did a good job of making it look like a suicide."

"You have a nice life—a nice house, a nice wife and kids, a good job. Why were you skimming?"

"In the beginning it was just fun money. Tipp and me used to play poker with a bunch of guys on Monday nights. And Tipp's wife would never give Tipp any money. So Tipp started skimming. Just a couple accounts for poker money. But then it was so easy. I mean, nobody knew the money was gone. So we enlarged until we had a nice chunk of Vito's accounts. Tipp knew Lipinski and Curly, and he brought them in." Shempsky wiped his nose again. "It wasn't like I was ever going to make money at the bank. I'm in a dead-end job. It's my face, you know. I'm not stupid. I could have been somebody, but nobody pays attention to me.

"God gives everybody a special talent. And you know what my talent is? Nobody remembers me. I have a forgettable face. It took me a bunch of years, but I finally figured out how to use my gift." He gave a crazy little laugh that sent all the hairs on my arm standing at attention. "My talent is that I can rob people blind, kill them on the street, and nobody remembers."

275

Allen Shempsky was drunk or crazy or both. And at the rate we were going he wouldn't even have to shoot me, because he was scaring me to death. My heart was pounding in my chest, echoing in my ears.

"What will you do now?" I asked him.

"You mean after I kill you? I guess I'll go home. Or maybe I'll just get in my car and drive somewhere. I have lots of money. I don't need to go back to the bank if I don't want to."

Shempsky was sweating, and under the flush on his cheeks his face was pale. "Christ," he said. "I really feel sick." He stood up and pointed the gun at me. "You got any cold medicine?"

"Just aspirin."

"I need more than aspirin. I'd like to sit and talk some more, but I gotta get some cold medicine. I bet I have a fever."

"You don't look good."

"I bet my face is all flushed."

"Yeah, and your eyes are glassy."

There was a scraping sound on the fire escape outside my window, and we both swiveled our heads to look. We saw only darkness beyond the broken pane.

Shempsky turned back to me and cocked the hammer on his revolver. "Now hold still so I kill you with the first bullet. It's better that way. There's a lot less mess. And if I shoot you in the heart, you can have an open casket. I know everybody likes that."

We both took a deep breath—me to die, and Shempsky to aim. And in that instant the air was pierced with a bloodcurdling roar of rage and lunacy. And Ramirez filled the window, his face contorted, his eyes small and evil.

Shempsky instinctively whirled and fired, emptying his gun in Ramirez.

I wasted no time running. I *flew* out of the room, through my living room, and out my front door. I sprinted down the hall, leaped down two flights of stairs, and almost bashed in Mrs. Keene's door.

"Goodness," Mrs. Keene said, "you certainly are having a full night. What now?"

"Your gun! Give me your gun!"

I called the police and went back upstairs with the gun in my hand. My apartment door was wide open. Shempsky was gone. And Briggs was still alive in my closet.

I ripped the tape off. "Are you okay?"

"Shit," he said. "I messed my pants."

THE UNIFORMS CAME first, then the paramedics and finally the homicide detectives and the medical examiner. They had an easy time finding my apartment. Most of them had been there before. Morelli had arrived with the uniforms.

It was now three hours later, and the party was winding down. I'd given my statement, and the only thing left was to get Ramirez into a body bag and haul him off my fire escape. Rex and I had set up camp in the kitchen while the professionals did their thing. Randy Briggs gave his statement and left, deciding his apartment without a door was safer than living with me.

Rex still looked perky, but I was exhausted. I was all out of adrenaline, and I felt like my blood level was a pint low.

Morelli wandered in, and for the first time all night we had a moment alone together. "You should be relieved," he said. "You don't have to worry about Ramirez anymore."

I nodded. "It's a terrible thing to say, but I'm glad he's dead. Any word on Shempsky?"

"Nobody's seen him or his car. He didn't go home."

"I think he's flipped out. And he has the flu. He looked really bad."

"You'd look bad too if you were wanted for multiple murders. We're leaving a uniform here tonight to make sure no one comes in through your window, but it's going to be cold in your bedroom. Probably you want to stay someplace else. My vote's for my house."

"I'd feel safe at your house," I said. "Thanks."

The gurney with the body clattered over the hall floor and rolled out my door. My stomach lurched, and I reached for Morelli. He pulled me to him and wrapped his arms around me. "You'll feel better tomorrow," he said. "You just need some sleep."

"Before I forget. You left a message on my machine that you needed to talk to me."

"We brought Harvey Tipp in for questioning, and he squealed like a pig. I wanted to warn you about Shempsky."

I WOKE UP to the sun streaming in through Morelli's bedroom window, but no Morelli next to me. I had a dim recollection of falling asleep on the ride to his house. And falling asleep again, next to Morelli. I had no recollection of any kind of sexual encounter. I was wearing a T-shirt and underpants. Since the underpants were on me and not on the floor that probably told me something.

I got out of bed and padded barefoot into the bathroom. There was a damp bath towel hanging on the hook on the door. A set of clean towels had been set out for me, neatly stacked on the tub. A note was taped to the mirror over the sink. "Had to leave for work early," the note said. "Make yourself at home." He also confirmed what I'd suspected—that I'd zonked out the minute my head hit the pillow. And since Morelli appreciated response to his lovemaking, he'd passed on last night's opportunity to collect on his debt.

I took a shower and got dressed and went to the kitchen in search of breakfast. Morelli didn't stock Pop-Tarts, so I settled on a peanut butter sandwich. I was halfway through the sandwich when I remembered the chauffeuring job. I'd never gotten around to reading the notecard, and I had no idea when I was supposed to get the sheik. I shuffled through the mess in my shoulder bag and found the card. It said Tank would drop the limo off at nine. I was to pick the sheik up at ten and drive him to Newark Airport. It was almost eight, so I finished my sandwich, stuffed yesterday's clothes into the tote, and called Mary Lou to bum a ride.

"Boy, you really get around," Mary Lou said. "When I dropped you off you were with Ranger. You must have had a busy night."

"You don't know the half of it." I explained to her about the kiss, and Ramirez, and Shempsky, and finally about Morelli.

"I can't imagine being too tired to do it with Morelli," Mary Lou said. "Of course, I've never been attacked by a homicidal rapist, held at gunpoint by a screwy banker, and had a guy killed outside my bedroom window."

Mrs. Bestler was waiting by the elevator when I walked into the lobby. "Going up?" she asked. "Second floor . . . belts, hand-bags, body bags."

"I'm taking the stairs," I told her. "I need the exercise."

I opened my apartment door and surprised a young cop who was feeding Rex Cheerios.

"He looked hungry," the cop said. "I hope you don't mind."

"Not at all. Feel free to join him for breakfast. Just poke around in the fridge until you find something you like."

The cop smiled. "Thanks. There's a guy here fixing your window. Morelli arranged it. I'm supposed to leave as soon as he's done."

"Sounds good."

I went into the bedroom and collected my chauffeur uniform of black suit and stockings and heels. I changed in the bathroom, added some lipstick and a swipe of mascara, and sprayed my hair. When I came out, the window man was gone, and my window looked sparkly clean. The cop was gone, too.

I grabbed my shoulder bag, said good-bye to Rex, and hustled down to the parking lot.

Tank was waiting for me when I swung through the back door at nine o'clock sharp. He had a map and directions.

"Should take you about a half hour from here," Tank said.

"Does he know I'm driving him?"

Tank's face creased in a wide grin. "We thought it would be a nice surprise."

I took the keys to the Town Car and slid in behind the wheel.

"You're carrying, right?" Tank asked.

"Right."

"And you're okay after last night?"

"How do you know about last night?"

"It's in the paper."

Terrific.

I gave Tank a little finger wave and drove away. I got to Hamilton and turned right. I drove several blocks and turned into the Burg. I had no intention of destroying another black car. I parked at my parents' house and went inside to get the garage keys.

"You made the paper again," Grandma said. "And the phone's been ringing off the hook. Your mother's in the kitchen, ironing."

My mother always irons during times of disaster. Some people drink, some take drugs. My mother irons.

"How's Dad?" I asked.

"He's out at the store."

"No problems left over from the stun gun?"

"Well, he isn't the happiest person I ever saw, but aside from that he's doing okay. Looks like you got another car."

"It's a loaner. I have a job as a chauffeur. I'm going to leave the black car here and take the Buick. I feel safer in the Buick."

My mother came out of the kitchen. "What's this about being a chauffeur?"

"It's nothing," I said. "I'm driving a man to the airport."

"Good," my mother said. "Take your grandmother."

"I can't do that!"

My mother pulled me into the kitchen and lowered her voice. "I don't care if you're driving the Pope, your grandmother is going with you. If she says the wrong thing to your father when he gets home, he'll go after her with a steak knife. So unless you want more bloodshed on your hands, you will fulfill your obligation as a granddaughter and get your grandmother out of this house for a few hours until things calm down. This is all your fault anyway." My mother snapped a shirt onto the ironing board and snatched at the iron. "And what kind of a daughter has shootouts on her fire escape? The phone's been ringing all morning. What am I supposed to say to people? How can I explain these things?"

"Just tell people I was looking for Uncle Fred, and things got complicated."

My mother shook the iron at me. "If that man isn't dead I'm going to kill him myself."

Hmm. Mom appeared to be a little stressed. "Okay," I said, "I guess I can take Grandma with me." Might not be a bad idea anyway. I didn't think the pervert sheik would be so fast to flash his johnson with Grandma on board.

"It's a shame we can't take that nice black car," Grandma said. "It looks more like a chauffeur car."

"I'm not taking any chances," I told her. "I don't want anything to happen to the black car. It's getting locked up nice and safe in the garage."

I loaded Grandma into the Buick, backed it out the driveway, and parked it on the street. Then I carefully eased the Lincoln into the garage and secured the doors.

In exactly thirty-five minutes I was at the address Tank had given me. It was in a neighborhood of expensive houses on two- and three-acre lots. Most houses were behind gated drives, tucked into yards filled with mature trees and professionally land-scaped shrubs. I pushed the button on the call box and gave my name. The gates opened, and I drove up to the house.

"I guess this is pretty," Grandma said, "but they aren't gonna get many trick-or-treaters up here. I bet Halloween is a big bust."

I told Grandma to stay put and went to the door.

The door opened, and Ahmed looked out at me and frowned. "You!" he said. "What are you doing here?"

"Surprise," I said. "I'm your driver."

He looked over at the car. "And what's that supposed to be?"

"That's a Buick."

"There's an old lady in it."

"That's my grandmother."

"Forget it. I'm not riding with you. You're incompetent."

I put my arm around him and tugged him to me. "I've been having a difficult couple of days here," I said in confidential tones. "And I'm running a little low on patience. So I'd appreciate it if you'd get into the car without a lot of fuss. Because otherwise, I'm going to shoot you."

"You wouldn't shoot me," he said.

"Try me."

A man stood behind Ahmed. He was holding two suitcases, and he was looking uncomfortable.

"Put them in the trunk," I said to the man.

A woman had come to the door.

"Who's that?" I asked the kid.

"My aunt."

"Wave to her and smile and get in the car."

He sighed and waved. I waved, too. Everybody waved. And then I drove away.

"We would have brought the black car," Grandma said to Ahmed, "only Stephanie's been having real bad luck with cars."

He slouched lower, sulking. "No kidding."

"You don't have to worry with this one, though," Grandma told him. "We had this one locked up in the garage so no one could plant a bomb on it. And knock on wood, it hasn't blown up yet."

I picked up Route 1 and followed it to New Brunswick, where I moved over to the turnpike. I got on the turnpike and headed north, barreling along in the Buick, thankful that my passenger was still fully dressed and Grandma had fallen asleep, mouth open, hanging from her shoulder harness.

"I'm surprised you're still working for this company," Ahmed said. "If I had been your employer I would have fired you."

I ignored him and turned the radio on.

He leaned forward. "Perhaps it's difficult to get a competent person to do a menial job like this."

I glanced at him in the rearview mirror.

"I'll give you five dollars if you'll show me your breasts," he said.

I rolled my eyes and raised the volume on the radio.

He slouched back in his seat. "This is boring," he shouted at me. "And I hate this music."

"Are you thirsty?"

"Yes."

"Would you like to stop for a soda?"

"Yes!"

"Too bad."

I had my cell phone plugged into the cigarette lighter and was surprised to hear it chirp.

It was Briggs. "Where are you?" he asked. "This is your cell phone, right?"

"Yeah. I'm on the Jersey Turnpike, exit ten."

"Are you shitting me? That's great! Wait until you hear this. I've been working all night hacking into Shempsky's files, and I've got something. Late last night he made plane reservations. He's supposed to be flying out of Newark in an hour and a half. He's flying Delta to Miami."

"You *are* the man."

"Hey, don't piss off a little person."

"Call the police. Call Morelli first." I gave him Morelli's numbers. "If you can't get Morelli, call the station. They'll get in touch with the right people in Newark. And I'll watch out for Shempsky on the road."

"I can't tell the police I hacked into the bank!"

"Tell them I got the information and asked you to pass it on."

Fifteen minutes later, I slowed for the tollbooth to exit the turnpike. Grandma was awake, looking for the tan Taurus, and Ahmed was silent in the back, arms sullenly crossed over his chest.

"It's him!" Grandma said. "I see him ahead of us. Look at that tan car that's just leaving the tollbooth all the way to the left."

I paid the toll and glanced at the car. It *did* sort of look like Shempsky, but it was the fourth time Grandma had been sure she'd seen Shempsky in the last five minutes. There were a lot of tan cars on the Jersey Turnpike.

I put my foot to the pedal and roared up behind the car to check it out. The car was a Taurus, and the hair color seemed right, but I couldn't tell much from the back of his head.

"You've got to get to his side," Grandma said.

"If I come up on his side, he'll see me."

Grandma pulled a .44 magnum out of her purse. "Everybody duck, and I'll shoot out his tires."

"No!" I shouted. "No shooting. You shoot one single thing, and I'll tell Mom on you. We aren't even sure it's Allen Shempsky."

"Who's Allen Shempsky?" Ahmed wanted to know. "What's going on?"

I was riding right on the Taurus's rear. It would be safer to put a car or two between us, but I was afraid I'd lose him in traffic.

"My father hired you to protect me," Ahmed said, "not to go off chasing men."

Grandma leaned forward, keeping her eye on the Taurus. "We think this guy killed Fred."

"Who's Fred?"

"My uncle," I told him. "He's married to Mabel."

"Ah, so you're avenging a murder in the family. This is a good thing."

Nothing like a little avenging to bridge the culture gap.

The Taurus took the airport turnoff, and the driver checked his mirror as he merged with traffic, then turned in his seat and took a quick, disbelieving look back. It was Shempsky. And I was made. Not many people in Jersey driving a '53 powder blue and white Buick. Probably wondering how the devil I found him.

"He sees us," I said.

"Ram him," Ahmed said. "Disable his car. Then we'll all rush out and subdue the murdering dog."

"Yeah," Grandma said, "plow this baby right up his behind."

In theory, that sounded like a reasonable idea. In practice, I was afraid it'd result in a twenty-three-car pileup, and headlines that read BOMBSHELL BOUNTY HUNTER CAUSES CATASTROPHE.

Shempsky swerved in front of me, jumping out of his lane.

He passed two cars, then swerved back. He was approaching the terminal, and he was panicking, determined to lose me. He changed lanes again and sideswiped a blue van. He overcorrected and crashed into the back of an SUV. Everyone stopped behind the accident. I was four cars back, and I couldn't get closer. No one was moving.

Shempsky was boxed in with his right front fender smashed into his right front wheel. I saw his door open. He was going to bolt. I hurled myself out of the car and hit the pavement running. Ahmed was behind me. And behind him was Grandma.

Shempsky pushed through the curbside check-in, dodging people with kids and bags. I lost him for a moment in the crowded terminal, then picked him out just ahead of me. I ran as fast as I could, not caring who I knocked over. I lunged when I was almost on Shempsky's heels, and I snagged his jacket. Ahmed grabbed Shempsky half a second after me, and the three of us went down. We rolled around a little, but Shempsky didn't put up much of a fight.

Ahmed and I had Shempsky pinned to the ground when Grandma came clattering up on her patent pumps. She had her gun in her hand and both our handbags tucked into the crook of her arm. "You should never leave your purse in the car," she said. "Do you need a gun?"

"No," I told her. "Put the gun away and give me my cuffs."

She searched through my bag, found the cuffs, handed them to me, and I clapped them on Shempsky.

Ahmed and I got to our feet, and we all did a high five with each other. And then we did a down low. And then Ahmed and Grandma did some complicated hand thing that I couldn't get the hang of.

———

CONSTANTINE STIVA STOOD at the entrance to the viewing room, keeping a close watch on the casket at the far end. Grandma Mazur and Mabel stood at the head of the casket, accepting condolences and making apologies.

"We're real sorry," Grandma Mazur said to Mrs. Patucci. "We had to have a closed casket on account of Fred was in the ground two weeks before we found him and the worms had eaten a lot of his face."

"That's such a shame," Mrs. Patucci said. "It takes something away when you can't see the deceased."

"I feel just like that, too," Grandma said. "But Stiva couldn't do nothing with him, and he wouldn't let us leave the lid up."

Mrs. Patucci turned and looked at Stiva. Stiva gave a small sympathetic nod and smiled.

"That Stiva," Mrs. Patucci said.

"Yeah, and he's watching us like a hawk," Grandma told her.

Allen Shempsky had buried Fred in a shallow grave in a little patch of woods across from the pet cemetery on Klockner Road. He'd claimed he'd shot Fred by accident, but that was hard to believe since the fatal bullet had gone dead center between Fred's eyes.

Fred had been exhumed early Friday morning, the autopsy had been done on Monday, and now it was Wednesday and Fred was having an evening viewing. Mabel seemed to be enjoying herself, and Fred would have been pleased by the crowd he got, so I guess everything turned out okay.

I was at the back of the room, to one side of the door, counting the minutes until I could leave. I was trying to be as inconspicuous as possible, staring down at the carpet, not especially anxious to engage in conversation about Fred or Shempsky.

A pair of motorcycle boots entered my field of vision. They were attached to Levi's-clad legs I knew all too well.

"Hey, Hotstuff," Morelli said. "Having fun?"

"Yeah. I love viewings. The Rangers are playing Pittsburgh, but that can't compare to a viewing. Long time, no see."

"Not since you went into a coma fully dressed in my bedroom."

"I didn't wake up fully dressed."

"You noticed."

I felt my face flush. "I guess you've been busy."

"I had to wrap up the case with Treasury. They wanted Vito in Washington, and Vito wanted me to go with him. I just got back this afternoon."

"I caught Shempsky."

This brought a smile. "I heard. Congratulations."

"I still don't understand why he felt it necessary to kill people. Wasn't he just doing his banker thing by opening accounts for clients?"

"He was supposed to pass the money through to a bank in the Caymans and establish tax-free accounts. The trouble was Shempsky was skimming the skimmers. When Lipinski and Curly panicked and wanted their money, the money wasn't there."

Shempsky hadn't told me that part. "Why didn't Shempsky just replace the money?"

"He'd spent it on venture investments that didn't pay off. I think it was just something that got away from him, and it got worse and worse, until it was so bad it was out of control. There were a couple banking irregularities, too. Shempsky knew it was dirty money."

I felt hot breath on my neck. Morelli looked at the person doing the breathing and gave a grunt of disgust.

It was Bunchy. "Nice collar, Cutie Pie," he said.

His hair was cut and clean and his face was freshly shaved. He was wearing a button-down shirt, crewneck sweater, and tan slacks. If it wasn't for the eyebrows I might not have recognized him.

"What are you doing here?" I said. "I thought the case was over. Don't you go back to Washington now?"

"Not all of Treasury works in Washington. I happen to be a Jersey Treasury guy." He looked around the room. "I thought Lula might be here since you two are such good friends."

I raised an eyebrow. "Lula?"

"Yeah. Well, you know, she looked like she might be fun."

"Listen, just because she used to be a hooker—"

He raised his hands. "Hey, it isn't like that. I just like her, that's all. I think she's okay."

"So call her."

"You think I could? I mean, would she hang up on me because of that tire thing?"

I dug a pen out of my bag and wrote Lula's number on the back of Bunchy's hand. "Take your chances."

"How about me," Morelli said when Bunchy left. "Do I get a number on the back of my hand?"

"You have enough numbers to last you a lifetime."

"You owe me," Morelli said.

A thrill skittered through my stomach. "Yes, but I didn't say *when* I'd pay off."

"The ball's in your court," Morelli said.

I'd heard that before!

Grandma was waving to me from the other end of the room. "Yoo-hoo," she called, "come here a minute."

"I have to go," I said to Morelli.

He took the pen from my bag and wrote his number on the back of *my* hand. "Ciao," he said. And then he left.

"The viewing is almost over," Grandma said. "We're all going over to Mabel's house to see her new bedroom set and have some coffee cake. Do you want to come with us?"

"Thanks, but I think I'll pass. I'll see you tomorrow."

"Thank you for everything," Mabel said to me. "I like this new garbage company you got me much better."

I PARKED THE Buick and took a moment to enjoy the night. The air was crisp and the sky was starless and black. Lights were on in my building. The seniors were watching TV. The bombers and rapists were gone, and this little part of Trenton felt safe again. I walked into the building and went to the bank of mailboxes to collect my mail. A credit card bill, a dental reminder, and an envelope from RangeMan. The RangeMan envelope contained a check for the chauffeuring job. A note was included with the check. It was hand-written from Ranger. "Glad the Lincoln survived, but locking it in a garage is cheating." I remembered his kiss, and I got another one of those skittery thrills.

I ran up the stairs, let myself into my apartment, locked the door behind me, and took stock. My apartment was nice and neat. I'd spent the weekend cleaning. No dishes on the counter. No socks on the floor. Rex had a clean cage, and the pine shavings smelled foresty. It all felt welcoming. And safe. And private. And intimate.

"I should invite someone over," I said to Rex. "After all, the apartment's all cleaned. I mean, how often does that happen, right? And my legs are shaved. And I have this great dress that I've never worn."

Rex gave me a look that told me in no uncertain terms he knew exactly what I was after.

"Okay," I said. "So what's the big deal? I'm an adult. I have adult urges."

I thought about Ranger again, and tried to imagine what he'd be like in bed. And then I thought about Joe. I knew *exactly* what Joe was like.

This was a dilemma.

I got two pieces of paper, wrote Joe's name on one and Ranger's on the other. I dumped the two names into a bowl, closed my eyes, mixed them up, and picked one. Let God decide, I thought.

I read the name and cracked my knuckles. I hoped God knew what he was doing. I showed the paper to Rex, and he looked disapproving, so I covered his cage with a dish towel.

I did the speed-dial thing before I lost my nerve.

"I have this dress I'd like your opinion on," I said when he answered.

A beat went by. "When would you like this opinion?"

"Now."

I SUPPOSE THERE'S a time and place for everything—and this was the time for the slinky black dress. I tugged it over my head and smoothed it out. The fit was perfect. I shook my head to fluff up my hair, and I sprayed some Dolce Vita on my wrist. I slipped my feet into the sexy ankle-strap heels and retouched my lipstick. Bright red. *Yow!*

I lit a candle on the coffee table and another in the bedroom. I dimmed the lights. I heard the elevator doors open down the hall, and my heart jumped in my chest. Get a grip, I told myself. No reason to be nervous. This is the will of God.

Baloney, a voice whispered in my head. You cheated. You peeked when you picked.

Okay, so I cheated. Big deal. The important thing is that I picked the right man. Maybe he wasn't right forever and ever, but he was right for tonight.

I opened the door on the second knock. Didn't want to seem overly anxious! I stepped back and our eyes met, and he showed no sign of the nervousness I felt. Curiosity, maybe. And desire.

And something else—maybe the need to know this was what I wanted.

"Howdy," I said.

He looked amused at that, but not amused enough to smile. He stepped forward into the foyer, closed the door, and locked it. His breathing was slow and deep, his eyes were dark, his expression serious as he studied me.

"Nice dress," he said. "Take it off."